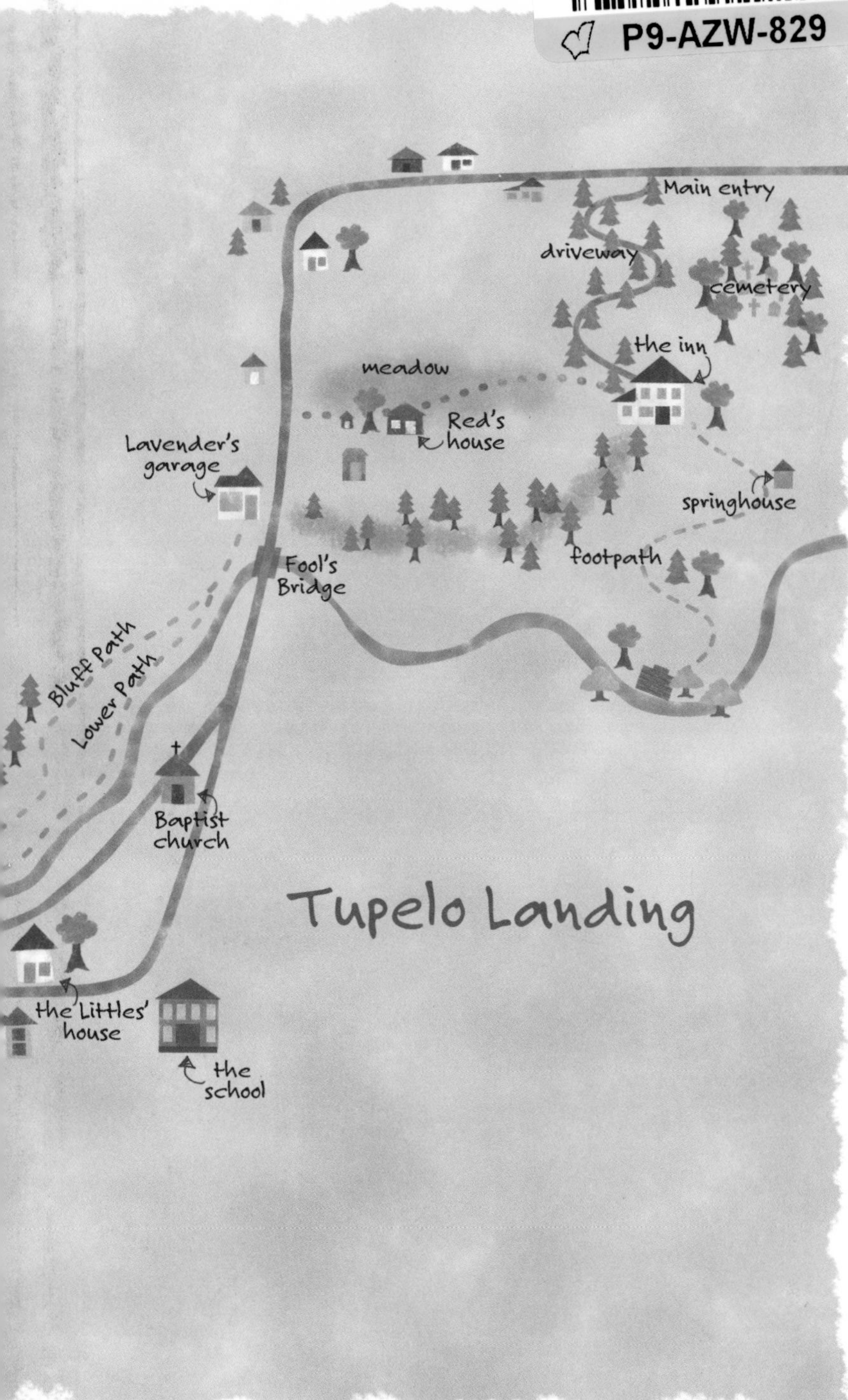
Main entry
driveway
cemetery
the inn
meadow
Red's house
Lavender's garage
springhouse
footpath
Fool's Bridge
Bluff Path
Lower Path
Baptist church
Tupelo Landing
the Littles' house
the school

The Law of Finders Keepers

Sheila Turnage

KATHY DAWSON BOOKS

KATHY DAWSON BOOKS
PENGUIN YOUNG READERS GROUP
An imprint of Penguin Random House LLC
375 Hudson Street
New York, NY 10014

Library of Congress Cataloging-in-Publication Data
Turnage, Sheila, author.
The law of finders keepers / Sheila Turnage.
Companion to: Three times lucky, The ghosts of Tupelo Landing, and The odds of getting even.
Summary: "A rumor that Blackbeard's buried treasure is somewhere near Tupelo Landing causes pirate fever to sweep through town just as clues about Mo's Upstream Mother surface and the Desperado Detectives—aka Mo LoBeau and her best friends Dale and Harm—take on the most important case of Mo's life"—Provided by publisher.
ISBN 9780803739628 (hardback)
[1. Mystery and detective stories. 2. Buried treasure—Fiction. 3. Pirates—Fiction. 4. Community life—North Carolina—Fiction. 5. Identity—Fiction. 6. Foundlings—Fiction. 7. North Carolina—Fiction.]
BISAC: JUVENILE FICTION / Mysteries & Detective Stories. | JUVENILE FICTION / Family / Orphans & Foster Homes. | JUVENILE FICTION / Humorous Stories.
LCC PZ7.T8488 Law 2018 | DDC [Fic]—dc23 LC
Printed in the United States of America
ISBN 9780803739628

1 3 5 7 9 10 8 6 4 2

Designed by Jasmin Rubero
Text set in Carre Noir Std family

For Rodney L. Beasley
and Patsy Baker O'Leary,
who've had Mo's back from the beginning

Table of Contents

Chapter One
The Odds-and-Ends Drawer

The Desperado Detective Agency's biggest case ever crept up on tiny Tupelo Landing in the dead of winter, and kicked off on the rarest of days. Unlike most of our borderline famous cases, it started with two things found.

One thing found by me, Miss Moses LoBeau—ace detective, yellow belt karate student, and a sixth grader in her prime.

One thing found by a stranger.

Before all was said and done, it plunged me and my fellow Desperados—my best friends, Dale Earnhardt Johnson III and Harm Crenshaw, the agency's newest detective—into a blood-thirsty chapter of our town's history, and an unspoken chapter of Harm's past. It put our lives in peril, tested our courage, and sent us racing for treasures of the world and treasures of the heart.

As for me, Mo LoBeau, it bent my rivers and scattered my stars.

As usual, I didn't see it coming.

In fact, I was dead asleep in the wee hours of January 11,

when my vintage phone jangled. I clicked on my Elvis in Vegas lamp. "Desperado Detective Agency, Mo LoBeau speaking. Your disaster is our delight. How may we be of service?"

I squinted at my alarm clock. Five thirty a.m.

The voice came through scratchy and worried. "Mo? It's Thes." Crud. Fellow sixth grader Thessalonian Thompson, a weather freak desperate to take me to a movie.

I yawned. "No movie."

"It's not that, Mo. I'm over you," Thes said. "It's going to SNOW. I'm giving a few special friends a heads-up."

SNOW? We haven't had *real* snow in Tupelo Landing since third grade!

"Really?" I said, kicking off my covers. "Is school out? Is this a snow day?"

"That's the problem. School's *not* out. Miss Retzyl makes that call, and she doesn't know my forecast because she's not answering her phone."

Our teacher, Priscilla Retzyl—tall, willowy, able to do math in her head—is the most normal person in my shy-of-normal life. I adore her. Secretly she likes me too, but ever since she got Caller ID she's been slow to pick up sixth graders' calls.

"Mo, will you go to her house with me?" Thes asked. "I'm an introvert and you're not."

True.

The gardenia outside my window shimmied in the moonlight. *What in the blue blazes?* Dale's face popped into view, his mama's flowered scarf pulled tight over his blond hair and knotted beneath his chin. Not a good look. "Mo," Dale whispered. "Wake up. Thes says it's going to snow."

"I know," I said, tapping on the glass. "Come to the door."

"Which door?" Thes asked.

"Not you," I replied into the phone as Dale crashed to the ground. I made an Executive Decision. "Thes, call Harm. Ask him to meet us at Miss Retzyl's house in twenty minutes for an Ensemble Beg. But you better be right about the snow."

I smoothed my T-shirt and karate pants as I strolled the length of my narrow, window-lined flat. I swung the door open and Dale bolted inside with his mongrel dog, Queen Elizabeth II, at his heels. "Hey," I said. "We got a snow mission. I'll be ready in three shakes."

"Sorry about the gardenia," he said. "I didn't want to knock, and wake up . . . anybody."

Anybody would be Miss Lana, who wakes up slow. Also the Colonel, who's moody thanks to an eleven-year brush with amnesia. The Colonel and Miss Lana are my family of choice and I am theirs. The Colonel saved me from a hurricane flood the day I was born. Together, we operate the café at the edge of town.

Dale unzipped his oversized jacket—a castoff from his

daddy, who won't need it for seven to ten years unless he gets time off for good behavior, which he won't. "Hurry, Mo. I'm sweltering to death," Dale said. "Mama made me layover."

"You mean *layer*," I said, sliding my jeans over my karate pants.

Dale, a co-founder of the Desperado Detective Agency, ain't a dead-ahead thinker, but he thinks sideways better than anybody I know.

I pulled on my red sweater and combed my unruly hair. I opened my filing cabinet, shoved aside unanswered Desperado Detective Agency letters, and snagged my orange socks.

"Get gloves too," Dale instructed as someone swished across the living room.

"Morning, Miss Lana," I called. "Dale and Queen Elizabeth are here. Can I borrow some gloves? It's going to snow."

"Snow? Really?" she said, peeking in. Miss Lana, a former child star of the Charleston community theater and a fan of Old Hollywood, gave me a wide, sleepy smile—the real one, not the one she keeps in her pocket for pain-in-the-neck customers at the café. "I love snow!"

She leaned against my doorframe, her *Gone with the Wind* bed jacket over her pink nightgown, her short coppery hair glistening in the lamplight.

"Hey, Miss Lana," Dale said, whipping his mama's flowered scarf off his head. "I hope you slept good. The scarf wasn't my idea. Mama said wear it or my ears would freeze off."

Dale's a Mama's Boy from the soles of his red snow boots to his scandalous good hair—a family trait. Because I'm a possible orphan, my family traits remain a mystery.

I tossed Dale my bomber cap and laced my plaid sneakers.

"Help yourself to my gloves, sugar," Miss Lana said. "They're in my odds-and-ends drawer." As she stumbled toward the smell of coffee, we raced to her room. I zipped to the curvy white chest of drawers. Her top drawer erupted in elastic and lace.

"*All* her drawers are odds-and-ends drawers," I muttered, opening them one by one and plucking a pair of blue driving gloves from the bottom drawer.

"Mo!" Miss Lana shrieked from the kitchen. "Don't open my bottom drawer!"

"Too late," I shouted as a note drifted to the floor. *For Mo When She's Ready.*

"Ready for what?" I murmured, uncovering a large white box. I touched a sticky spot where the note used to be as Miss Lana skidded through the door. The Colonel eased in behind her, his bottle-brush gray hair dented on one side, the plaid robe I gave him in first grade cinched at his thin waist.

"What's in here?" I asked, hoisting the box. "Can I open it? I feel ready."

"No," Miss Lana said, grabbing it. She looked at the Colonel and gave him a soft nod. He nodded back. "Tonight, sugar. When we have time to talk," she said, her voice going tinny.

Weird. Miss Lana's a theater professional. Her voice never goes tinny.

"But it has my name on it *now*."

"It's waited almost twelve years," the Colonel said. "It can wait until the end of something as rare as a snow day."

Our snow day!

"Come on," Dale said, pounding for the door.

We grabbed our bikes and blasted down the blacktop, into tiny Tupelo Landing. But with every pump of my pedals, my curiosity tapped at the lid of that mysterious box.

What's *in* it, *in* it, *in* it?

Chapter Two
A Second Thing Found

Dale and me zipped across Miss Retzyl's yard and thundered up the steps to Harm, who sat on the porch rail, one black loafer flat on the floor, the other on the bottom rail. Lately Harm practices looking good sitting on different things, in case the big-haired twins are watching. At nineteen, the twins ain't looking his way.

Harm flipped his scarf over his shoulder and nudged his dark hair from his eyes. "Hey LoBeau," he said, very cool. "What's cooking?"

Dale snickered. "Café humor. Smooth."

"Café humor, *lame,*" I said as Thes's dad, a preacher, pulled to the curb in his faded old sedan. Reverend Thompson says if Jesus rode a donkey, he's not driving a new car.

Thes hurried toward us. "What's our plan?" he asked as the porch light clicked on.

"Ad-lib," I whispered.

Miss Retzyl opened the door. "Why are you on my porch?" she asked.

"Because you don't answer your phone," I replied, very

polite. "Thank you for taking our meeting. I'm glad to see you in warm pajamas on a snow day but just between us, I always thought you'd wear a gown. I yield the floor to Thes."

Thes stepped forward. "My forecast today: five inches of snow in Tupelo Landing."

Harm leaned close. He smelled like Old Spice. Lately, he pretends to shave, in case girls like that. "Won't the town's snowplows handle that?" he whispered.

Like I said, Harm's new. The Tupelo Landing learning curve starts at the edge of town. "We don't have a snowplow because it never snows," I said. "Sometimes Tinks Williams cleans a lane with his tractor, but only if he wants to go somewhere."

I smiled at Miss Retzyl. "After declaring an Official Snow Day, please drop by the café for complimentary snow cream. Detective Starr too, if he ain't busy with traffic accidents, which he will be. Nobody in Tupelo Landing can drive in snow, but we still try."

Miss Retzyl's boyfriend, Detective Joe Starr, is the Desperados' main competition. She looked into our first flurry and smiled. "Thanks, Thes. I'll call the mayor and cancel."

"Really?" Harm said. "But it just started. In Greensboro it snowed all the time. We used to . . . Never mind," he added, shoving his hands in his pockets and grinning—a good look.

Not that I care.

"Enjoy your snow day," she said as winter breathed a curtain of snow across the sunrise. "And Mo, tell Lana I'll take her up on that snow cream."

Like I said, secretly Miss Retzyl likes me.

The sky went silver-blue with snow as we pedaled back to the café—me and Dale on our old bikes; Harm on his sleek silver ten-speed. Thes had gone home to monitor the snow.

I pushed open the café door and the radiators' steam wrapped me in a warm hug. So did Miss Lana. She'd dressed for Hollywood Snow—in her long, red velvet dress with white trim, and blond Marilyn Monroe wig. Bing Crosby crooned from the jukebox. Our Christmas lights still twinkled over the windows, and our antique aluminum tree dozed in the corner.

"Miss Retzyl hopes you'll make snow cream," I said, ditching my coat.

"Got it, sugar," she said, pointing to the window. Outside, she'd arranged pans along the hood of the Colonel's Underbird—which used to be a Thunderbird until the *T* and *H* fell off.

"Grab your aprons," the Colonel said, muscling in with a tray of coffee cups. "The town will be here soon as they find their snow gear." Harm and Dale snagged aprons. They help out at the café. In return the Colonel keeps them in pocket change and eats.

"We'll use a snow theme today," Miss Lana told me, unrolling a cotton sheet around the cash register. Miss Lana loves themes. Without a theme, she says, life feels pointless and hollow as an old tin can. "Mo, could you get the snowman salt and pepper shakers? Harm, put cinnamon in the steamer, if you don't mind. Nothing awakens memories like aroma. And Dale, enlighten the Winter Tree, please sir."

Dale looked at me. "Plug it in," I whispered, and he nodded.

Dale trotted to our aluminum tree—a memento of Miss Lana's childhood. In a few weeks, we'll switch out snowflakes for glittery red hearts, for Valentine's Day. Miss Lana can't abide an unadorned winter.

The phone rang and I scooped it up. "Café. We ain't open yet."

"What time does Miss Thornton come in?" a stranger asked. If his voice went any greasier, I could fry an egg in it.

"Who is this?" I demanded, and he slammed down the phone.

"Weird," I muttered.

The Colonel tossed a handful of mail on the counter, all of it addressed to the Desperados. We get mail from everywhere, thanks to newspaper stories on our cases and my borderline odd life.

"I hope all those folks are looking for detectives," Harm said, eyeing the envelopes. "We could use a paying case."

Lately, Harm worries about money. His granddad Mr. Red gave up moonshining when Harm moved in last summer, which means Mr. Red ain't burying any new jars of money in his woods. Instead he's digging up his life savings, jar by jar.

Harm fanned out the letters as Tinks Williams parked his tractor and slouched in with a box of groceries from the Piggly Wiggly. Tinks is Tupelo Landing's Do-It Man. He delivers things, fixes things, helps out at the café. Nobody notices him much; he's part of the town.

"Hey, Tinks," Harm muttered. "We got leaky pipes and Gramps won't even call a plumber. He's using an old dogwood branch to find the leaks. He calls it dowsing, but I call it crazy."

"Crazy ain't crazy if it works," Tinks said, heading for the kitchen.

"Choose a letter, LoBeau," Harm said. I picked one as my archenemy for life, Anna Celeste Simpson, blasted in wearing a ski outfit the color of chlorine gas.

"Morning, Harm," she said, practicing her Boy Smile.

"Harm's busy," I told her, and snapped the letter open to scan it. "Here's a long-lost niece case in Georgia, two states away—outside our Bicycle Radius," I reported.

Attila unzipped her jacket. *"A lost family member,"* she said. "How fitting. Another piece of unclaimed luggage on the baggage carousel which is your life."

"*Excuse me?*" Miss Lana said, rocking to a stop and raising her eyebrows. The Colonel says Miss Lana's eyebrows should be registered as weapons. They can stop you dead, back you up, or cut you down.

Attila shook the snow out of her perfect blond hair. "I just mean somebody's lost and so is Mo—ripped from her lost mother's arms, as you people tell it, washed into town during a hurricane. On the cul-de-sac we say you're an angel for taking her in, Miss Lana."

"Mo's *not* lost," Miss Lana said, her voice icy enough to frost a mug. "She's where she belongs. At home, with the Colonel and me."

"If you say so," Attila said, claiming a window table. "By the by, the mayor's asked *certain* families to select music for our new Sunrise Serenade Series. As a first family of Tupelo Landing, we Simpsons are leading the way. Our choice plays from the Episcopal church's steeple tomorrow morning. Miss Lana, are your people involved, I hope?"

We ain't and she knows it.

Attila's family is a first family. So are Harm's and Dale's, but they're still a shoo-in for Not Invited. Like I said, Mr. Red's an ex-moonshiner. Dale's people are mostly awaiting trial. Our family is a last family of Tupelo Landing. I washed into town, the Colonel wrecked his car and stayed, and Miss Lana showed up on the Greyhound a few days later, looking for him.

"No?" Attila said, giving Miss Lana a smile. "Pity."

Attila's a weasel. She'll bite your head off just to watch you bleed.

The door slammed against the wall and tall, thin, borderline-Gothic Skeeter MacMillan and sweet Sally Amanda Jones blasted in. Sal's the second-shortest kid in sixth. Though shaped like a tube of lipstick, she's mastered the art of strategic ruffles and curls. Dale blushed to his roots. "Hey, Salamander."

"Hello, Dale," Sal said, her eyes glowing.

Dale's blushing? Odd. Usually Sal does the blushing.

Harm opened another letter. "Here's a case in Milwaukee. Also too far."

Dale frowned. "Are you sure? Isn't that near Tarboro?"

Sal shrugged out of her plush lavender jacket. "Dale, Milwaukee's in Wisconsin—nine hundred eighty-three miles from here. You'd never make it on your bicycle," she said as Grandmother Miss Lacy Thornton eased in.

"Good morning, dears," she said, snow glistening in her blue hair. Her usual greeting, only flat. I turned her coffee cup up as she took her place at the counter.

"What's wrong?" I asked.

"Oh, a salesman of sorts is trying to hunt me down and he's getting on my nerves. He knows who my friends are, but he won't say how. He knows where I go and what I do. And I don't know who *he* is, beyond what he told me over the phone."

Dale frowned. "You got a stalker."

My legendary senses went on red alert. "He called here a little while ago, looking for you. As the richest nice person in town, you got to be careful. I'll pro bono you the Desperado Bodyguard Division until we catch him," I said. "We'll watch you twenty-four/seven."

"We have a bodyguard division?" Dale said, his face lighting up.

"Us," Harm told him. "I'll start tonight."

"Dale and me will check the rest of our correspondence at headquarters," I said as he shoved our mail beneath the counter.

"*Headquarters?* Oh. The closed-in side porch you call a flat," Attila snipped from behind her menu. "I'll have a water to start, Mo."

"Sorry, we're out," I told her as Dale sloshed by with waters for Sal and Skeeter.

The snow drifted down as the regulars drifted in, excited as kindergartners watching their first snow. The Uptown Garden Club, aka the Azalea Women, tumbled from their van and rumbled in like a chatty avalanche.

"Welcome, I'm Mo LoBeau, a possible orphan, and I'll be taking care of you today," I said as they bumped two red Formica tables together.

I glanced at the Specials Board. "Today, we're offering our Avalanche Delight—a landslide of French toast beneath a blizzard of powdered sugar. This comes with bacon and coffee for six ninety-nine."

"We'll take it," they chorused. Outside, as the snow went bigger and stronger, a restored 1955 GMC pickup truck eased into the parking lot.

Lavender!

"Specials for the Azalea Women," I shouted as Dale's big brother sauntered in like a big golden cat, snowflakes kissing his eyelashes and hair.

I shot to his side. Lavender, a race car driver on NASCAR Sabbatical while he opens his own garage, unbuttoned his denim jacket. "Hey, Mo," he said. "Snow agrees with you."

Everything about Lavender agrees with me, and he knows it. I've been asking him to marry me since first grade. "Bacon and egg sandwich for Lavender," I shouted. Lavender, who I will go out with in just seven more years, doesn't have to order out loud; I know him by heart.

"Mo!" an Azalea Woman called. "We need silverware and water!"

The first rule of being a waitress is never lose control of your table. "In a minute," I bellowed, polishing Lavender's napkin holder.

The phone rang and I grabbed it. "Café. Eat in or take out, no deliveries. This is Mo LoBeau, a possible orphan poised to earn your tip. Please tell me how."

"Mo? Gabriel Archer the Tenth. Give me Lacy Thornton. It's urgent."

The stalker. The hair on my arms stood up.

"This is her bodyguard," I said, and the café looked up. "You may speak with me."

"Tell her I have the clue of a lifetime. And Mo, I know you're only ten years old, like your friends Harm and Dale. So drop the bodyguard act."

Ten years old? Is he mad?

"For your information, Dale and I are twelve-ish," I said, very cold. "And Harm just had a birthday, making him thirteen."

"The clue's worth millions. Ask her to take my call."

I covered the mouthpiece. "Grandmother Miss Lacy, it's the stalker, Gabriel Archer the Tenth. He says he has the clue of a lifetime and it's worth millions."

The café went so quiet, I could hear the snow fall.

Grandmother Miss Lacy clattered her cup to her saucer. "Oh, for heaven's sake. It's that blasted treasure hunter again."

Treasure hunter?

She headed for the phone, her gray galoshes squeaking. "Mr. Archer? Who told you I was here? And *what* clue do you have?" she demanded as Mayor Little bustled in, stomped the snow from his tasseled loafers, and smoothed his ice-blue tie over his plump belly.

"Good morning, citizens," he said. "Tomorrow's our first Sunrise Serenade."

"Shhhhh," the Azalea Women said.

"You found *what*?" Grandmother Miss Lacy said into the phone. "Remarkable. And in Boston, of all places." She drummed her fingers on the cash register. "Very well, Mr. Archer, I'll meet with you. But not today. We're snowed in. I'll be in touch," she said, and hung up.

"*What* treasure?" I demanded as she slipped back on her stool.

"Blackbeard's treasure, dear," she said, her old eyes sparkling.

"Turkey feathers," the mayor snapped. "There's no such thing."

"Oh, but there is," she said. "Blackbeard lived in Bath, just fifty miles away. For a brief time, anyway. Terrifying man, rich as sin. Buried his treasure three hundred years ago, and no one's found it—yet. Apparently Gabriel Archer has a new clue."

Mayor Little scowled. "Mother won't be pleased."

Myrt Little, the mayor's mother, is the oldest, richest, meanest person in Tupelo Landing.

"If you ask me, she's never pleased," Sal said, very soft. People hardly ever ask Sal, but she's usually right.

Grandmother Miss Lacy picked up her fork. "Well, I'm curious and Myrt won't keep me from investigating. You

Desperados will meet with Gabriel and me, of course. If you have time. Blackbeard's treasure is one of history's greatest mysteries. I'd love for you to solve it."

If we have time? I looked at Harm, who was nodding like a yo-yo.

"We'll try to work you in," I said as Miss Lana ferried breakfast plates to Sal's table. The crowd went into full Treasure Talk as we settled in with our friends.

"That makes two things found today," Dale said, handing the blueberry syrup to Sal. "Mo's mystery box, and a clue to a treasure we didn't even know we had." He smiled at Sal. "I hope you'll still like me when I'm rich."

"Me too," she said, and he blushed again.

I looked at Grandmother Miss Lacy's dreamy little-girl smile. "She knows something she ain't telling," I whispered to Harm.

He looked over, into Mayor Little's flashing gray eyes. "And whatever it is," Harm whispered back, "the mayor doesn't like it. Not one little bit."

Chapter Three
We Open the Mystery Box

Thes nailed the forecast. That afternoon, with five inches of snow on the ground, we hit the slight slope at the ancient inn Miss Lana and Grandmother Miss Lacy own, just outside town. The hill meanders across the inn's grassy lawn, funnels through the woods, and spreads onto the vacant field next to Mr. Red and Harm's place.

Attila inched along on Tupelo Landing's only snow skis. The rest of us spun down on hubcaps and cookie sheets. During the trudge up the hill, we found Blackbeard's treasure a hundred times, and spent it a thousand ways.

Tinks roared over on his tractor around four, and Sal hitched a ride to town. A little later, the rest of us piled into Lavender's truck—the Desperados and Queen Elizabeth in the front. "Sorry, we're full," I told Attila. "Hop in the back with the rest of the sixth grade."

Lavender, who smelled like Ivory soap, muscled his old pickup along the lane as the sun slid toward the horizon. I smiled at him. "I have a once-in-a-lifetime mystery box at home. As my Intended, you're welcome to the Opening."

"Thanks, Mo," he said. "But I have a date."

Lavender spends time with the big-haired twins. A lesser person might feel threatened, but like Miss Lana says, you don't compete for love. It's either yours or it ain't.

"You're invited too, Desperados," I said.

"You don't have to ask *me* twice," Dale said as Lavender swerved into the café parking lot.

"Me either," Harm echoed as we all tumbled out.

Attila slid out of the back of the truck. Her perfect blond hair had blown up like an angry porcupine. She pushed past us, to the truck's passenger door. "I want a ride to my home on the cul de sac, Lavender," she said, climbing in. "I hope you enjoy the Sunrise Serenade tomorrow."

"Sunrise?" Lavender said. "I love music, but isn't that a little early?"

"I chose the Hallelujah Chorus." She glanced at Harm, and lowered her voice. "It's so sad about Mr. Red going broke. Of course *somebody* has to be poor, and Harm's mother *did* abandon him, so . . . well, mothers know best," she said, like that made sense.

My temper jumped. "Hey!" I shouted, grabbing the door as she tried to close it. "You can't talk about Harm like that."

"Mo's right," Lavender said. "Apologize to my friend or walk."

"I'm sorry if I misspoke, Harm," she said, and slammed the door.

A faux apology. I hate Anna Celeste Simpson.

"Ignore her, Harm," Dale said as Lavender chugged away.

Harm nodded and ambled off, but not before I saw the hurt in his eyes.

Dale looked at me. "I don't know what you're thinking, Mo, but Mama says always take the high road."

"I try to, Dale," I said. "But there's a reason they invented off-ramps. And I'll get even with Attila for hurting Harm if it kills you and me both."

After supper, Miss Lana flipped the café's sign to CLOSED and we trooped around the café and up the graceful wooden steps to the back half of our building—our home place. "Thanks for the box, whatever it is," I said, very subtle.

The Colonel sank into his chair and kicked off his boots. "Let me read Harm in on some background before we open it." He pulled a paper from his pocket. "Mo was three when I wrote this for her," he told Harm.

"Your baby letter," Dale murmured, settling in with Queen Elizabeth at his feet.

"Mo was such a cute thing," Miss Lana said, her eyes misting. "Chubby little wrists . . ."

"I wasn't chubby," I said as Harm made a note on his clue pad.

"Well," Dale said, "there was that time in third grade. Your tall did sort of go sideways."

The Colonel cleared his throat. By now I know the letter by heart, but I love to hear him read it more than I love to breathe.

Dear Soldier,

I know you wonder how we came to be here, in Tupelo Landing.

You were born during a hurricane. I imagine your mother did what people do on hurricane days: She bought food, tied the porch furniture down, fell asleep listening to the wind. No one expected a flood.

Like others, she awakened in darkness, startled by the bump of furniture against her walls. She swung her legs over the side of the bed and screamed. The floodwater lapped against her knees. She splashed across the porch and scaled the trellis as bits of other people's lives drifted by: an easy chair, an oil drum, a chicken coop with a drenched rooster perched on one side. You were born as the water crept up the roof and her world shrank smaller and smaller.

In the distance, I believe, she caught a glimmer of hope: a broken billboard spinning crazily on the tide. She wrapped you in her gown as the sign skidded across the roof. Gently, she placed you there, then cried out as the makeshift raft slipped from her hands. You spun away, my dear. And you were not afraid.

I, on the other hand, was scared out of my mind.

I awakened in a wrecked car, in a raging storm, my head howling. Winds roared. Trees fell. Worlds drowned.

Who was I? I couldn't remember. Where had I come from? I didn't know.

I slid down the bluff by the creek, grabbing great handfuls of kudzu to break my fall, and crouched by the water. My leather shoes sank into the mud. I locked my arms around my knees and rocked to keep from screaming.

I didn't know there was a dike upstream. I didn't know it would break.

"Why God?" I cried. "What do you want from me? Give me a sign."

In that instant, your billboard crashed ashore on a wall of water, cracking the back of my head. I reached for balance and touched what I thought was a puppy. Then you grabbed my finger. My God, I thought. It's a baby. I fainted dead away. That's how Macon found us the next day—me unconscious on half a billboard, you nestled in my arms, nursing on the pocket of my uniform.

"Macon. My daddy," Dale said, like Harm didn't know.

The half billboard said: ". . . Café . . . Proprietor."

Our path seemed clear.

I will always love your mother for letting you go, Soldier. And I will always love you for holding on.

Love, the Colonel

PS: I apologize for naming you Moses. I didn't know you were a girl until it was too late.

I'd read that letter a thousand times, but the Colonel's gravelly voice sent the words straight through me. "So," the Colonel said, folding it. "Questions?"

Dale and me shook our heads. Not Harm. "Yes, sir," he said, careful as walking barefoot through sandspurs. "Just . . . Well, the hurricane's fact. But you don't *know* Mo's mother climbed on a roof. Do you?"

Good question. One I'd never asked before.

"Informed supposition." The Colonel glanced into Dale's baffled eyes. "A good guess based on facts. The rivers flooded, the countryside flooded, and people climbed to their roofs for safety. Most were rescued. Some weren't."

"And the wall of water?" Harm asked.

"Fact," the Colonel said. "The dams broke, or were opened by cities upstream."

Harm pushed his hair back. I used to think he needed a haircut. Now I know he keeps it long so he can think without looking like he's thinking. "You said Mo's mother couldn't swim."

"Because a mother would have swum beside her baby. And she . . . didn't," Miss Lana said, her voice sad.

Harm nodded. "Did you keep the sign?"

Rookie questions, but sweet. "Of course not," I said. "I'd know."

"It's under the porch," the Colonel said.

Under the porch? My heart dropped like a truckload of bricks. I grabbed my jacket. "Let's check it out."

"Tomorrow, Soldier," the Colonel said. "It's dark, and the sign's become . . . a staging platform." Dale looked at him, frowning. "I piled stuff on it," the Colonel admitted.

Harm tapped his pencil. "A baby on a billboard. Why didn't Mo slide off?"

"Good question," Dale said. "I love Mo, but she's clumsy."

Miss Lana placed the box the long way on my lap. "We decided we'd give this to you when you were ready, sugar. That day has come. Open it."

I lifted the lid and pushed aside brittle tissue paper. *"A sweater?"*

"You were wrapped in the scrap of a gown, with this over top," she said as I gently lifted out an indigo sweater. "She . . . or *someone* tied you in place with its arms. You can see how they're stretched."

My heart hammered as I lifted the sweater to my face. It smelled like a lost river and forgotten rain.

It's small, I thought. She was thin, like me. This is how big my mother was, this is how wide. She fit in this space. Her arms went here. This collar touched her neck.

My breath felt far away. Harm's voice brought me back. "Did you check it for DNA?"

The Colonel sighed. "DNA tests were too expensive back then."

"They're not now," Harm said. "And they could prove whether Mo's biological mother wore it. And if she had a police record, DNA could identify her," he added, his voice quick.

"We can ask Starr to run it," Dale said. "Or Skeeter, but she's expensive."

Test it? I just found it! This was moving fast. *Too fast.*

Dale studied the box top's raised letters. "Mo, your mom shopped at Belk's."

"No," Miss Lana said. "That's my box, Dale. I put the things inside."

Something in the box glinted. "This is yours too," she said, lifting a golden, tear-shaped pendant with an engraved initial: *J*. I let its delicate chain flow over the back of my hand.

"The letter *J*. Was it hers?" I squeezed the necklace so tight, it bit my hand.

"Perhaps. I found the chain looped around your ankle," the Colonel said.

Dale cleared his throat. "It probably got caught in the rolls of . . . chubby."

"We couldn't get a good fingerprint," the Colonel said.

"J. First name? Last?" Harm asked, making a note.

Miss Lana shrugged. "First, probably. We made calls, placed ads, sent messages, but . . ." She looked at me. "We thought you'd like to wear it someday."

My feelings fluttered like startled birds. "Thank you. I love these things. But . . . but why didn't you tell me before?" I asked, trying to sand the ragged from my voice.

Miss Lana's voice held steady and calm. "I thought of giving you the necklace earlier. But I was afraid you'd lose it. And the sweater would have swallowed you alive—until now."

"We decided we'd give it to you when you were old enough. Today you are, and we have," the Colonel said, very firm. "There's one more thing in that box."

Excitement tightened iron bands around my chest as Miss Lana moved the last layer of tissue. "The ads we placed, looking for your . . . other people. And newspaper articles about the hurricane, and flood."

"Great background," Harm murmured. "If you decide to look for her again."

I stared at the sweater, and waited to drift from the ceiling and settle in my body. "Is there anything else you forgot to mention? I mean, I only been looking for her my entire life."

"Yes," Miss Lana said. "I forgot to mention how much we

love you and how grateful we are to have you in our lives."

The Colonel stretched. "My bubbly nature is losing its fizz. Who wants snow cream?"

"Me," Dale said. "Queen Elizabeth gets brain-freeze."

I looked at Miss Lana and then the Colonel, and searched for the right words for people that saved you and raised you, and packed your past in a box until you were old enough to hold it in your hands. The words ain't been made. I hugged Miss Lana, who's warm and soft as a feather bed. Then I squeezed the Colonel, who hugs like a bag of confused bolts.

It's funny how two hugs can feel so different, and still be true.

An hour later, Dale settled on the couch and Harm hurried to Grandmother Miss Lacy's to bodyguard her. I slipped into bed and opened Volume 7 of the *Piggly Wiggly Chronicles* on my lap. Volumes 1–6 sit in a bright line across my shelf—spiral notebooks filled with a lifetime of letters to my Upstream Mother.

I used to think she would write back, or find me. One day, I knew she wouldn't. I kept writing anyway, to stay in step with my heart. Tonight, for the first time in a long time, I felt like I might actually find her. I picked up my pen.

Dear Upstream Mother,

I got your sweater beside me, so close I can

almost feel it breathe. And your necklace, with its tear-shaped pendant.

Touching them is almost touching you.

Your lost girl,

Mo

I snuggled in and waited for sleep, but my thoughts whirled like the lights on Miss Lana's Winter Tree: the sign, the sweater, the pendant . . . New clues. But what if I *still* can't find her? What if I do find her, and she doesn't want me?

I sat up, my heart pounding.

I had too much new in my life. I needed something familiar. I grabbed the phone and dialed Grandmother Miss Lacy's number.

"Hello?" Harm murmured, and I pictured him clutching her avocado-green phone.

"It's Mo. I got a plan for Attila." I whispered quick instructions, hung up, and settled back into bed.

There's comfort in the familiar, I thought, dozing off. Even when the familiar is revenge.

Chapter Four
Revenge Plus a Slimeball

At five o'clock the next morning, I slipped into the living room primed for action. Nobody hurts my people and gets away with it, especially not Anna Celeste Simpson. Dale slept flung across the settee, his arms wide open to dreams. "Wake up," I whispered.

"Where?" he demanded, sitting up. Queen Elizabeth growled.

"Mo's living room," I whispered. "We got to meet Harm. Now."

He looked around like a flustered blond owl. "Is it still dark again or is this yesterday?"

Dale doesn't wake up good.

Moments later Dale, Harm, and me trudged down Last Street, the moonlight soft as a baby's kiss on the snow. Harm stuffed his hands in his pockets. "Sunrise is at six thirty. We should be in and out of the steeple, but if we're not, you did bring an Emergency Exit Plan, right, Mo?"

I squeezed the package beneath my jacket. "Right."

Dale plucked a branch from the snow and side-armed it

into a six-inch drift. "Liz! Fetch!" Queen Elizabeth tossed her head and trotted in the opposite direction.

"So," Harm said, walking backwards to face me. "New clues about Upstream Mother. When do we start?"

My stomach swayed like a hammock full of monkeys.

"We have better resources now," Harm said, breath steaming. "We have Miss Lana, Detective Starr, and Lavender. Skeeter and Sal, with their genius and connections. That sign could hold a thousand clues, Mo. We can DNA-check the sweater. Plus, Mo, you've got the best-looking detectives in Tupelo Landing," he said, grinning.

"We *are* nice-looking," Dale said. "And Mama says I haven't even bloomed. She says I'll be tall as Lavender when I blossom, and better-looking too."

Nobody will ever be better-looking than Lavender. Still, as a best friend, I nodded.

"This is what you always wanted, Mo," Harm said. "Right?"

"Right," I said, trying to settle the swirl inside me.

Dale studied my face. "Take your time, Mo," he said. "Sometimes you got to wait for your heart to catch its breath before you know which way to go."

Dale reads me like footprints across snow.

We crunched to a halt before the tiny Episcopal church. A small sign by the door read: FOUNDED 1726.

"Around back," I said, the snow squeaking as I led the way to the back door.

"Breaking and entering a church," Dale muttered. "Mama won't like this."

"You can't break and enter if it ain't locked, and they never lock the back door," I said, slipping inside.

As we scaled the steeple's narrow stairs, Dale tugged a flashlight from his red snow boot. He tilted the beam to a giant sound system as Queen Elizabeth plunked down.

"Wow, this system's huge," Harm said. He examined the switchboard and flipped a switch. "Let's see. This is the mic, and . . ." He lifted a vinyl from the turntable. "The Hallelujah Chorus. What did you bring, Mo?" he asked, setting Attila's selection aside.

I slid a vinyl from beneath my jacket. "Elvis. 'Blue Suede Shoes.'"

Harm grinned, rocked his slim body to the side, and rose onto his toes à la Elvis. "Well it's one for the money, two for the show . . ." he sang, going into a graceful, knee-wobbling dance. Dale grabbed the dead microphone and joined in, mugging to the mic as their voices flowed together like rivers twirling toward the same happy sea.

Dale and Harm are musical. I ain't.

As Harm slipped Elvis onto the turntable, Dale and me went to the window and gazed out over the curve of our river, and our sleeping town.

Harm flipped a switch and the mic screeched, its cry piercing the first hint of day.

A light clicked on, over on First Street. "Sorry," Harm whispered.

Dale pointed to the snowbank beside the river. "Who's *that?*" A broad-shouldered man stepped from the pines, his long black cape flowing. He swept off his wide-brimmed hat and waved it at a low-flying airplane as a smaller figure stepped up beside him, hand on hip.

"Clowns," Dale whispered, his voice shaking. Dale has a terror of clowns.

"Nah," Harm said, glancing out the window. "Just a couple of strangers. Only . . . who's that woman?" he asked. "She reminds me of . . ."

"Of who?" I asked as she melted back into the woods.

"Nobody," he muttered. "I think this thing's set up. Let's get out of here."

The man turned like he could feel Dale's stare, raised his arm—and pointed straight at us. Dale screamed into the mic, blasting his terror across the town. I staggered back, slamming into Harm—whose elbow hit the play switch. Elvis went spinning: "Well it's one for the money, two for the show, three to get ready, now, go, cat, go but don't you step on my blue suede shoes . . ."

House lights blinked on all over town.

Harm snatched up the needle, scratching Elvis silent. A bird chirped. A siren sounded in the distance and the man disappeared into the pines.

A blue light swirled across the snow—coming straight for us. Only one man in town owns a blue light and siren: Detective Joe Starr.

"I told you we shouldn't break into a church," Dale said, his eyes filling with tears. "*Now* what are we going to do?"

"Run," I said, shoving him toward the steps. "Run!"

As Harm, Dale, and Queen Elizabeth fled in a wild tangle of paws and shoes, I yanked my Emergency Escape Plan from my jeans pocket. I tossed the note to the floor and thundered behind them as Detective Joe Starr's Impala wheeled into the back parking lot, blue light spinning. "You're surrounded," Starr shouted. "Come out with your hands up!"

"Like he can do a Solo Surround," Dale said, very scornful.

"This way," I said, pushing into the sanctuary. We pelted across the ancient stone floor—clap, clap, *clonk*. My foot went off-balance against a wide, flat stone as it gave slightly beneath my foot. I slammed into Harm.

"Graceful, LoBeau," he whispered.

Miss Lana says grace may come with puberty, but I ain't holding my breath.

We jetted through the door and across the snowy lawn. "We'll never make the café," I gasped. "Grandmother Miss Lacy's house. Go!"

Moments later we skidded across Grandmother Miss Lacy's icy porch and pounded on her door. "What on earth?" she cried, swinging it open.

We zipped inside. Harm turned out the foyer light as Dale and Liz crouched beneath a window. I edged the draperies aside, breathing hard.

"What's going on?" Grandmother Miss Lacy looked at us, her old eyes huge behind her bifocals.

"Nothing," we said as Starr's patrol car purred by.

She burst out laughing. "I was just wondering who played Elvis in the steeple. I don't suppose *you* know."

"We plead the fourth," Dale said, wiping the snow from Liz's whiskers.

"He means the fifth," I told her as someone stomped across her porch and knocked.

"Hide," she whispered. I stepped behind a drapery as the boys dove for cover, Queen Elizabeth at Dale's side. Grandmother Miss Lacy swung open the door. "Yes?"

The man from the river swept off his hat: black curls, high cheekbones, gray eyes. A razor-thin scar ran from the outer edge of his right eyebrow, down his jawline, to his square chin. He flashed a megawatt smile and dropped a briefcase on the floor. "Miss Thornton? Gabriel Archer the Tenth, at your service."

Gabriel Archer the Tenth? The treasure hunter?

Miss Lana says always make an entrance. I waited a beat and swept the drapery aside. "Greetings," I said, and weighed my next move.

Dale, who babbles when nervous, didn't weigh nothing. He popped up from behind a fern. "Yes, she's Miss Lacy Thornton. I'm Dale, and that's Mo LoBeau, Miss Thornton's honorary granddaughter. I'm glad you're not a clown," he added as Harm casually rose from behind a chair.

"And you must be Harm Crenshaw," Gabriel said, smiling like we were normal.

Every red flag I own went up. "How do you know Harm?"

"You Desperados are in the newspapers. The photos don't do you justice."

Flattery. Even when I hate it, I like it.

"Charming town," he added. "Love the old church. Miss Thornton, I just happened to be in Tupelo Landing, with that clue of a lifetime—"

"No one just *happens* to be in Tupelo Landing, Mr. Archer," she interrupted. "But as long as you're here, take a seat in the parlor. I won't be a minute."

He walked into the parlor like he owned it and tossed his hat on a table.

"Keep an eye on him while I dress. If he tries anything, use this," she whispered, handing me her walking stick.

Excellent.

We followed him into the parlor, which is prim and

neat, and I sat on her swoop-back sofa, her cane across my knees. Gabriel explored the mantel—my school photos, a black-and-white of a very young Grandmother Miss Lacy. "Stylish," he said. He wandered to the window, took out his cell phone, and held it up. Like we got reception in Tupelo Landing.

"He needs to wash his hair," Dale whispered.

"That's product," Harm told him. "We should try it." Lately Harm thinks about his hair.

"I hate to be nosy," I lied, very casual, "but how did you get here?"

"A red Jaguar pulling a trailer of very expensive gear. I parked it at the bridge, and explored your river. Lovely waterfront."

Dale frowned. "A Jaguar with a trailer hitch? Lavender won't like that."

"Lavender," Gabriel murmured, leafing through Grandmother Miss Lacy's photo album. "The race car driver." He turned a page. I glanced over to see a photo of Tinks in an old-timey band uniform, maybe from high school. "And here's Tinks Williams as a boy," he said, the hint of a smile in his voice. "Looks like he was in an awkward stage."

"He still is," Dale said, tipping the album shut. "How do you know Tinks?"

"And how do you know Lavender?" I glanced at Harm.

"And who was that woman you were with this morning? And how'd you get that scar on your face?"

Gabriel perched on a delicate chair. "I do my research. The woman's a friend from the city. And I got the scar in a sword fight, in Madagascar," he said as Grandmother Miss Lacy bustled in, her navy suit trim, her pale hair shimmering. She took her usual chair.

"Tell me, Mr. Archer: What can I do for you?"

"The question is, what can I do for *you?*" Gabriel leaned toward her, Zorro handsome. "But before I explain, perhaps the Desperados could be excused."

"There is no excuse for us," Dale said, very steely.

"The Desperados stay," she agreed, and I took out my clue pad. "We were on our way to breakfast, so please be succinct."

Dale looked at me. "Make it snappy," I whispered, and he nodded.

Gabriel hesitated like a card player reshuffling his hand. "Very well. We all know of Blackbeard's treasure. Gold, silver, jewels—much of it from Spanish treasure ships. Scores of treasure hunters have looked for it. Have they found it? No. Why?"

"They're wrong?" Dale guessed.

"Exactly," Gabriel said. "They've looked in Bath, where Blackbeard lived. They've looked on Ocracoke, where he died, or around Beaufort, where he sank his own ship. They've looked in Canada, where people say he mingled his treasure with Captain Kidd's. They haven't found it simply because the treasure's in Tupelo Landing. And I have the clue that proves it."

He snapped open his briefcase and pulled out a paper.

"Is that your clue?" I asked. He ignored me.

"Miss Thornton, I use the latest equipment—Ground Penetrating Radar, metal detectors, aerial photography." He smiled. "Here's my resume. Duke University, and a treasure hunter ever since: Madagascar, Spain, the Florida Keys. And here's your contract," he said, putting both papers on her end table.

"You own the land around Tupelo Landing, and I own the clue. Let me search your property and I'll give you *half* of my find. I'll set up in that old fishing shack on the river—I won't be even a shade of trouble. This is a fair offer based on bona fide information."

Dale looked at Harm. "Bona fide," Harm whispered. "It means good faith."

Sometimes I think Harm and me are subtitles for Dale's life.

"And the clue?" she asked.

"That's between me and a pirate," he said. "And you, after you sign my contract. One last thing," he said. "I don't do business with children other than my niece, Ruby. It's too dangerous. Six men have died hunting for this treasure—which is guarded by a curse."

"A curse?" Dale said, going pale. Dale's not good with curses.

"Piffle," Grandmother Miss Lacy replied. "I don't believe in curses, Mr. Archer, and I hope you won't waste any more time trying to scare me. To be clear, I own *most* of the land around Tupelo Landing. Not all of it. Leave your contract and your resume. Call me at two p.m. for my answer. Harm," she said, "would you show our visitor out?"

Harm, who's practically her grandson if her and Mr. Red ever get married, walked him out. We watched Gabriel stroll toward the river, a stark black figure against the snow.

"You don't like him," I said, watching Grandmother Miss Lacy's face.

"Not really. He's pushy," she said, walking to her mantel and plucking an old book. "But I often do business with people I don't like. Here's a book you Desperados might enjoy. I did, at your age. It's called *Pirates: Their Blood-Curdling Symbols and Very Short Lives*. Chapter three is particularly chilling."

"Thank you, but I feel like I just read one," I said. Dale backed away like she was holding a spitting, coiling serpent, but Harm took the old book.

"Thanks," he said. "I like to read when I can't sleep."

"I'm sorry you can't sleep, dear," she said, and hesitated. "I've offered to lend Red money to repair your home and his truck, but . . . ." She shrugged delicately. "You're always welcome here. Both of you." She headed for the door. "Let's go to breakfast."

"Wait," I said. "Grandmother Miss Lacy, if you sign Gabriel's contract, he'll keep us out of the hunt. Harm and Mr. Red need that money. And Dale and me could use a treasure too."

She slipped her clear plastic bonnet over her blued hair and tied it under her chin.

"You may not be treasure hunting with Gabriel Archer if I sign," she said, very easy. "But trust me: You'll be in the hunt with *another* client by day's end, or my name's not Lacy Thornton."

Dale looked at her, his face thoughtful. "But your name *is* Lacy Thornton."

"Bingo," she replied, and led the way to her car.

Chapter Five
A Narrow Escape

I briefed Grandmother Miss Lacy on my new Upstream Mother clues as we inched to the café in her Buick. After she parked, I leaned forward to show her my pendant.

"It's lovely," she murmured, cupping it in her hand. "*J* makes such a beautiful sound. Jasmine, Jennifer, Joslyn . . ."

"They kept the sign I rode into town too. We're clue-checking it after breakfast. And I got her sweater. I want to wear it but so far, I ain't."

Her old eyes went soft. "It looks like we have two treasure hunts on our hands. One of the world and one of the heart." She scanned the packed parking lot. "I'd say Elvis has shaken up the town," she said, smiling.

She was right. Elvis in the Steeple was the Topic du Jour as we swaggered in.

Attila Celeste Simpson stood by the jukebox, red-faced. She stomped her foot. "For the last time, my family did *not* choose 'Blue Suede Shoes' for the Sunrise Serenade," she shrieked. "Father is a dentist, for heaven's sake. We've been sabotaged." She pointed at us. "Confess."

"I'm not allowed to confess," Dale said, heading over to give Lavender a hug.

A blast of cold swept across the room as Mayor Little stalked in. "Lawlessness in the spire," he fumed. "Dale, if your father weren't a long-term guest of the state, I'd suspect him."

"Yes," Dale said, very serene. "Hard time is an excellent alibi."

"I'm sad Anna Celeste has come to this," I said. "I had such hope for her."

"Manners, sugar," Miss Lana whispered, swishing by. Thanks to Miss Lana, I got professional-level manners. Thanks to my yellow belt in karate and the Colonel, I also possess wolverine-level fighting skills.

Yin and yang.

The mayor plopped onto a stool. "Welcome," I said, scanning the Specials Board. "Today we got the Colonel's Rock-and-Roll Casserole—a popular upbeat of eggs, cheese, and sausage, served with Hunka Hunka Steaming Grits. For vegans, we got Tofu Tender, Tofu True."

"Two Rock-and-Roll Casseroles. One for here, one to go—for Mother," he said as Detective Joe Starr stomped in.

Crud. I went innocent as snow.

"Greetings, Detective Starr. Are you off-duty?" I asked. "I hope so, because we have a blue-light special, free to off-duty cops only. All you can eat for two ninety-nine."

"Break-in at the Episcopal church," he said, tossing his hat on a table. "Thoughts?"

"I'm blank," I said.

Dale went inscrutable as long division. "I'm blank too. So is Queen Elizabeth. Harm hasn't known anything since he moved to town."

"So true," Attila murmured.

"Really? I'm surprised since I followed your tracks across the churchyard." He flipped open his notepad. "A pair of girls' sneakers, a pair of snow boots, a pair of slick-soled loafers."

The café gaze went from my plaid sneakers, to Dale's snow boots, to Harm's loafers. Starr flipped the page. "And a set of dog tracks." The café looked at Queen Elizabeth.

"Footprints are circumstantial," I said. "We maybe visited the church yard *yesterday*."

"And there's this," Starr said, pulling my Emergency Escape Plan from his pocket. "The intruder dropped a sixth-grade math paper in the steeple. Somebody made an A-plus."

"Automatic alibi for me," Dale said, relaxing.

"Mo makes A's," Attila said, smiling like a spider with a web to spin. "So does Harm."

Starr swaggered toward me. Harm looked out the window. Dale closed his eyes. Starr veered and dropped the paper on Attila's table. "Yours, I believe, Anna Celeste."

Attila stared at the math paper I'd tossed as we ran down the steeple stairs. "I didn't! I never!" she sputtered, going red. "I mean, that's my old math paper, but somebody stole it from my desk weeks ago. Or . . ."

"Arrest her!" I cried, and the café gasped.

"Whoa," Harm said, dark eyes twinkling. "I'd hate for Anna to have a criminal record, even if she is . . . well, Anna."

"Thank you," Attila said, blinking back tears. "But I didn't . . ."

"Harm's right, Detective," Grandmother Miss Lacy said, buttering her toast. "Besides, Elvis is practically medicinal. He certainly invigorates me." She smiled at Attila. "Thank you."

"But . . ." Attila said.

"As for the Desperados," Grandmother Miss Lacy continued, "I can vouch for them. They spent the morning with me."

Nothing says *I love you* like an alibi.

The Colonel spun Lavender's sandwich down the counter. I rushed over with the black pepper. "Thanks, Mo," Lavender whispered.

I love it when he whispers.

"An arrest might be unpopular, Mr. Mayor," Lavender said. "And this *is* an election year."

The mayor froze. He fears elections like Dale fears clowns.

"What the hay," he said. "All is forgiven, dear Anna

Celeste. No charges, Detective Starr. Vote for Mayor Little, the mayor who cares."

Anna stomped her foot. "But I haven't *done* anything."

A white van pulled up and the Azalea Women rolled in, Gabriel Archer bobbing among them like a happy cork.

"Everyone, meet Gabriel Archer," an Azalea Woman cried. "A treasure hunter."

Silverware clattered to plates. The big-haired twins stood up to get a better look.

Gabriel swirled his cape over the back of a chair and winked at Miss Lana.

"I do the cooking, wink at me," the Colonel growled. The Colonel hates strangers. Also most of the people we know. "What's your business here?"

"Blackbeard's treasure," Gabriel replied, and smiled around the room.

"Balderdash," the mayor said. "Pirates never came this far inland," he added as sixth grader Jake Exum—short, no-neck, jeans—swaggered to Gabriel like a pirate himself.

"Need crew? My brother Jimmy and me have shovels."

Unlikely. I flipped open my pad and made a note: *Lock Miss Lana's toolshed.*

"Thanks," Gabriel said, "but I have a crew. A friend, and my niece, Ruby. This is too dangerous for amateurs. This treasure's cursed." He made his voice swirl dark as his cape: *"Surge of blood, Snap of bone, Loss of mortal breath. Seek my treasure, Scurvy Dog, and trade your life for death."* He flipped back to his regular voice. "So, what's good here?"

"Everything," I said, grabbing my order pad. Miss Lana says to know a person's soul, see how he treats a waitress. "I'm Mo, a possible orphan, and I'll be taking your order. For you, I recommend the Silver-Dollar Pancakes. This comes with unlimited water and air for sixteen ninety-five, not including tip—which I suggest thirty percent. Coffee and bacon run extra."

Gabriel looked at the mayor. "I thought you said pirates didn't come this far inland."

"A treasure hunter. This is *your* doing," the mayor said, glaring at Grandmother Miss Lacy. "I warn you, if you betrayed Mother . . ."

A betrayal? In Tupelo Landing? Even the Colonel froze, his cloth in mid-swipe.

The mayor dropped a twenty by his cup. *A six-dollar tip!* "Mo, wrap my special with Mother's. Bring my change with our delivery," he said. Crud. No tip, as usual.

I gave him my Professional Smile. "I'd love to deliver for free, but my bike doesn't have snow chains, plus we don't deliver. I hate to turn you down, but no," I said as he scrawled a note: *Come to my house. Mother will make you rich beyond your wildest dreams.*

"On the other hand, we'll be there in five minutes," I said as he stomped out the door.

Attila's mother's Cadillac swerved around the mayor and tootled the horn. "You framed me, Mo," Attila said. "You embarrassed me in front of *my* town."

"It's my town too," I said, my ears going red.

Her eyes went narrow and mean. "You act like a hotshot detective, Mo, but you're scared to solve the only mystery that matters in your life. Of course, I understand why." She sighed, zipping her jacket. "Your Upstream Mother probably doesn't want you any more than we do. So sad to be a throwaway girl like you."

The café gasped.

"Wow, Anna, that was vicious—even for you," Harm said.

Dale looked at me. "Count to ten," he said. "One, two . . . "

But my temper hit my mouth like Lavender's car hits the racetrack—tires smoking. "I ain't a throwaway girl, you grits-for-brains," I shouted. "And she does too want me, and I ain't afraid to look. For your information, the Desperados reopened her case last night. With new clues. We'll find my mother. Soon."

Miss Lana gasped. She looked like Dale when a football knocks the air out of him. She breathed in sharp, and set her chin. "You can count on me, sugar. And the Colonel too."

I nodded. I been counting on Miss Lana and the Colonel all my life.

Miss Lana strolled across the room like the café royalty she is, and opened the door. "Mo has *never* been thrown away, though she was most gratefully found," she said, zeroing in on Attila. "Don't come back without some manners." She slammed the door behind her.

My heart was still pounding as Attila's beige Cadillac pulled away.

I gave Miss Lana a hug, and Dale slipped up beside me. "I know your temper's your life's work and you just crashed and burned with that, but Mama says you don't lose until you stop trying. Let's go check your sign, Mo. We need your baby clues. All of them. We got to find your Upstream Mother or deal with Attila's mouth the rest of our lives."

Lavender dropped a ten. "Good luck, Desperados. I'm going to Harm's."

"Right. Our stupid truck," Harm muttered. "Any idea what's wrong with it?"

"Probably the transmission," he said.

"That's three hundred dollars easy," Harm said, looking sick.

"Don't worry, Harm. Red and I'll work it out," Lavender said, and sauntered away.

The Colonel says a good leader leads with her brains and her heart. I pulled the mayor's note from my pocket: *Rich beyond your wildest dreams.*

My sign's been waiting for me all my life. But Harm needs a paying job now.

I snagged the mayor's delivery. "Mount up, Desperados," I said. "Get ready to meet your wildest dreams."

Chapter Six
Beyond Our Wildest Dreams

Two shakes later, as we eased through Mrs. Little's Thorny Plant Collection, the mayor's door swung open. "Mother's in the parlor. Leave your shoes by the door," he said, snagging his takeout and fading down the hall. We kicked off our shoes.

"Greetings," I said as we filed into the parlor.

Mrs. Little sat in a rocker facing the moth-bitten settee, her face sallow, her yellow-streaked gray hair swept up in a tight bun. "Sit," she said.

"As you may have seen on our website, our initial fifteen-minute consultation is free. Please begin," I said, taking out my clue pad.

Dale looked at me, his eyebrows sky-high. "We have a website?"

"No," I whispered. Then louder: "The mayor mentioned riches."

She nodded. "You'll start today. We'll pay you fifteen percent."

Dale looked at me. "What's she talking about?" Dale kills me. How would *I* know what she's talking about?

"We understand completely," I said, very smooth. "As borderline professionals, we need our standard fee of . . ." I hesitated. We have no standard fee.

"Sixty percent," Harm said, very smooth. "Plus nine hundred dollars in advance."

Is he mad? Who would pay us that much?

"In cash," I said.

"Plus snacks," Dale added.

"That's piracy, Desperados," the mayor said, bustling in with Fig Newtons and milk. "We'll give you twenty percent of Blackbeard's treasure and not one doubloon more."

Blackbeard's treasure?

"Fifty percent," Harm said. "Same as Gabriel Archer's fee."

She adjusted her black shawl. "Gabriel Archer is an adult with a track record. He's found treasures all over the world. You are nosy children with gall. Forty percent."

"We're the best detectives in Tupelo Landing," I said. "Fifty percent plus our advance. *If* we take your case. I hate to rush you, but we have another client."

"*Fifty percent then,*" Mrs. Little snapped. "That Mosquito person can draw up a contract. And we'll sign it in blood," she added, eyes glittering.

Dale reached for his milk. "You mean Skeeter. No blood. Mama wouldn't like it."

"How do I know I can trust you?" she demanded as Dale stuffed a cookie in his mouth.

"Ooo ha far urd," Dale said.

"And our word is gold," I added.

"Fine. But if Gabriel Archer and that goody-two-shoes Lacy Thornton find the treasure first, the nine hundred dollars come home to me. Son, get the cash."

The mayor went to the mantel and thumped a panel. It swung open on a small safe. Inside sat a heap of oddly shaped coins. Also a jumble of diamond rings and a stack of cash. "Mother's engagement rings," he said, following my gaze.

He counted nine hundred dollars out on the table. "I hope I have your attention," he said.

"You do," we chorused.

"Then here's our story," he said, his round face earnest. "And it cannot leave this room."

He turned a carved chair to us and sat down. "The treasure begins with Mary Ormond—Blackbeard's fourteenth wife."

Dale whistled. "Fourteen wives. That's a lot of alimony. Mama says—"

Mrs. Little stomped her foot. "He didn't *divorce* his wives. He killed them, or left them to starve. Or worse. And he soon planned to kill Mary—who was pregnant with his child. Mary and her friend Peg-Leg caught wind of his murderous plan. They loaded a treasure into a skiff in the dead of night, rowed upriver, and built a house. *This* house."

Harm gasped. "Mary stole Blackbeard's treasure?"

The mayor frowned. "*Stole* is such a harsh word," he said. "Let's say she set it free and it didn't come home to him. Mary and Peg-Leg settled down, and she had her baby. Sadly, Blackbeard's cut-throats came one day without warning, and Mary and her little family were forced to flee—leaving the treasure behind."

Harm whistled. "Then the treasure really is here, just like Gabriel Archer said."

"Yes," the mayor said.

Mrs. Little hunched forward. "Mary left one clue. I looked into it myself, years ago. Lacy Thornton and Red Baker helped me." She tugged a scrap of paper from her pocket: *"Here's our oath: We—Myrt, Lacy, and Red—solemnly swear to find Blackbeard's treasure, share and share alike."*

"Incredible," Harm said as she passed it to him. "This really *is* signed in blood."

"Take our case and you'll have Mary Ormond's clue, *and* access to her old home. This house," the mayor said, padding to the bookcase and taking down a small box. He lifted a note from the box and read Mary's clue:

Look to my roof for clues to lost treasures:

Death's trail, upon reflection, leads to rich pleasures.

"*Death's trail?* That doesn't sound good," Dale said.

Harm ignored him. "Mrs. Little, the clue says *look to my roof.* Did you search it?"

She hacked into a black hankie. "Do I look stupid?"

"Rhetorical," I whispered, and Dale nodded.

"Father had the wooden shingles removed so Lacy, Red, and I could examine them one by one. He would have helped, but a tree fell on a windless day, crushing him like a bug."

"*Blackbeard's* curse," Dale whispered, the blood leaving his face.

"There is no curse, short boy!" Mrs. Little shrieked. "The shingles are stacked in the attic. Maybe you'll see the clue we missed. Find my treasure and you'll be rich. Fail and you get nothing."

"Excuse us while we vote," I said, and we filed into the hallway.

"Yes," Harm said before I could ask. "My three hundred dollars will repair our truck."

"No," Dale said. "The treasure's cursed, and Upstream Mother's more important. Two cases, plus school, plus Queen Elizabeth, plus chores—it's too much."

"Dale, we'll be rich," Harm said. "You can hire somebody to do your chores. And buy Miss Rose a car that cranks *every blessed time*."

Still, Dale shook his head. "You know how my life's been so far. Add a curse . . ."

Harm turned to me. "Mo, you'll have enough money to search for Upstream Mother no matter *what* it takes.

Television ads, radio, travel . . . This is the chance of a lifetime, don't let it get away. Everybody vote. I say yes."

Excitement and curiosity rustled like a baby dragon inside me. With a treasure, I'd set up an Upstream Mother search that could not fail. "Yes," I said.

Dale sighed. "I'll say yes to make it monotonous, but my heart says no."

"You mean unanimous," I told him.

"Okay, but only if we start *tomorrow,*" he said. "Today we check Mo's sign."

"Deal," Harm and I said. We filed into the parlor. "We can start tomorrow."

"Wonderful," the mayor replied, slipping the cash into an envelope. "I'll deliver this to your guardians, for your college funds."

"College fund?" Harm yelped. "That wasn't our deal. I want my money now."

"Fine print," Mrs. Little snapped. "Double-cross us, and you'll rue the day you met me."

I opened my notepad and clicked my pen. *Look up "rue."*

"Back at you," I said, very professional. I plucked Mary Ormond's clue from the mayor's fingertips, and we headed for the door.

Chapter Seven
Hideous, In Fact

A little later, Dale peered beneath my back porch. "Doesn't the Colonel ever throw anything away?"

"*He* does," I said, loading film into my old-timey camera. "Miss Lana doesn't. Things are like people to her. She doesn't want to hurt their feelings."

I snapped a photo of Harm sitting on the steps, *Pirates: Their Blood-Curdling Symbols and Very Short Lives* open on his knee. "Listen to this," he said, pushing his hair back. "Blackbeard's treasure includes Spanish jewels, a famous silver cup, gold coins, and pieces of eight."

"Pieces of eight what?" Dale asked, grabbing a stick and raking a spiderweb away.

"Silver coins they broke into eight bits, for change. That's why old people say a quarter's worth two bits. Get it? Two-eighths equals a quarter."

"Pirate fractions," Dale muttered. "That's just wrong."

Harm turned the page. "Blackbeard died at Ocracoke Island, on North Carolina's Outer Banks. But most of his crew was hanged in Virginia. Check out his flag," he said, turning the book toward us. On the flag's black background, a milk-white skeleton held a goblet in its right hand, and speared a red bleeding heart with its left.

"He was ambledextrous," Dale said. "Both-handed."

"You mean ambidextrous," I said as he crawled beneath the porch.

Dale yelped and backed out. A sliver of glass glinted in his palm. "The curse," he said as I teased the glass free.

A moment later he sailed back under, bumping and thumping beneath the porch. "Out-coming," he called. My baby bike skidded out, its front wheel crumpled. A broken ice cream freezer. The Colonel's old boots. "Found it!" Dale called. "Pull!"

A cobwebby piece of a sign skidded across the snow—a white sign with faint red letters:

. . . Café

. . . Proprietor

Dale rolled out and shook the dirt from his hair. "So this is a birth sign," he said, hopping up. "I always wanted to see one."

Harm frowned. "Dale, a birth sign is . . ." He looked into Dale's eyes. "Never mind. Look at that trim," he said. "It's ugly. Hideous, in fact."

Understatement.

I touched the sign and tried not to think how Upstream Mother felt, grabbing hold.

Dale studied the trim. "Cows plus cars plus fish and crabs, all roped together like a nightmare rodeo. You rode into town on an ugly piece of ordinary."

A voice sounded off in my mind: *What did you expect, Mo? A return address?*

"Mo, we need photos of this trim for our files," Harm said. We heaved the sign upright. I lined up the shot, Harm and Dale on each side, smiling. *Click, click, click.* I walked around.

"This sign's useless," I said, trying not to cry.

"Useless?" Harm said, shocked. "Mo, it's great. It's so ugly, somebody will know it. And it says exactly what the Colonel says it did. Which tells us he's a reliable witness, even if he did hit his head that night. And that means we can trust the rest of his letter too."

Smart, I thought, turning the sign into a lie-detector test.

"Listen, I'd like to take the lead on this case," he said, muscling the sign beneath the house and spanking his hands clean. "Sometimes the best thing for an old mystery is a new set of eyes."

Harm? Taking the lead on the mystery that is my life?

"Thanks, but I got it," I said, and waited for Dale to back me up. He didn't.

"Harm asked great questions last night and we didn't, because we heard your story so many times it all sounded true," Dale said. "He asked for your birth sign, and we didn't. And he lie-detectored the sign and we didn't. He's right, Mo. Vote. All in favor of Harm."

They raised their hands. Crud. I did too. I love democracy, except when I lose.

"Thanks," Harm said. He took out his clue pad and drew up a quick checklist. Harm is organized. He likes straight lines, creased slacks, socks that match. I'm more of a throw it and see where it falls kind of person.

"Mo," he said, "you develop the photos and I'll make flyers featuring this trim. We'll paper the town with them first, and move out from there. Somebody will know it. I'm going home to make a Master Plan, and ask Gramps about Myrt Little's first treasure hunt. Mo, you ask Miss Thornton. We'll talk at school tomorrow."

"What about me?" Dale asked. "I'd planned to get in some snow time and then wire the chicken house for sound, but I could do different. We're having trouble with coyotes again, and coyotes hate NPR."

Harm didn't miss a beat. "You're our big-picture man, Dale. Stay open to inspiration on both cases—the treasure, and Upstream Mother. And enjoy the snow."

As Dale and Harm headed off, I framed a few more black-and-whites. A lick of snow on a gardenia leaf. *Click.* A skirt of snow around our sycamore. "Miss Lana," I shouted as I biked past the café door. "I'm going to Grandmother Miss Lacy's."

"Be home in time for supper," she called.

I pedaled to Grandmother Miss Lacy's Victorian two-story in two minutes flat—a possible record. I photographed Gabriel's red Jaguar, and headed toward the steps.

"Hey, Tinks. What's *Gabriel* doing here?" I asked as he rounded the corner. Like me, Tinks has a background job. Unlike me, he's so quiet, people sometimes mistake him for furniture. He knows everything going on in Tupelo Landing.

"Hey Mo," he said. "Gabriel's shouting, mostly. Your name's come up." He slung a handful of fertilizer on the steps. "Fertilizer melts ice and doesn't kill the pansies. I don't want Miss Thornton slipping. Old bones are like hearts: They break quick and heal slow."

As I scampered up the steps, Gabriel's voice boomed through the door. "I didn't spend three years researching Blackbeard's treasure to compete with a pack of juvenile delinquents!"

"The Desperados are *not* delinquents," Grandmother Miss Lacy said. "They're smart, funny children. I'm surprised you're threatened by them."

"I *demand* exclusive access to your land," he said, going louder.

"Don't try to bully me," Grandmother Miss Lacy said, calm as well water. She's no taller than me, but she lives tall.

"If you wanted exclusive access to my property, you should have put it in your contract. You didn't, we've both signed, and that's that."

"They'll stay out of my way if they know what's good for them," he said, and yanked open the door. "You," he said, glaring at me.

I went inscrutable. "You too."

He stomped to his car and roared away, tires screaming.

"He has temper issues," I said as I trailed Grandmother Miss Lacy to her old-timey kitchen, where tea sat steaming.

"Eavesdropping is unattractive," she said. I hung my head and counted to three. "Stop pretending to feel guilty," she said. "And don't push Gabriel, Mo. He's . . ."

"A bully?" I said, settling into a chair.

"He's hot-headed, and very smart." She looked at me, her glasses sliding down her nose. "I've seen his clues and they're excellent. Dawdle and you'll lose this race." She poured the tea. "You must be working with Myrt by now."

Grandmother Miss Lacy's pumping me for information?

"I'm sorry, our cases are totally confidential unless we tell people," I said.

"Be careful, this tea is hot," she said, bringing it to the table. "Mo, everyone in town knows you visited Myrt Little today, and I assume she gave you Mary Ormond's clue. She'd be a fool not to. You're the best detectives in town."

"True," I said, very modest.

"Let me lay out my rules, just in case you didn't hear them through the door. Gabriel can hunt for treasure on the land I own, and so can you Desperados. But Lana and I own the inn together, as you know. We have decided *no one* will search there unless they have definite clues taking them there. We don't want random people digging up the inn's lawn."

"Why are you in this race anyway?" I asked. "You don't need the money, and . . ."

"You're right," she said, sliding my cup to me. "I have enough money to get me from this world to the next. But a treasure! Myrt's been sitting on Mary Ormond's clue for eighty years. She'd *still* be sitting on it if Gabriel hadn't come to town. I don't care who finds the treasure, Mo. But I do want to see it before I die."

I grinned. "You're betting on both horses in a two-horse race."

"I'm not just another pretty face, dear," she said. "And I couldn't stand to search with Myrt again. She's so literal. She hasn't an ounce of imagination in her.

"Mo, there's one more thing. Our friendship means more than gold to me. Let's promise we won't lie to each other or let treasure come between us. You may ask me anything, and if I can't tell you, I'll say so. And vice versa. That way we can compete as friends."

"Excellent," I said, and sipped my tea, very sophisticated, trying to think how to get Gabriel's clue. Pain unfurled in my mouth like a scarlet flag. I spit the tea in the cup.

"And Mo, please don't ask me for Gabriel's clues. I won't betray his confidence any more than I would betray yours." She handed me a napkin and changed the subject. "How's your search for Upstream Mother going?"

"Funny you should ask. We just photographed the sign. If you have time . . ."

"I can't wait," she said, her smile making her young again. "It was so smart of Lana to save that sign for you."

"No ma'am, the Colonel put it under there," I told her. "I got one more question. We saw a woman with Gabriel the morning he came to town. Who is she? And where's his niece, Ruby? Doesn't she hunt treasure with him?"

"That's three questions," she said. "I asked the same things, and I'll tell you what he told me: Absolutely nothing. But time will tell, I'm sure."

Time always tells in Tupelo Landing, if you wait long enough.

"Grandmother Miss Lacy?" I looked into her eyes. "I love you. But just so you know, we ain't cutting you any slack on this treasure race. We'll find that treasure before you and Gabriel do. So brace yourself for heartbreak."

She lifted her teacup. "May the best team win," she said, and the race was on.

That night, sweater beside me, I opened Volume 7 and grabbed a pen.

Dear Upstream Mother,

Good news! Tupelo Landing's top detectives are on our case. Grandmother Miss Lacy and me developed my photos, to make a flyer. The Ugly Trim on it just might bring me home to you.

Also the Desperados are in a treasure race worth millions.

I'm saying this so you know I'm not looking for you because I need anything. I got my own money. I'm just looking to find you, and the piece of my heart you held on to the night the rest of me slipped away.

Mo

PS: I am of normal height with unruly hair and hot temper, which I been working on the temper all my life. I gave up on the hair some time back. School tomorrow.

Chapter Eight
What We Ain't Got

Inspiration hit like a freight train the next morning as I pedaled to school. I slapped my bike into the bike rack and zipped to Dale and Harm. "What's Gabriel got that we ain't got?"

"Experience," Harm said. "Equipment. Three years' research."

"And he can search full-time and we're stuck in school," Dale added as Sal strolled over sipping hot chocolate.

"We can't get equipment and experience, but we can do three years' research in a few days," I said as the bell rang. "I've got a plan."

Attila grabbed us at the door. "Desperados, Thes lost a pet last night," she said, her voice tragic. "Is that part of the curse? Dale, didn't he adopt one of Queen Elizabeth's puppies?"

Dale's face went pale. Liz's pups are family to him.

"Anna, it was *Spitz,*" Thes said, walking over. Thes's orange cat Spitz goes missing twice a week. He's the only pet on our Do Not Search For List. "I told you that."

"My mistake," she murmured, and walked away.

"Thes," Dale said, catching his breath. "Queen Elizabeth is planning a puppy reunion for March. You and King are invited." He looked at me and Harm. "As the puppies' godparents, you're invited too. Queen Elizabeth loves the puppy portraits you gave her for Christmas."

"We'll come," Hannah Greene said, shooting in loaded with books. She and her little sister co-adopted a pup.

"We're in," Sal said. "Little Ming can't wait, Dale. Neither can I."

Dale blushed crimson.

"Hey Dale, what's up with the blushing?" Harm asked. Dale pretended not to hear and scooted to Miss Retzyl, who'd also adopted a pup.

"Queen Elizabeth is planning a family reunion. You and your pup are invited."

Miss Retzyl smiled. "We'll be there. Take your seats, class. We'll start with history."

"Here goes. Follow me," I whispered to Dale as he sat down. "Pirates are history, Miss Retzyl."

To my shock, Attila backed me up. "Mo's right. Invite Gabriel Archer to class," she said. "He's handsome and rich and from an old Virginia family. Plus he drives a Jaguar. Detective Starr, on the other hand, drives an Impala. Mother says trade up if you can."

Miss Retzyl went fire-hydrant red. "I don't trade my friends," she said, cool as sliced cucumbers. She has off-the-charts temper control. She studied us like Oprah trying to decide whether to surprise us with new cars or makeovers. "Who'd like to write pirate reports?" she asked.

We went quiet as half-past-dead.

Sal raised her hand. "We lack incentive since we're not beneficiaries."

Dale looked at me. "She wants a cut of the treasure," I whispered. Beneath Sal's bobbing curls lurks a finely tuned business brain.

Dale nodded. Harm looked over and shrugged.

I hopped up. "Thank you for that introduction, Miss Retzyl," I said, strolling to the front of the room. "Sal, as you know, the Desperados have taken on maybe the biggest mystery in pirate history: the hunt for Blackbeard's treasure. As fellow sixth graders, we hate to get rich without you. Any kid who reports on Blackbeard and his friends gets a cut of the treasure. This only pays off if we find the treasure, but we're confident in your research skills."

"Very confident," Dale said. "Way beyond anything that makes sense."

The classroom turned to Sal. "You'll cut us in for how much?" she asked.

Harm scribbled some quick calculations and held up his notebook. "One one-hundredth of one percent. Each," I said. "That's only *if* the Desperados find the treasure."

Harm jumped in. "It may not sound like much, but if we

find a treasure worth a million dollars, that's . . . one hundred dollars each. For one report."

Sal drummed her fingers on her daily planner. "Throw in extra credit and no footnotes, we'll take it," she said, and the class wheeled to Miss Retzyl.

Crud. Miss Retzyl's normally warm brown eyes had gone cold as fish eyes. "We don't pay students to write reports in Tupelo Landing, Mo," she said.

"I couldn't agree more," I replied. "Only this isn't so much a public school report as it is a once-in-a-lifetime Independent Study Opportunity of a private-school caliber."

I waited. Independent Study is to Miss Retzyl as catnip is to kittens.

Jake took out his notebook—a first. "How deep did pirates bury their treasure?" he asked, rummaging for a pencil. "Because our shovel handle broke."

Miss Retzyl pounced on it. "Extra credit, bonus for footnotes. Class, whatever agreement you and the Desperados make after school is up to you."

"Deal," Sal said, and the class cheered.

"Now, who has a topic in mind?" Miss Retzyl asked.

Ideas zinged around the room thick as threats around a pirate den. "Where to dig!" "Pirate fashion!" "Treasure ships!" "How to swear like a pirate!"

Dale raised his hand. "What do parrots talk about while we're sleeping?"

Harm chimed in. "Blackbeard's death. Shot, stabbed, beheaded—and people say he still walks around, looking for his head."

I love it when school and real life overlap, which is mostly never.

"Let's finish our study of Rome and start on pirates," Miss Retzyl said, and we dug out our books. "Who knows why the Roman Empire fell? Dale?"

"Gravity?" he guessed.

I raised my hand. "Rome fell because of a barbarian. *Attila* the Hun," I added, and the class laughed.

Attila, who went red, raised her hand. "It also fell because of pointless battles. Like Mo's search for a mother who doesn't want her."

"Take that back, Cadillac brat," I shouted, and Miss Retzyl snapped her book closed.

"That's enough, girls. Let's finish our study of Rome with a pop test."

After school, we dropped our bikes at the Littles' door. "*Western civilization*?" Dale said. "*That's* the best thing Rome did? Are you sure? Because I put pizza."

Mrs. Little opened the door. "You're late," she snapped. "Did you bring the clue?"

"Of course," I said. "We secured it in our state-of-the-art transport unit."

Dale gave her his social smile. "Mo stuck it in her math book. You're old, but you might have a lot of visitors," he continued, very smooth. "May we put a flyer on your door?"

Harm slipped our Ugly Trim flyer from his backpack. He'd designed it during science, and Skeeter had run copies during lunch.

HELP SOLVE A REAL-LIFE MYSTERY!
RECOGNIZE THIS UGLY TRIM?
KNOW WHERE THE BILLBOARD STOOD?
GOOD INFORMATION EARNS A CASH REWARD
(PAYABLE AFTER WE FIND THE TREASURE)
CALL HARM AT 252-555-7338

Mrs. Little snorted and handed the flyer back. "It's ugly. Don't put it on my door. Mary's roofing is in the attic. Damage anything and . . ."

"We know," Harm said, smiling. "You already told us. We'll rue the day we met you."

"What's wrong with roux?" Dale whispered as we headed down the hall. "Bill Glasgow makes it for me and Mama. We eat it on dirty rice."

Miss Rose's boyfriend, Bill, is from Louisiana. He plays his mandolin like he cooks: hopped up and spicy, with a nice in-between of smooth.

"Roux and rue. Homonyms. Same sounds, different words," Harm said, opening the attic door. "Bill's roux means Cajun gravy. Mrs. Little's rue means regret. We'll *regret* the day we met her."

"But we already do," Dale said, peering up the staircase. "Are those spiderwebs?"

"Scared of spiders, short boy?" Mrs. Little snapped behind us and we jumped. She handed me a battery-powered lantern. "If you open windows, close them. Heat costs money and money doesn't grow on trees. Get cracking."

We clattered up the dusty stairway and bumped to a halt. The attic stood rafters-high in three hundred years of hideous castaways, broke-downs, and whatsits. Harm picked up an old ukulele and strummed. "Put that down," Mrs. Little screeched from below.

"She has dog ears," Dale whispered.

Harm ditched the ukulele and trotted downstairs. His voice drifted up to us. *"Mrs. Little, I noticed a radio on your bookcase. May we borrow it? Music gets us cracking."*

Harm's polite. Miss Lana says it proves somebody spent time with him. He's also smart. He came up and turned the radio on just loud enough to hide our voices.

"We need more light," I said, wiping the grime from a gable window.

"This one won't come clean," Dale said, raising the other window. "Found the old shingles," he called, scrambling over a mountain of dusty quilts to pick a long, thin wedge of wood from a stack against the wall. "What was Mary Ormond's clue again?"

I slipped the note from my math book. *"Look to my roof for clues to lost treasures . . ."*

"*Lost treasures.* Sounds good," Harm muttered. "Gramps managed to get the truck fixed, but he still hasn't found our leaks. He's getting discouraged." He eyed the stack of shingles, which ran the length of the attic and stood shoulder-high. "We need a process," he said.

"We'll stack the rejects over here," I said, shoving a pile of moth-ravaged taxidermy projects aside. "Search each shingle for a map, a code, a message . . . anything woman-made."

In a blink we found our process: Grab a shingle, search the face. Flip it, search the back, scan the narrow sides. Restack. Repeat, repeat, repeat.

Two hours later Dale tossed the last shingle into the reject pile. "We got nothing."

"Grandmother Miss Lacy said Mrs. Little was too literal and lacked imagination on the first search," I said, studying Mary's clue again. *"Look to my roof . . ."*

"Right," Harm said. "They only looked at the shingles. But if you're downstairs looking up, you're looking *to* the roof. The clue could be anywhere in here—or in the walls, the floorboards." He pushed a stuffed possum aside. "We'll start mining the rest of the attic tomorrow."

"Okay, but we better work fast," Dale said as we tromped downstairs. "Sal says Gabriel's setting up his fancy equipment. And we know he has clues. And so far we got silt."

"*Zilch,*" Harm said. "But we've eliminated the wrong path, which sets us free to find the right path."

"Very Blackbeard Zen," I said, and he grinned. He looks happy, I thought as we zoomed toward the café. But he didn't look happy for long.

The spicy scents of stroganoff and the boom of cannon fire met us at the café door. Dale ducked. I pulled him to his feet. "It's Russia Night. Miss Lana's playing Tchaikovsky's *1812 Overture,*" I said as Miss Lana swirled over in her red snow dress.

"Thank heavens you're here," she said, giving me a quick kiss on each cheek—very European. "We're standing room only. Grab your order pads, my babushkas."

I checked out the Specials Board and scouted the lay of the café. Three strangers stood by the Winter Tree, waiting for a table. Attila and Mrs. Simpson sat cheek-to-jowl with the Azalea Women. Mr. Red and Grandmother Miss Lacy sipped waters at a center table.

"Flyers," I whispered. Harm tugged a handful from his backpack. I went table to table. "Welcome, comrades. Identify this Ugly Trim and receive a free dessert. Thank you."

"Order up!" the Colonel called, and I zipped over to snag some fries.

I smiled at Grandmother Miss Lacy and placed the fries by her menu. "Please enjoy a Fried Spud-nik appetizer on the house," I said as Dale trotted over with ketchup.

Dale watched Harm swagger to the big-haired twins. "That's sad. Lavender says the twins don't even know Harm's alive," he said.

"Welcome to Russia Night," I told Grandmother Miss Lacy. "Tonight we got our From Russia with Love Special. This starts with a deep red Beet Soup . . ."

"Borsch," Miss Lana called from across the room.

"Bless you," I replied. "Plus the Colonel's Stroganoff. We're also offering a All-American Melting Pot Special—Mexican Chili and Swiss Cheese Toast."

"Thank you, but Red and I are Gabriel's guests tonight," she said. "We'll wait for him."

"Speak of the devil," I muttered as Gabriel swirled in and took a seat.

"Evening," he said. "Find a treasure, Mo?" He glanced at the Azalea Women and cranked up his volume: "Sadly, I've suffered a setback. My young niece can't join me. Terrible loss. Good news too. The old fish camp where I'm setting up positively *reeks* of treasure."

"That's vintage fish guts you're smelling," I told him.

He plowed on. "The camp's on the low side of the river—the best place for a pirate to unload a heavy treasure."

My stomach dropped. *Why didn't I think of that?*

"I thought of that, and we've found an even *easier* place to unload," I said.

"Do tell," Gabriel said as Harm strolled toward the big-haired twins, his tray high above his head. The café door swung open, catching his eye. His face went dishwater gray. His tray wobbled and tipped. The soups slid. A twin screamed.

Time clicked into slow motion.

"Nyet!" Dale cried, hurtling for Harm. The bowls ricocheted against the table. The deep red soup bounced like acrobats across the twins' identical white blouses and surprised faces.

The café went silent. Dale looked at Harm. "Good news. The twins know you're alive."

Life clicked back into real time. "Cleanup on the twins," I called, but Harm's gaze stayed riveted on the door.

I turned, following his stare. A dark-haired woman unzipped her purple faux-leather jacket and smoothed her black slacks and blouse. She squared her shoulders and made an entrance Miss Lana would be proud of, red stilettos click-click-clacking.

"Mom," Harm said, his voice thin as his smile. "What are *you* doing here?"

*****

"Baby, you've grown a foot since I saw you," she said, slicing through the crowd. She pushed her hair back exactly the way Harm pushes his, and kissed his cheek.

She's pretty, I thought. Eyes like Harm's, one-side dimples like Harm's, a smile with a quick on-off switch. Like Harm, only Nashville fancy.

I stepped to his side.

"Mom, these are my friends . . ." Harm said, and his face went blank.

He forgot our names?

Dale smiled. "Dale Earnhardt Johnson III," he said in a move straight out of *Manners Girls Like*. "I'm Harm's best friend who is a boy. My dog Queen Elizabeth II would have come too if we'd known you were in town. Harm's like a brother to her."

"Hey, Dale." She gave him a smile to dazzle the sun, and turned to me.

"Mo LoBeau," I said. "And that's my family over there—Miss Lana and the Colonel."

"Call me Kat. Kat Kline. Stage name."

She rumpled Harm's hair. "I swear, you're as good-looking as I am. Look at you! You'll be tall as your daddy. The girls must be crazy about you."

A delicate blush spatter-painted Harm's cheeks.

"Not me," Attila faux-whispered to the Azalea Women.

I stepped up beside Harm before I could think why. "You're right," I said, very loud. "*I'm* crazy about Harm, and so's every other *smart* girl in sixth grade."

Hannah and Sal nodded from their tables. Harm gave me a gentle elbow.

"I hate to break up a mother-son reunion, Kat," Gabriel interrupted. "But we have some business to discuss." He looked at Miss Lana. "You know, Kat could perform here while she's in town. It would be good for you and great rehearsal time for her."

"No," Harm said, very quick. "I mean, Mom's professional. She doesn't do cafés."

"Call me Kat," she said. "*Mom* makes me sound so old." She surveyed the café, her eyes finding the Azalea Women. "Ladies, good to see you. What's it been . . . ten years?" She smiled at the twins. "Crissy and Missy. You've sure grown up good."

"Thank you. I and Crissy are hair professionals who drive a Mustang," Missy said as Miss Lana cleaned up the last of the splattered soup. "Welcome home."

"Thanks," she said. "Hey Tinks. You're looking good too."

Tinks's stare trailed her to Gabriel's table.

"May I present the soon-to-be-famous Kat Kline," Gabriel said. "My partner in our treasure hunt."

Kat is Gabriel Archer's partner? She was the woman by the river?

My world stopped spinning for one quick breath. *Kat's* the reason Gabriel knows all about Tupelo Landing, and the people in it. *She's* the reason Gabriel thought we were ten years old the first time he called: That's how old Harm was when she left him in Greensboro.

"Fascinating," Attila's mom said. "*I* thought you left Tupelo Landing to start a new life with some good-looking man and then headed off to Nashville to become a star. And now you're back as a treasure hunter. What *will* you think of next?"

"Betsy Simpson," Kat said, making the words sound like a curse. "Since I know you're dying to ask, I'm a gnat's hair away from making it huge. This treasure will finance my big break." She zeroed in on Mr. Red, and took a deep breath. "Hello, Pops."

Mr. Red rose and walked out the door.

Kat reset her smile. "Hello, Miss Thornton."

Grandmother Miss Lacy nodded. "Hello . . . Kat. It's been years. Please do sit down."

As dinner clattered on, Kat charmed everybody within charming distance—everybody except Harm. Grandmother Miss Lacy offered her a room at the inn, and Kat said yes. Miss Lana invited her for breakfast, and she said yes again.

"Your mom's good-looking," Dale said as we bused tables at the end of the supper rush.

"Runs in the family," Harm said. He winked at me, but his wink lacked voltage.

"What's wrong?" I asked as we lugged dishes to the kitchen.

"Kat makes me nervous. She changes things," he said. "You'll see."

Dale heaved a tray of dishes onto the counter. "You never talk about your people."

"Not much to say," Harm answered. "Dad's on an oil platform in Louisiana. She's a great singer, and he's a great guy. They just aren't right together."

I hesitated. As a friend, I didn't want to ask. As a Desperado, I had to know. "What about the treasure? Are you on Kat's side, or . . ." I went tactful. "On Mrs. Little's?"

Harm eased a stack of dishes into the sink. "I'm with you guys, Mo. I haven't seen Mom in three years. And I wish I hadn't seen her today."

Jealousy sliced through me like a sling blade in the dark.

Harm doesn't want his mother and here she is, big as life. I been wanting my Upstream Mother all my life, and I can't even find her.

Dear Upstream Mother,

Harm's mother blew into town tonight. I wish

it had been you walking through the café door. I think Harm does too.

We're papering the town with our Ugly Trim flyer and we search the Littles' attic crud tomorrow.

Wish me luck,

Mo

Chapter Nine

Beyond the Known World

The mayor met us at his door the next morning, which was a Saturday. "Sorry I missed your mom last night, Harm. She was a pistola in her day. I hear she came to town with Gabriel Archer. That must be tough for you—your mom on the opposite side of the treasure fence."

I went professional. "If you're asking which side of the fence Harm's on, he's Desperado to the bone," I said, heading for the hall. "We're searching attic crud today. We need a storage room for non-clue items. I hate to rush you, but dawdle and you lose."

"Mother," the mayor called. "I'm giving the Desperados the Dingy Room."

"I'll start bringing things down," Harm said, bounding away.

Mrs. Little bellowed from deep in the house: "Tinks is driving me to Bingo. Tell the Desperados to stay out of my taxidermy supplies."

The mayor led us to a dusty room of faded yellow wallpaper. "It was a guest room until Mother realized she hates guests," he said.

Harm rambled in with a basket of yarn.

The mayor staggered back, his hand over his heart. "Mother's knitting," he whispered, his eyes going glassy. "Mother's an expert technically, but her sense of style . . . Those sweaters . . ." He reached over to touch the door.

"Post-traumatic sweater disorder," Dale said. "He's grounding himself."

The mayor shuddered. "You'd never know it to look at me now, but I was an unfashionable child."

"She's a *knitting* expert?" Harm said. "Mo, we can show her your sweater!"

Mrs. Little's claws on Upstream Mother's sweater? Unlikely.

The mayor drew a jagged breath and jangled his keys. "I'm sure Mother would be glad to share her expertise. But burn that knitting. Sometimes the past looks best in ashes."

As the day spun by, we dug through the Littles' attic crud century by century. Even with the window up, it was hot work. We shed our jackets and worked in our T-shirts.

By day's end, we'd dug down to the eighteenth-century clutter. We decided to break.

"Mo, about your case," Harm said, sitting on an old milking stool and crossing his arms. He's lifting Lavender's weights again, I thought. "I mapped out a plan for us last night, when I couldn't sleep." He tugged a paper from his pocket and spread it on a mountain of quilts.

FINDING MO'S UPSTREAM MOTHER
CLUE #ONE. The Sign
1. Develop the photo of the sign (Mo) and show it around (All). CHECK
2. Plaster the town with it. (All)
3. Contact area Chambers of Commerce to see if anybody recognizes it. (Harm and Skeeter.)
CLUE #TWO. The Sweater
1. DNA-check the sweater—Starr (free) or Skeeter ($$$).

He added a note to the bottom of his list.

2. Ask Mrs. Little to look at the sweater, and follow up on any clues. (All)

"That's nice," Dale said. "I mapped my thoughts too," he added, and tugged a wad of paper from his pocket. He smoothed the wrinkles out and placed it on the quilts, by Harm's.

Queen Elizabeth's Puppy Reunion

× Get Party Hats. No! Ears! 

- Lemon meringue pies for humans
- LIVER meringue pies for Liz + pups
  - crumble dog biscuits for crust

Invite Newts? They are sensitive
GAMES! Fetch, tricks, running.
Photos? Ask Mo.

DNA, what is it made out of? ~~[crossed out]~~ what if it says Mo's Mother is a criminal at large with a brain like Mo's? Agh!

DANGER!

THOUGHTS by Dale some details

IDEA!!

Good!!

FLYERS!

free! Put up everywhere!

****Flyers also = airplanes!! I have heard a little plane at night but where does it land? FIND OUT!

can it do SKYWRITING or BANNERS?

How to Find Upstream Mother

(A) Advertise! Blitz!!!
Radio → costs $
Newspaper → $
Television (*Ask Mo to come her hair or use product!) → $$$

Ads Cost $$$

How to get $$ –

idea Hold a Ruffle!

Ruffle off –

1. cakes! (Mama, Harm, Miss Lana)
2. a ride in Lavender's race car when he gets one?
3. On the verge gig?
4. Attila's bike. (No wrong nevermind.)

"Great, Dale," Harm said, looking startled. "Lots of new directions to consider."

"I try to keep it fresh," Dale said, very modest.

"I like the advertising blitz, but you're right, that takes money," I said, leaning into the stack of quilts to read a sideways scribble. The bedding slumped, and I kneed it back into place. The quilts toppled, sending up a cloud of dust.

Three trunks peeked out. Two large wooden trunks and a smaller, carved trunk—all latched.

"Treasure chests," Dale said, his eyes shining. "Thank you, Mary Ormond."

I grabbed my camera from my bag. We popped the latch on the first trunk and lifted the lid, the old hinges creaking. Dale reached in and lifted out . . . *Click* . . . an old bonnet.

He scowled. "Clothes," he said, like he'd found bird droppings. "A dress, gloves, and a handbag that smells . . ." He sniffed and frowned. "Like gunpowder."

Click, click, click.

Harm lifted a rectangular package and stripped away its cloth wrappings. A painting of a young woman peeked out—short brown hair, sallow cheeks, and ski-slope nose. She wore a plain brown dress with a white collar. Harm flipped the portrait. In Mary's flowing handwriting: Tupelo Mother, 1727.

Dale opened the second trunk.

"This is better," Dale murmured. "Beautiful old woodworking tools—chisels, planes, hammers. Knee britches and a vest. And *one* boot?" he said, lifting it.

Click, click, click.

"One boot? These are Peg-Leg's things!" he cried.

We turned to the last trunk, its lid carved in a comet-burst of circles and Xs. Dale tried the latch. "Locked tight as a tick. Not like the others."

I floor-checked the clutter. "I saw a pry bar somewhere."

"A pry bar?" a voice said from the top of the stairs. "On an *antique*? Good grief. You people wouldn't know a treasure from a hole in the ground." Attila walked in wearing state-of-the-art safari gear. "Where's Mrs. Little?" she asked as I threw quilts over the trunks. "I want to speak with her."

A lie. No one wants to speak with Mrs. Little.

"Breaking and entering *again?*" I said.

She flipped her hair. "The door's unlocked. Besides, the mayor invited me to drop by."

She cased the attic and smiled at Harm, who used to like her before he knew her. "I guess you know Gabriel's niece didn't show. She usually handles the metal detector for him."

"So?" Harm said.

"So, I'm Gabriel's new intern."

I snorted. "That explains the getup. But why would Gabriel throw in with you?"

"Everybody knows Mr. Red's broke," she said, ignoring

my question. "It just breaks Kat's heart. She wants to help—we all do. Work for us and we're on the same team. We can pay minimum wage. Take it or leave it."

"Leave it," Dale said. "Go away."

Sometimes I could kiss Dale, except Dale's Dale and I don't kiss.

She shrugged and looked Harm up and down. "If that's how you feel. *I* hope Kat makes it big. A *good* son would help her."

"Harm is a good son," I said, stepping toward her. "You heard Dale. Go."

She fled down the stairs and out the front door, me on her heels. "Don't come back," I shouted. I slammed the front door, locked it, and ran back upstairs. "We better open that last trunk quick because—"

"She'll be back. We know," Harm said. "Listen, I like the mayor, but he blathers. Let's keep our discoveries quiet. I don't think he meant any harm inviting Attila over, but . . ."

"Social skills can be a blessing or a curse," Dale said, very wise. He picked up a wire, knelt before the third trunk, and slipped the wire into the lock. "Come on, open for Dale," he whispered, closing his eyes and jiggling the wire.

The lock popped.

We lifted the lid and peeped in. "Empty," Harm said. "Why would somebody lock an empty trunk?"

"They wouldn't," I said, tapping the trunk's floor as Dale backed away, watching.

Tap tap tap. Tap tap tap. Tap tap *thonk.*

"Your fingers are only ankle deep, Mo," Dale said.

Harm tilted his head and studied me. "He's right." Dale's usually right, once you figure out what he's saying. "The trunk has a false bottom. Dale, you're a genius."

"I know," he said. "Sal told me."

Outside, the mayor's Jeep backfired. "They're back. Hurry," Harm whispered. As my hands flew across the bottom of the trunk, Harm checked the corner guards. "This one's loose . . ." He twisted it as the Littles bumbled in downstairs and slammed the door.

"Bingo," Dale said as a door slid open in the trunk's floor.

"Don't mock me!" Mrs. Little shrieked. "We can't all win!"

Harm lifted our lantern over the trunk's secret compartment. Inside lay a sheet of heavy parchment, folded, and sealed with blood-red wax. A horned skeleton glinted up from the wax, one hand holding a cup, one spearing a heart. "Blackbeard's seal," Harm whispered.

I flipped the parchment to find a note. Gather your courage and act. Mary. I gathered my courage and popped the bright red seal. A hateful scrawl shouted up at me:

YOU FILTHY SCURVY DOGS.
TOUCH MY TREASURE AND I CURSE YOU FOR ETERNITY.
BLACKBEARD

"Cursed for eternity," Dale said, looking worried. "Mama's gonna kill me."

"And there's Blackbeard's seal at the bottom of the note—*in blood!*" Harm said.

"Yoo-hoo," the mayor called from the steps. "Who locked the door?"

"Hide the trunks!" I whispered, stuffing Blackbeard's note in my messenger bag. The quilts' dust had just settled when the mayor burst in.

"Hello, Desperados. What's that?"

"Old quilts," I said. "I may have seen knitting too."

He backed away. "We stopped at the café on our way home. Lana needs you. I'll give you a ride. Chop-chop!"

Not likely. The mayor's Jeep is a pile of dents held together by Lavender's genius and the prayers of scattering pedestrians. "Thank you, but we have official transport," I said. "I hate to give you bad news, but you had an intruder tonight: Anna Celeste—Gabriel's intern."

The mayor gasped. "Gabriel's *intern*?"

"She tried to buy us off, but we handled it," I said.

"We'll secure the attic for you, Mayor," Harm offered, herding him downstairs. Harm locked the attic door and slipped the key in his pocket.

I went steely. "It's hard to predict the behavior of the criminally insane, but I believe Anna Celeste will be back to steal your clues—and your treasure," I told the mayor. "Guard this door with your life."

"And try not to babble," Dale advised, and we stalked into the night.

A crescent moon peeked through scurrying clouds as we peeled toward the café. Harm rode no-hands beside me, tall and slender, hip-guiding his fancy silver bike from side to side.

"About your sweater, Mo," he said. "I think we should take it to Joe Starr or to Skeeter, to check the DNA. How about it?"

We skidded to a halt at Dale's turn-off. Fear whirled inside me like glitter in a snow globe. Suppose the sweater isn't even hers? Suppose it is, and her DNA's in the system, and she's in jail?

What if she's like Dale's daddy? Hard and mean. Or like Kat, or Mrs. Simpson?

What if I was a mistake and she wishes I'd never happened?

I pictured Mary's latest note. *Gather your courage and act.* I took a deep breath. "Skeeter made reservations for Monday morning. If Starr won't check the sweater's DNA for free, I'll ask Skeeter then," I said, my heart pounding.

Harm grinned. "Great. But since when does the café take reservations?"

"Since never. Skeeter likes to practice for when she lives in a city. I penciled her in for a window table, seven a.m."

"That's sweet Skeeter reserved," Dale said. "Because I thought I'd come for breakfast Monday too." He pointed to me like a king knighting a soldier. "I reserve."

"Me too," Harm said. "I'm sick of Gramps's cooking."

I looked up at the stars, and then at my friends. Dale already told me he'd promised Liz a bath Monday before school. And Mr. Red doesn't cook breakfast. Harm does.

"I owe you, Desperados."

"Come to dinner with Kat and me one night and we're even," Harm said. "I'll cook. I was thinking—I acted like a little kid last night. I mean, it's been three years . . . I want to get to know Kat and I want you to know her too. Dale, you and Sal too." We nodded. "I'll let you know when I have a time and a place. Kat may not be much of a mom and I might not be much of a son, but we're in this life together," he said, and pushed off toward home.

That night, I tiptoed through the Colonel's ragged curtain of snores, to Miss Lana's door. "Miss Lana," I whispered. "Are you sleeping?"

She clicked on her light and pushed up her sleep mask. "Say it again in English?"

"Harm wants to DNA-test my sweater," I told her.

"Send it away? *So soon*? That's a big step, sugar." She

scooched over and threw her bedcovers wide. The smell of her Noxzema rolled over me like a comforting tide.

"We'll ask Starr first," I said, slipping in beside her. "As a civil servant, he can't charge. Skeeter's associates work good, but they charge sky-high. Only . . . Miss Lana, if somebody loses that sweater or hurts it, I feel like I might die."

She smoothed my hair. "I know. I'm scared too. Fear of the unknown, I suppose." She looked at me. "What would you tell me if it was *my* sweater, sugar?"

"That's easy. Starr and Skeeter know their stuff. The chance is pretty much zero anything bad would happen."

My fear drifted away. Miss Lana says we have all the answers locked inside us. The hard part is finding the right questions to unlock them.

"Mo, are you sure you want to do this?" she asked. "Because you don't have to. There's nothing wrong with leaving things alone. The unknown is . . . so unknown. Like those old maps sailors used to draw. They'd map what they knew of the world, and at the edge they'd write 'Here be dragons.' Dragons can fascinate—or they can breathe fire."

I waited for my heartbeat to fall in rhythm with hers.

"That's the thing about dragons," I said. "You don't ever know until you meet them eye to eye."

Dear Upstream Mother,

Bad news: I am cursed for eternity. On a

lighter note, we have new clues to the treasure—things from Mary Ormond's trunk and Peg-Leg's. We just have to figure out how to use them. Also, Gabriel's desperate enough to take Attila for an intern—which is odd. If work's involved, Attila is dead weight.

Dale sings in church tomorrow, and Harm and me will go. We're sending your sweater off for DNA testing Monday. I hope you like dragons.

Love,

Mo

Chapter Ten
Sweater Day

Monday morning Harm and Dale flew through the café door. "Hey Miss Lana, hey Tinks. Did you bring it, Mo?" Harm asked, and I pointed to my sweater box on the counter. "I'm proud of you. That's brave." He tossed his scarf over a chair. "Really brave."

Dale zipped behind the counter. "Mama says if I may please have breakfast, she'll be by to settle up," he told Miss Lana, and she smiled.

Miss Lana and Miss Rose are best friends. There ain't no settle up between them. "Help yourself," she said, and Dale popped two pieces of Wonder Bread into the toaster.

As I dropped a flyer by Tinks's coffee cup, I eyed his skinny red tie, white shirt, and navy church suit. "Sharp outfit. Who you driving for, Tinks?"

"Al's Florist, in Ayden. Valentine's Day is coming. Love is big business. Of course, I get a lot of flowers thrown back in my face too. Love's risky."

My stomach rolled. Valentine's Day—the curse of middle

school. A jungle of social anxieties—what-if's swinging through the treetops, should-I's hiding in the shadows, told-you-so's ready to eat you alive.

Dale's toast popped up. "Queen Elizabeth would like cards this year. Mama says she's got post-puppy depression. Something sweet, nothing with cats or clowns. Mama says it sounds a little crazy, but . . ."

"Crazy ain't crazy if it works," Tinks said. "I'll get her a card, Dale." He smiled at Miss Lana. "I put that pork chop delivery in the kitchen for you. Give me the special, Mo," he added as Joe Starr swaggered in and settled on a stool.

Here goes my sweater, back into the world, I thought.

Dale and Harm vaulted onto stools flanking Starr as I leaned against the counter and gave him my waitress smile. "Glad you dropped by." I slid the milk pitcher toward him. "Have some half-and-half minus a half. On me. Professional courtesy."

"Thanks," Starr muttered as Miss Lana splashed his coffee cup full.

I slipped my sweater box to his place. "I'm hoping you'll DNA-check this sweater. It would mean a lot to me."

Starr lifted the box top with his fork. "Is it evidence?"

"It could be evidence of a missing person—my Upstream Mother."

"Right," he said, lowering the box top. "Sorry, Mo, if

it's not from a crime scene, I can't help. Besides, the lab's backed up for months. And Skeeter has better connections."

Crud.

Miss Lana put our biscuits down. "Joe, what do you know about Gabriel Archer? He waltzed into town talking treasure, but I get a bad feeling about him. He's charmed the Azalea Women out of their collective mind. Betsy Simpson's even invested in his hunt."

"Anna practically broke into the mayor's house for him," Harm said.

"Anna's gone roach," Dale added.

"He means rogue," I said as Starr flipped his pad open.

"Actually, I checked on Gabriel when he first came to town," he said, thumbing through the pages. "Thought he might be a con after Miss Thornton's fortune. Here we go. Gabriel Smith 'Smitty' Archer. From Charleston, West Virginia."

"*West* Virginia?" Miss Lana said. "He told me he's from Virginia."

Starr turned a page. "He went to Duke on a scholarship, and flunked out."

"Smart but stupid," Dale said.

"Bankrupt twice. No family. Credit cards maxed out. He and his partner got expelled from Madagascar for trying to swipe national treasures—to sell," he said as Skeeter and Sal strolled in. He snapped his pad closed. "No charges, though. He's clean."

Interesting.

"Excuse me," I said, and headed for Skeeter, who stood by the door practicing looking aloof. "Welcome to Chateau Café," I said. "Do you have a reservation?"

"Skeeter MacMillan, Esquire. Table for two."

"Right this way."

Dale hurried to hold Sal's chair. "Hey, Salamander. Can we join you?"

"*May* we join you," Miss Lana corrected.

"I was thinking Harm and me and maybe Mo, but I'll get you a chair too," Dale told her as I tossed a paper napkin in Skeeter's lap.

"Today our chef's offering his famous Heartbreak Hotel Biscuit—a buttermilk biscuit filled with a fried egg and orange cheese. We pair this with our deep-fat-fried Vintage Fruitcake. For the faint of heart we offer a tofu scramble with a delicate collard slaw—locally sourced."

"Heartbreak Hotel," Skeeter said, and Sal nodded.

"And cranberry juice, please," Sal said.

Harm scooted up with our own Heartbreaks and smiled, his dimples set to impress. "And while you're here, ladies, I'd like to discuss a case."

As Sal and Skeeter polished off their fruitcake, Harm plunked my sweater box on their table. "We need this DNA-tested. It's part of a cold case—nearly twelve years cold."

"So it's true," Sal said, her eyes glowing.

Miss Lana waltzed over. "Send your bill to me, girls."

"Done," Skeeter said, lifting the lid with her knife. "Did anyone touch it?"

"Mo did," Harm said. "Miss Lana. The Colonel. Dale. Me."

"Queen Elizabeth may have sniffed it," Dale added as Gabriel whooshed in. Gabriel took a central table, checked his reflection in a spoon, and smoothed his hair.

Harm lowered his voice. "We want to know if this belonged to Mo's Upstream Mother. And if it did . . . we want her name. And contact information."

Sal's nod set her short curls bobbing. "My cousin works in a forensic lab in Charlotte. I can make a call. But we'll need a DNA sample from you, Mo."

I spit on a napkin. "Will that do?"

"Very elegant, LoBeau," Harm said, grinning.

Skeeter folded the napkin. "Nicely," she said, scooping up the sweater box.

Dale grabbed her hand. "If somebody could knit a portal to another time, which I'm not saying they can, that's what's in that box. We got to have that sweater back, and it has to look good. Don't cut it or lose it. Don't put in stains that won't come out. It's a family heirloom."

A family heirloom. The words warmed me like Miss Lana's chili on a cold day.

The warmth lasted all the way to class, when Jake and Jimmy Exum walked in wearing their brown Sunday suits. Last time they wore their suits to school, they blew up the classroom.

Miss Retzyl went pale. Dale slipped to the edge of his seat, ready to run.

"Jimmy and me got our Extra Credit Pirate Report. It's based on a library book," Jake said, and we gasped. Exum boys are to library as vampires are to sunlight.

Miss Retzyl's color came back, sort of. "Go ahead, boys."

Jimmy pulled a shaggy black beard from inside his coat and hooked it over his ears. Jake unfolded a paper and read: *"People used to be short like Dale, but Blackbeard was a giant. He stood six and a half feet tall with black flashing eyes. Blackbeard tied slow-burning fuses in his beard to terrify enemies and light bombs."*

Jimmy tugged matches from his pocket.

"No fire," Miss Retzyl said, snatching the matches so fast, her hand blurred.

"Blackbeard smelled like gunpowder," Jake continued. *"In his free time he enjoyed blowing off his friends' kneecaps, taking hostages, and sinking ships—even his own. His famous friends included Israel Hands, Anne Bonney, and Stede Bonnet."*

Jimmy stepped up. "Mama's tall. Her back hurts if she bends over. This tells us tall pirates like Blackbeard buried their treasure shallow."

"Ridiculous," Attila snapped. "Blackbeard was management. He wouldn't bury his own treasure, he'd make underlings do it."

He ignored her. "Jake and me specialize in shallow digging. If we can dig in your yard, let us know." They bowed and we applauded them to their seats.

"Ten points for using the library, boys," Miss Retzyl said. "I believe that's a first."

"Ten points?" Attila gasped. "For *that?*"

"We start where we are," Miss Retzyl said, very Zen. "Take out your math books," she added as Harm sauntered to the pencil sharpener. I took out my book and turned off my brain. On his way to his seat, Harm dropped a note on my desk. Gabriel alert. Sharpen your pencil. Now.

I snapped my pencil lead and headed for the window. I cranked the sharpener and watched Gabriel strain to push a heavy metal contraption across the schoolyard.

"Mo," Miss Retzyl said, "sit down. You'll sharpen that pencil to a nub."

"Yes ma'am," I said. "Thank you for that intervention. Over-sharpening is a terrible habit, hard to admit, harder to break. Gabriel's up to no good by the monkey bars."

"He is not," Attila said. "He's using a *very expensive* Ground Penetrating Radar to check for pirate things. They're unlikely on this side of the river, but it never hurts to look. We've already found a sword across the river. We're having it appraised."

"A sword?" Thes croaked, rising to peer out the window.

The class rumbled.

"Settle down," Miss Retzyl said, strolling over to me.

We stood side by side, watching Gabriel pluck something from the dirt and drop it in his collection bag. He leaned against the heavy machine and pressed on.

I smiled up at her. "Do you ever feel like we're equals from a past life and so it's odd that you're now the teacher and I'm a mere student?" I asked, my voice low.

"No," she said. "Go to the office and call Detective Starr. We're being robbed."

An hour later, Attila slammed her Mean Cuisine onto the table next to ours. "Calling Starr was wrong. My parents pay taxes. Gabriel can take things off public land if we say so."

Sal slipped in by Dale. "Public land belongs to everyone, Anna. That's why he *can't* take things. It's stealing from all of us. It seems like he'd know that." She smiled at Dale. "Mama says thank you for the fresh eggs."

Dale blushed. "You're welcome," he said. "The chickens are laying good now that the coyotes aren't howling so close. Coyotes sing like police sirens, only glittery and dangerous as knives. I couldn't lay an egg either, if they were howling around me."

Sal nibbled her sandwich. "I'd love to hear them sometime."

"Sometime *later*," I said. Too late.

Dale threw his head back and yodeled like a fleet of police cars. The lunchroom went silent. Jake and Jimmy jumped up and ran for the door.

"Impressive," Sal said, scooting closer to Dale.

"Stupid," Attila muttered as the lunchroom chatter picked up again.

"Sal," Harm whispered, out of Attila range, "can you and Skeeter meet with us this afternoon? If Gabriel's already finding artifacts, we need to step up our game. We could use your research skills and your fashion sense. We have two trunks full of clues."

"Will you be there, Dale?" she asked, and he nodded. "I'll check our schedule and let you know, Harm."

Skeeter and Sal couldn't work us in until Thursday. We spent the next afternoons plastering the town with flyers, and combing the last of the attic crud for clues. When we finally stepped into the attic Thursday, to set up for our meeting, it was like stepping into a deep freeze.

"Oh no, I forgot to close the window," Dale said, running

to the gable. "And it *rained.*" He touched the plaster beneath the window. "This wall's soaked!"

"Ruined!" Mrs. Little shrieked behind me and we jumped like cats. "I told you not to leave the windows open!"

I wheeled to face her, but Dale went statue-still. He's not good with authority figures.

"Unless I'm wrong, Anna Celeste left that window open," I said, luring Mrs. Little's attention from Dale. I stepped to my right. She turned with me, her gaze glued to mine.

I stepped right again. She turned with me, putting Dale behind her.

Dale sprang to the window, grabbed the crosspiece, and tugged. The rain-swollen window stuck fast. He lifted his feet and bounced by his fingertips, his face going red as Harm slipped up the stairs and bounded over to help him.

Miss Lana says when in doubt, compliment.

"I love what you've done with your hair," I said. "Taxidermy skills are hard to translate to the human experience, but somehow you've managed." The window screamed down, and Mrs. Little whirled to face the boys.

Behind them, the soggy plaster beneath the window slowly bulged. It did a slow-motion backflip off the wall and thudded to the floor at their heels.

"There," I said, very smooth. "That couldn't have worked out better. May we show you out?" I asked, taking Mrs. Little's elbow.

"Unhand me," she snarled, and slammed her cane against the quilts covering the third trunk.

Something clicked.

"What was that?" she demanded.

"Nothing," we chorused.

"Fix that wall or pay for it," she snapped. "I came up to say the mayor and I leave tomorrow for the Thorny Plant Convention. Here's the house key," she said, forking it over. "And if anything's amiss when we return . . ."

"We know," I said as she clunked downstairs. "We'll rue the day we met you."

She slammed the door at the bottom of the stairs.

"Why did we take her case?" Dale muttered as Harm and I tore for the pile of quilts covering the third trunk—and that mysterious click.

"Why did you take my case? Greed!" Mrs. Little shouted from downstairs. "Harm needs money. Red's broke. And you have guests. Tall girl, short girl."

"Skeeter and Sal," Harm said, dropping the quilts back in place and turning our radio on.

The puzzling click would have to wait.

"Good news, Mo," Skeeter said, walking in. "Your sweater's at the lab. Mother's cousin was airlifted to Charlotte this morning for surgery. No charge for the upgrade. But you're on the clock starting . . . now," she said, glancing at her watch.

"We'll be brief," Harm said, noting the time. "Dale?"

Dale swaggered over, grabbed the quilt on the first trunk, and swept it away. "Pesto!"

"You mean *presto,* Dale," Sal said as he opened the trunk. She peered in and caught her breath. "A calico dress—*real* calico," she said, lifting out a dress and examining the tiny flowers woven into the fabric. "The stitching is beautiful." She draped the long skirt over the trunk and gasped. "Someone snipped a square from this skirt! That's criminal . . . Ouch!" she cried, pulling her hand back and slipping her finger into her mouth. "Straight pins," she murmured. "Odd ones, made of brass. Hope they're not cursed."

She dipped in again. "A bonnet. Gloves. . . . A tapestry purse!" She wrinkled her nose. "It smells funny."

"That's gunpowder," Dale said as she unwrapped the portrait.

"This woman looks familiar," Sal said, studying the painting as Dale opened the second trunk. Sal peeked in. "Homespun britches, tools . . . *One shoe?* And the sole's tacked on—that's Colonial technology." She looked at us, her eyes glowing. "I'd love to price these things for you."

"Skeeter, we need your internet skills too," Harm said.

"To track down that Ugly Trim sign," Skeeter guessed, and he nodded.

"You'll want our consultant bundle, Desperados," Sal said. "It gives you access to Skeeter's research skills, my business and fashion genius, and our complete confidentiality package. I suggest it because Gabriel has top-of-the-line equipment *and* connections *and* Anna Celeste's nose for gold. And you've got . . . us."

Sal has a depressing way with summary. I nodded.

"Excuse us while we confer," she said, and they stepped away to whisper.

Dale edged over. "How much money do we have?"

"Not counting the cash we have to give back if we can't find the treasure and subtracting repairs to the plaster wall we just ruined?" I asked. "About *minus* fifteen dollars." I gave Sal a smile. "Feel free to pro bono us. We send a lot of business your way."

"I'm sorry, Mo, but curses drive our cost up," she said. "We'll do it for ten percent."

Dale whistled. "So if we find a billion-dollar treasure, we give you . . ."

We waited. Math is to Dale as water is to evaporated.

"A lot," he concluded.

"That's *if* you find the treasure," Sal said. "If you don't, ten percent of nothing is zip."

"Deal," I said, and they headed downstairs.

Harm zipped to the quilts hiding the third trunk. "The click," he said. We dragged the quilts away, lifted the lid, and tapped along the floor and walls. A wall panel swung open.

A small book belly-flopped onto the trunk's floor.

"Lavender and me talked about it, and I don't believe in curses," Dale said, backing away. "But you open it, Mo. Just in case. Out of the three of us, the devil would be most worried about going toe to toe with you."

I hesitated. Sometimes it's hard to know what to say.

"Thank you," I replied, and opened the book. "Mary's handwriting," I reported, and read: *"Blackbeard's curse is a shark. It circles back. Love, Mary."* I thumbed through the pages—all of them blank.

Dead center of the volume, Mary had pressed a daisy.

I read the words beneath its withered petals. *"A rose by any other name smells as sweet. William Shakespeare."*

"What the devil does a daisy have to do with Blackbeard?" Harm muttered.

"Is my wall fixed?" Mrs. Little bellowed from below.

"We're working on it, Mrs. Little," I shouted. "Don't worry, we're handy."

Harm felt the plaster beneath the window. "This wall has to dry before we can repair it." He tossed a chunk of plaster to me. "Think fast, LoBeau." I snagged the plaster with my left and flipped it into my right.

"Mo would have made Little League MVP," Dale said, "only she got excommunicated for trying to curveball Attila to death."

The plaster had landed upside down in my hand. I

stared at the faint purple hieroglyphs covering the back of the plaster—squiggles, lines, triangles. "What's this? Code? Or . . ." I knelt and peeled a chunk of damp plaster from the wall.

Behind it lay a thin ghost of white paper, its ink pulled away by the plaster.

"Mary's clue," I said, my heart pounding. "She plastered it inside this wall. We found it! The treasure's practically ours!"

Chapter Eleven
She's Coming Here?

Twenty minutes later we muscled our bucket of clues up Harm's back steps onto his porch.

"Wow," Dale said, staring at a shelf over the washing machine. "That's a lot of money jars." True. Beside the dented cans and off-brand laundry detergent sat six soil-caked Mason jars, all of them empty.

"Withdrawals from the First Bank of Gramps," Harm said. "Life's expensive. Christmas, repairs, plumbing . . ."

"How many more jars are buried out there?" I asked, looking to the woods.

"Maybe ten," he said, heading into the kitchen. "A couple of these came up empty."

Harm's mom, I thought. Kat has access to a metal detector, and she'd know Mr. Red's banking habits. I looked away, ashamed of thinking bad of her.

Harm dropped the heavy bucket by the kitchen table and opened the yellow checked curtains. Outside, Mr. Red rounded the side of the shed, holding a Y-shaped branch in front of him, one branch of the Y in each hand.

"He's dowsing for water," Dale said before I could ask. "Still looking for those leaky pipes. Daddy used to dowse too." The branch tip bobbled, and dipped hard. Mr. Red marked his spot. "Like Tinks said, crazy ain't crazy if it works."

Harm opened the fridge. "If we eat supper now, we can take our time putting our plaster puzzle together."

"I'll call the Colonel," I said, darting to the phone.

He picked up on the second ring. "The Colonel. Speak to me."

"I'm invited for supper at Harm's," I said, and whispered, "We found a mega-clue."

I could hear his quick nod. "Hang on a second, Tinks," he said. And then to me, his voice low: "Right-o, Soldier. Supper and a mega-clue. Rose happens to be here. I'll tell her too. Be home by eight."

He hung up. The Colonel hates long good-byes.

We had the table set in two shakes. Harm went to the back door: "Gramps! Supper!"

Mr. Red sauntered in. Lately he's been combing his white hair up in front. "You look nice," I told him, and he winked. Him and Harm wink identical.

"Hope Lacy thinks so too," he said, rolling his shirtsleeves and reaching for the soap. He staggered back, yelping in pain. "Dang it," he said as a bloody knife clattered to the floor. He bent forward and squeezed his hand.

"Gramps!" Harm grabbed Mr. Red's hand and jerked the faucet wide open. The old spigot spit like a cat and water dribbled over Mr. Red's hand.

"Get the bandages out of the bathroom, Mo," Harm said. "Run!"

"Maybe we are cursed," Harm said after supper. He smiled and made his voice spooky. "*Leaky pipes, spitting water, cold showers instead of hot . . .*"

I laughed and studied the odd-shaped chunks of plaster on the table. "Let's do this like a jigsaw puzzle," I said. "Turn the purple marks up. We'll start with the pieces that show the edges of Mary's paper. You can see where the plaster overlapped the paper's edges, if you look."

Harm grabbed a cookie sheet. "Maybe we can frame it."

We worked near an hour, matching faint purple lines. The edges took shape, and we worked inward, toward the heart of the puzzle.

We added pieces, shuffling and turning them. "This wavy line could be a river—only not our river, it curves the wrong way," Harm said, frowning. "These purple triangles could be rooftops, but not Tupelo Landing's: They're on the wrong side of the river."

"And what's wrong with that corner?" Dale asked, hovering over the puzzle. "Looks like a shark bite—jagged around the edges, like teeth prints."

Mr. Red padded in, headed for the tea pitcher. "Hold it, Gramps," Harm said, hopping up. "Your hand might start bleeding again. Hey, you know this river?" he asked, pouring the tea.

Mr. Red studied our map. "Nope, but whoever drew it didn't like you very much. That purple ink's poisonberry ink. Myrt Little used to make it in high school—family recipe. Touch it to your lips or let it stay on your skin and you'll be sick as a dog."

"*Poisonberry*?" Dale gasped, jumping away from the map.

We bolted for sink and soap.

I washed up, and turned to find Mr. Red studying the map. I went subtle. "Hunting treasure with a poison maker like Mrs. Little must have been . . ."

"Miserable," Mr. Red said. "I only put up with her because I was trying to catch Lacy's eye. Of course, Lacy was too rich and I was too . . ."

"Good-looking," I said, and he laughed the way Harm laughs.

"Do you have plastic wrap?" Dale asked, and Harm opened a cabinet door. Inside, everything stood at attention—Harm's work. Mr. Red's more a Leaning Tower of Dishes man.

"Let's wrap the puzzle up, to keep the poison away."

Dale is to plastic wrap as Houdini is to straitjacket. He

always gets out of it, but it takes time and death-defying struggle. As he battled the wrap, I spotted a spare piece of plaster under the table. I tore off a ribbon of plastic and wrapped it. "Here's the map's north point and a bunch of squiggles," I said, and nudged it into place.

Dale frowned. "That *N* is like my second-grade N. Backwards." His eyes went wide. "Your room, Harm," he said. He grabbed the map and zipped down the hall.

I stepped into Harm's room—a first—and took a look around.

It runs opposite Dale's boy pit. His trim single bed sits beneath the room's lone window, his blue-plaid bedspread tucked in neat.

"Nice," I told him, and he relaxed.

Dale carried the puzzle to the mirror over Harm's dresser and tilted it forward. "I thought so," he said. "This sign's backwards to forward."

Harm smacked his forehead. "Of course. Mary told us in her clue: *Death's trail, upon reflection* . . . She knew the ink would fade into the plaster and make a reverse image," he said as the dogs outside yipped. "But why does she say *Death's trail*?"

Mr. Red stomped to the back door. "Hush, you dogs!"

"Turn it so the *N* points up," I said, and Dale turned the map.

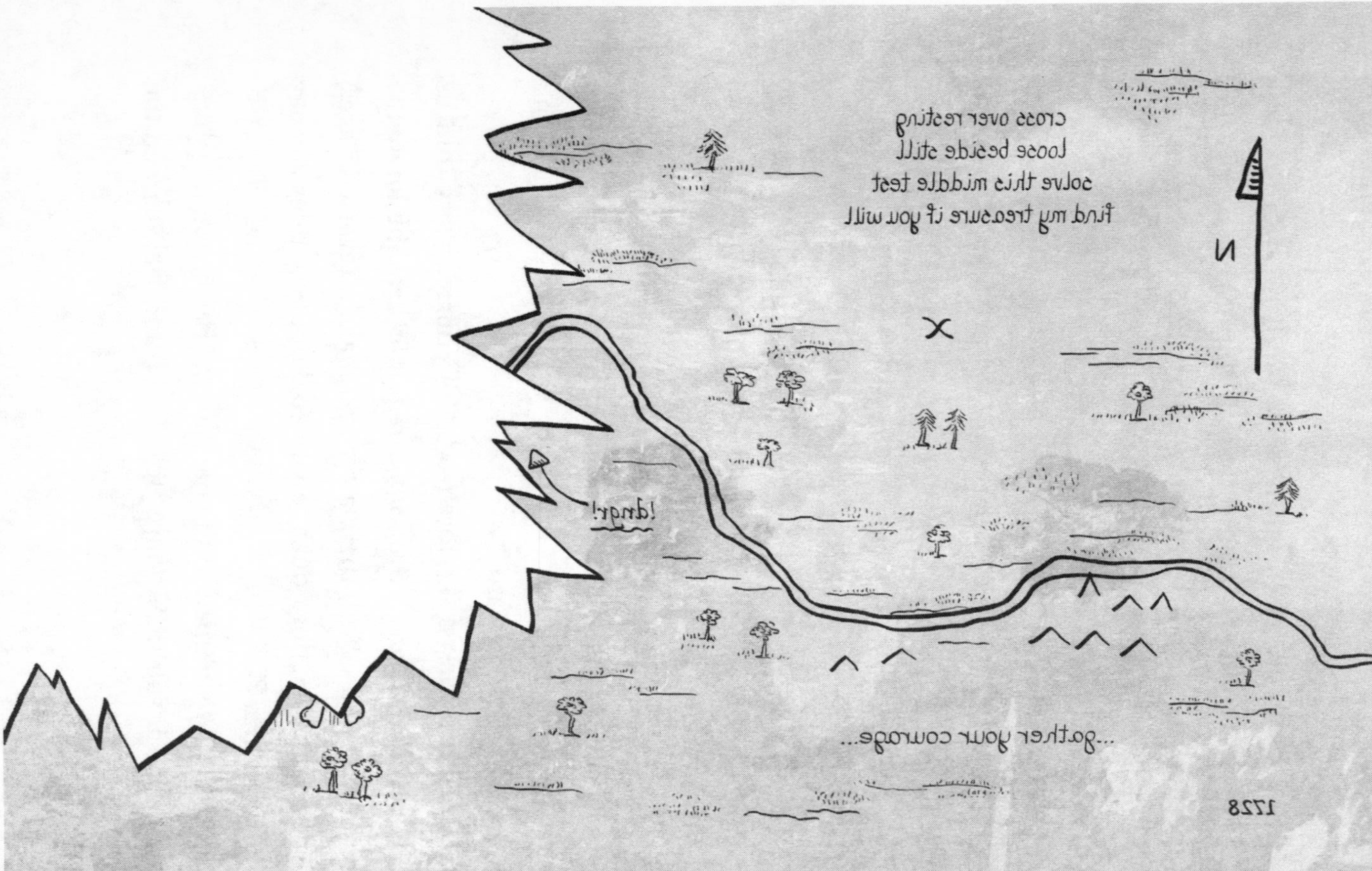
cross over resting
loose beside still
solve this middle test
find my treasure if you will
N
X
!dngr!
...gather your courage...
1728

"That has to be our river," Harm said. He opened his notebook and sketched it as the dogs quieted down. "And there's a date: 1728. And Mary's motto: Gather your courage."

"If that's the town, this *X* is near the fish camp," Dale said. "Where Gabriel set up."

I leaned to study the map. "*D-N-G-R*. Danger." I read the lines by the north arrow. *Cross over resting, loose beside still. Solve this middle test, find my treasure if you will.*

"Middle test. We're halfway there," Harm said, leaning so close, I could almost feel his blood pumping.

The phone in the hallway rang. Mr. Red shouted, "Harm, telephone."

"You two are the only ones who ever call me. Unless . . ." His dark eyes glimmered. "Hey Gramps, is it a girl?" he called, his voice hopeful.

"Some people might say so," Mr. Red said, and let the phone clatter.

Harm mirror-checked his hair. "It could be a twin."

"No. They're out of your league," Dale said. "Lavender told me."

"You never know when you'll get called up from the minors," Harm said. He strolled to the phone as Dale and me drifted into the living room and perched on the balogna-colored sofa to pretend we weren't eavesdropping. Harm picked up the phone, ducked his chin. His voice came out unnaturally deep and smooth. "Crenshaw, Harm Crenshaw. How are you this evening?"

Harm dropped his cool like a little kid drops a jacket. "Mom?" he said, his voice climbing like a monkey scaling a tree. "I know, I mean Kat. . . . Well, sure I do, but . . . *now?*"

Harm skidded into the living room. "Kat's coming *here,*" he said, his voice laced with panic. "And this place is a wreck."

"So what?" Mr. Red said from the doorway. "She's seen it a million times. Besides, she's not welcome. Call her back and tell her not to come."

Harm swallowed hard. "Come on, Gramps. I haven't really talked to her in a couple of years. And you haven't talked to her in—"

"In not long enough," he muttered.

Dale broke in. "Mama says Kat used to sing in church and she sings like an angel."

"Did she? Well, the Devil used to be an angel too," Mr. Red snapped.

"Hey!" Harm said, very sharp.

They stood glaring at each other, hands on hips. Harm blinked first. "Kat couldn't make a living in Tupelo Landing. Singing in church won't pay the bills," he said, turning away as a car wheeled into the yard, sending its yellow beams flickering across the curtains.

"That's true," Dale said. "Church work mostly pays in the next life."

The headlights died and a car door slammed. The dogs yelped. "Blast it," Mr. Red said. He whirled, stomped through the kitchen, and slammed the back door.

Kat's quick footsteps tattooed the porch. Harm swung the door open. "Hey," he said, stepping aside for her. "I'm glad you stopped by."

An easy hour later, we sat at the kitchen table watching Kat polish off a ham sandwich. She licked her fingertips. "You're a good cook," she told Harm.

"Harm *is*," I said. "Miss Lana says it's not cookbook cooking either. It's talent cooking—a feel for tastes and textures. She says he's a poet with spices. He helps at the café when she's doing something fancy."

Harm glowed. "Thanks. I'll cook dinner for you one night. For all of us."

"I'd love it," she said, and I settled back and watched them, waiting.

So far, they'd discussed the weather, Nashville, and school. I'd showed her my pendant with the letter *J*, and our flyer. "That's some trim," she'd said. "Mind if I keep it?"

"Sure, we got plenty. Skeeter's sending them to Chambers of Commerce upstream of us. And we're waiting on the

DNA from my sweater to come in," I said, and went for a change of subject. "Check these out," I said, dragging a few photos from my bag—Lavender laughing, Harm sitting on my steps with the pirate book.

"You have a good eye," she said, and smiled sudden as sunshine in rain. "Hey, I need some new publicity photos. Maybe we can work something out. How's Myrt Little?" She laughed. "Don't look so surprised. Your friend Anna told me you'd taken her case. Cleaned up her attic for her too, I hear."

"Anna's not exactly a friend, Kat," Harm said, hopping up to take her plate to the sink.

"No," she said, her face going thoughtful. "She wouldn't be. She's too much like her mom. I went to school with Betsy Simpson, you know. She's a weasel, but I'll say this for her: She's an honest weasel. Not a lying bone in her stuck-up little body."

She cranked up the Mother Vibe. "Listen kids, I don't want to scare you, but Gabriel says this treasure's cursed. "*Surge of blood, snap of bone, loss of mortal breath* . . . You aren't worried, are you? Dale?"

"Come on, Kat. You don't believe in curses," Harm said.

"No, I don't. Still . . . Anna cut her leg with the metal detector. That child has zero rhythm. And Gabriel walked into a branch and near cracked his skull while he was pushing his GPR around. *Surge of blood, snap of bone* . . ."

Harm made a chat-zone U-turn. "How did you meet him, anyway? He's sort of . . . not your type. I mean, Dad's low-key and kind of cool . . ."

"Like you," she said.

"I think I know why you and Gabriel are together," Dale said. "Opposites attract and you're sweet. Is that it?"

Kat's laugh was practiced this time. She's buying time to think, I thought.

"We're not a couple, if that's what you mean," she said, studying Harm. "We're partners in this treasure hunt. That's it."

If she heard the back door open behind her, she didn't show it. Mr. Red eased in.

"Gabriel swirled into a club where I sing, talking about the Treasure of Tupelo Landing," she said. "What are the chances of that?"

"Zero," Mr. Red snorted.

"Hey Pops," she said, turning. "I'm glad you came in. I want to make things right with you. I mean it." He waited. "After we cash out the treasure, I'll make my demo tape. I'll be set for life—and if I am, you are. We can get you a new truck—whatever you need. How about it? Miss Thornton would like you to be rich. She thinks the world of you, but I can't see her marrying a poor man. Can you?"

"Grandmother Miss Lacy ain't like that," I said, but Mr. Red had already walked out the door, setting the dogs barking again.

Silence settled over us like a delicate net. "Well, I tried. I better go," she said.

Miss Lana doesn't like me to brag, but I have killer sensitivity. "Dale, we should leave first. Harm probably has questions about why Kat deserted him, and Kat may want to express guilt or beg forgiveness. They could bond. Excuse us," I said, very polite.

"No," Harm said, quick as a rifle shot. "I mean, sit back down. Kat can give you a ride home. That is . . . if you're going anyway, Kat."

Harm doesn't want to be alone with her, I thought. Odd. It's the thing I want most in the world, to be alone with Upstream Mother.

I waited for Harm to ask the important questions. The ones I'll ask Upstream Mother: Do you miss me, do you want me, is my heart the same as yours?

"Do one thing, and I'll take everybody home. Sing for me," Kat said. "Anna says you're great. Please? You and Dale. I haven't heard you sing since you were a little bitty boy."

Dale stepped up neat as a pin, but Harm rose head down, the way he did when he first started singing. "Don't worry," I whispered, lining them up in front of the stove. "You'll be great. Sing 'Amazing Grace.' It's the one I love best."

They sang the old hymn rich and sure, their voices rolling easy as fog along a rocky trail home. Their last note drifted away, and Kat and me clapped.

She jumped up and kissed Harm's face. "You sing like an angel, baby. I swear you've gotten so good, you remind me of me. Sing it with me? Just once? Please?"

Harm shook his head, but she'd already stepped up beside him. He closed his eyes, and they inhaled like they shared one breath between them.

They sang wide-open and full, their voices wheeling and dipping like birds across a white winter sky, fitting together in ways I never knew voices could fit. Their voices faded away and they opened their eyes.

"Wow," Dale said. "I never heard anything like that. Like your voice got born out of hers, Harm, they fit so smooth."

"Like an angel, baby," Kat said, swishing to the door. She turned and gave him one last smile. "Nashville would eat you up. Good luck with that treasure hunt, kids. Watch out for the curse, Dale. I'd hate for Harm to lose you."

She slammed out, and we went to the window to wave her good-bye.

"You sounded great," Dale said again. "But I don't want you going to Nashville."

"I won't. She means the things she says, but she forgets them fast as she says them."

We watched her taillights bounce out of the yard.

"Happens every time," he said. "I believe every word she says—right up until she's gone."

Dear Upstream Mother,

Kat forgot to give us a ride home. Dale called Lavender, who came for us.

I rode in the middle. Lavender smelled like Ivory soap and dust. He asked about you and I gave him your regards. When he knows you better, I'll give him your love.

Kat and Mr. Red scrape against each other like a bicycle chain against a bent guard. So far, I don't know what happened between them.

But Mr. Red said there was zero chance of Gabriel Archer <u>happening</u> into Kat's club in Nashville, talking about Tupelo Landing, and he's right. Either Gabriel tracked her down—or Kat was flat-out lying.

All I know is if she's the one emptying Mr. Red's money jars, Mr. Red's going to be broke faster instead of slower, and once he's broke Kat's help will look better and better to him. Not that I would say that to Harm.

Sadly we have school tomorrow, so the day is pre-wasted.

Mo

PS: We found Mary Ormond's map! We're halfway to rich—and halfway to funding a mega-search for you.

Chapter Twelve
We've Been Robbed!

The next morning, a Friday, started out normal as cornflakes and went crackers by eight a.m.

Attila dropped a bag on the café counter. "*I* found Colonial musket balls," she said. "Gabriel's going to have them appraised. What have *you* found, Mo?"

Only the treasure map, I thought. "Nothing," I said.

"Start my three-minute eggs, loser," she said, and tossed her hair.

"Soft-boiled for the half-baked," I shouted to the Colonel, who was filling the coffee urn.

"Kat says I'm a whiz with a metal detector," Attila told the Azalea Women. "I've found a sword hilt, these musket balls, and a fancy shoe buckle—all of it Blackbeard's."

"Or else it belonged to another dead person," Dale said, sloshing by with water for Queen Elizabeth. "The unfamous lose stuff too. They're famous for it. Right, Colonel?"

The Colonel, who was counting scoops of coffee, kept counting.

"Colonel," an Azalea Woman fluttered, "what *are* your

thoughts on Anna's luck with history's knickknacks? Perhaps she's a reincarnated pirate," she said, and tittered.

Miss Lana believes in reincarnation. Also auras, chakras, and tarot cards. The Colonel believes in stars, cash, and Miss Lana and me. As their kid, I walk a fine line.

The Colonel snapped the urn closed, turned it on, and marched to the kitchen.

"His hearing comes and goes," I told the Azalea Women, very diplomatic. Mostly when they come, it goes. But like Miss Lana says, you don't have to say everything you know.

Jake Exum hopped a counter stool. "Hey, Miss Lana," he whispered. "Jimmy and me will dig up a treasure for you after school, only we forgot our breakfast money."

She speed-wrapped two biscuits and popped them in a bag. "No digging. Scoot," she whispered. Miss Lana says the day she can't feed a hungry child is the day she wears a plain brown dress and flat hair. Meaning never.

Attila perked up as Gabriel bustled in. "Morning, Gabriel," she sang out. "Where's Kat? I'm ready with my artifact report."

"Later," he said, not looking at her. "Mo, put my cheese biscuit on Miss Thornton's tab. Or give me credit."

"Cash only," the Colonel shouted from the kitchen.

"The Colonel's hearing is back," Dale reported.

Gabriel patted his pockets. "Anna, do you have cash? Help me out, sweetie."

"Don't call her sweetie," I said. "You don't know her good enough. Attila deserves respect even if she is her."

"No credit? Hicks," Gabriel muttered, his face going dark.

My temper popped. "If you need credit, go to a McDonald's and beg for credit at the drive-thru. Me and my co-hicks ain't covering you."

"Mo!" Miss Lana cried. "Manners!"

Gabriel scooped up Attila's musket balls and stomped out as the phone rang. I grabbed it, my temper still simmering.

Harm's voice came through thin and scared. "Mo, is Detective Starr there?"

"Starr?" I said. "No. What's wrong?"

"Joe's in Ocracoke, sugar," Miss Lana whispered. "On business."

"He's out of town," I told Harm. *"What's wrong?"*

"We've been robbed," Harm said as Gabriel roared out of the parking lot. "Our map's gone, Mo. Get over here, quick. We need help."

Harm met us in the front yard, shivering in his pale blue pajamas and black loafers.

"I'm sorry," he said as we dropped our bikes. "I put the map on the kitchen table with my books before I went to bed. I was going to bring it by the café this morning, and ask the Colonel to keep it for us. I locked the doors. I *know* I did. I double-checked, because of Attila." His breath shook. "I'm sorry."

"If you didn't steal it, it's not your fault," Dale said. "What else is missing?"

"Just our map, I think," he said. "A couple closet doors were open, but Gramps might have done that. There's something else," he said, leading the way to his window as thunder muttered in the distance and an airplane puttered overhead. "On my windowsill. It looks like a bloody handprint—but no handprint I've ever seen. No fingerprints, a weird lifeline . . ."

"He was tall, to lean here," Dale said, going onto his toes to look at the handprint. "Wonder how long he stood here, watching you sleep."

"Jeez, Dale," Harm said.

"Gabriel Archer's tall," I said. "He just left to have some artifacts appraised. I'll bet our map was one of them."

"Whoever it was wears strange shoes," Dale said, dropping to one knee to check the prints. "These have tacks in the soles. Like Peg-Leg's boot, in the Littles' attic," he said as Mr. Red slammed out the back door, scowling.

"Starr's not coming back 'til Monday," Mr. Red fumed, stuffing his pajama shirt into his work pants. "Just like a lawman. Gone when you need him, stuck to you like a cocklebur when you don't."

I made an Executive Decision. "With Starr gone, we got

borderline jurisdiction. I'm claiming this as a Desperado crime scene. Harm, we need a blood sample from the windowsill and we need some evidence bags."

"Freezer bags work good," Dale told him.

"I'll get them, and a paint scraper to pry up paint chips," Harm said, heading inside.

"Mr. Red, we need a note saying why we're late for school. Dale, you handle footprints. I'll shoot the crime scene photos."

Lightning flashed in the dark clouds boiling toward us.

"You got thirty minutes before the storm hits," Mr. Red told us, and the race was on.

"More weird footprints," Dale shouted, checking by the door. "Going in and out."

I lined up my photos: windowsill, footprints. I backed up toward the dog pen for an establishing shot. "There's footprints over here too," I called, and Dale hurried over.

He studied the yard. "My big-picture thought: Gabriel stood at the window, walked in, grabbed the map, and came here, near the dogs—who barked their heads off."

"They did bark—around four a.m.," Mr. Red said, strolling over. "I shouted them quiet."

"The thief did some whirling in these weeds," Dale said. "See how they're pressed down? Then he ran for the woods. But why?"

"The dogs barked again, maybe," I said, clicking off a few

photos. "He was afraid Mr. Red would come out or shoot out the window."

The wind barreled across the yard, bending the broom-straw low. Something glinted by the shed.

"Our map!" I shouted. "Gabriel must have dropped it. It's all here but the riddle." I photographed it, peeled off my jacket, and wrapped it up. "We'll check it for fingerprints."

The wind gusted again, setting something twisting in a privet at the edge of the woods. Dale rocketed to it and plucked it up. "Plastic wrap!" he called. "The strip you used to wrap the North Arrow piece. Our riddle's out there naked," he said, his voice grim.

Harm hurried over, dressed for school. "We still have the riddle even if we don't have the plaster. I wrote it in my notebook."

I looked into the boiling sky. "Good. We got to cast those footprints now, or lose them."

"I saw plaster of paris by the money jars," Dale said, and hurried off with Harm.

"What are we missing?" I muttered, walking over the crime scene again. I photographed the muddle of footprints by the door—the weird boots with the tacked-on soles walking in, and walking out. I followed the prints to the dog pen. Mr. Red's dogs watched me like a ragtag choir, ready to howl. "Smile," I said, focusing my camera. *Click.*

What's that?

A tremble of blue caught my eye—a sliver of royal-blue fabric dangling from a strand of barbed wire. I bagged it as Harm and Dale headed back—Dale carrying Harm's unopened umbrella, Harm beating a bowl of plaster of paris like pancake batter.

They knelt by the footprints. I held the umbrella over us as the raindrops splatted down.

"Rain. Great. At least things can't get any worse," Harm muttered.

Wrong.

First, Mr. Red's truck stalled out. Second, Grandmother Miss Lacy, who picked us up, needed gas.

Last but not least, we broke the Cardinal Rule of Note Presentation: Read it before you hand it in. As Miss Retzyl scanned the note Mr. Red had penned for us, her face went a detention shade of red.

We took a step back. I smiled. "Whatever the problem is, I can explain."

She read the note out: *"Dear Priscilla, The kids are late due to a break-in at my place. If your boyfriend Joe Starr had been on the job they would have been on time, so blame him. It's just middle school anyway. Cordially, Red Baker."*

The classroom went quiet as death. Possibly ours.

"We share your disappointment," I said as Dale's stomach rumbled. "Thank you for that reminder, Dale," I added. "Miss Retzyl, it may cheer you to know Dale and me left the café without our lunches this morning. Starvation is harsh punishment. I only hope it teaches us a lesson."

"Sit down," she snapped, and we slipped into our seats.

At lunchtime, Harm opened his pack of orange, four-corner Nabs. "Have one," he offered, and glanced at Attila. She sat bragging to a pack of seventh graders about the musket balls, shoe buckle, and sword hilt she'd found.

"She found all those artifacts for Gabriel?" Harm muttered. "Incredible."

Before I could answer, the Colonel marched in with white takeout bags.

Our lunches!

"Colonel!" I shouted. "Over here!" He waved and headed for the lunchroom lady.

I rushed for him as Attila jumped up and grabbed at a seventh-grade boy who'd swiped her dessert. "Give that back," she said, zigging as I zagged.

We shoulder-slammed hard enough to send my Upstream Mother pendant swinging.

"Watch where you're going, Slow-Mo," Attila said, bumping me again. The seventh graders laughed, and I felt my neck go red.

"I *was* watching, zit-wit," I said, bumping her back. "And don't you ever . . . push . . . me . . . again," I said, giving her a shove. Attila stumbled, clawing for balance. Her fingers hooked my necklace. She snatched it to the floor and her eyes went narrow and mean. She slowly raised her foot—and stomped my pendant.

It crunched like a pecan does—loud and helpless.

Attila smirked and took her foot away.

No, I thought, looking at the broken pendant. Please, no.

The lunchroom disappeared and the days between kindergarten and sixth grade melted away in a red-hot lava of rage. It was me and Attila on the kindergarten playground, alone, enemies to the death, our baby venom flowing.

I lowered my head and charged. The round of my head hit the soft of her belly. She wheezed, crumpled, and skittered backwards into Thes's lap.

I scooped up my necklace and my treasure fell open in my hand. Harm's shocked face and Dale's worried eyes went to blurs.

My knees sagged. I sat down on the floor. Hard.

I looked at the Colonel, across the room. As if he heard my heart scream, he turned to me. "Soldier!" he shouted, and sprinted toward me, shoving empty chairs aside. "Are you okay?" he asked, sliding up beside me. "Are you hurt?"

I held my necklace to him the way I used to hold a broken

toy for him to fix. The fine chain rained across my hand and I felt my face crumple. He cupped his hand beneath mine and stared into the locket.

From inside the tear-shaped pendant, a photo stared up at us.

Breathe, I heard Miss Lana whisper in my mind. Breathe.

Dale bumped down on the floor. "A picture?" he asked. "Is it Upstream Mother?"

"It can't be," Harm said, kneeling beside me. "That's a man."

Chapter Thirteen
A 911 Darkroom Situation

That afternoon, Miss Lana leaned against the counter, studying the photo of the curly-haired man pumping gas. "He's a handsome somebody," she said, and I felt as proud as if I'd breathed life into him myself.

"I looked twenty times today to make sure it was real," I said. "Of course he could be anybody to Upstream Mother. A brother or an uncle or a friend . . ."

"Whoever he is, he's a heck of a clue," Harm said as the Colonel cracked a roll of quarters like an egg and clattered the coins into the cash register. "Colonel, you said you checked the pendant for fingerprints. But you *couldn't* have looked inside."

My breath caught. Upstream Mother's fingerprints.

"Maybe Joe can check. Priscilla says he'll be back Monday," Miss Lana said, sliding the pendant to me.

"This photo's so small," Harm said, studying it. "If a picture's worth a thousand words, we're missing nine hundred of them here. Can you enlarge it, Mo?"

Brilliant! "Let's ask Grandmother Miss Lacy."

"We need to fingerprint it first," he said. He tapped his fingers against the countertop. "Starr's going to have a lot to deal with when he comes back. The crime scene at our house, plus whatever he's working on out of town. I say we pull the prints ourselves. That way we can enlarge the photo now, without damaging the fingerprints. And we only have to ask Starr to run the prints—which makes it easier for him to do us a favor. What do you say, Mo? I know how. Gabriel Archer isn't the only man who does his research."

Pull the print ourselves?

I searched for words that supported Harm as a fellow detective, yet expressed doubt in a subtle, non-threatening way. I failed. "Are you insane?" I asked. "We never lifted a print before and this is the most important clue of my life."

Dale helped himself to cake. "If Joe Starr can do it, it can't be that hard," he said.

Harm hopped up. "It's not. But we'll practice first. We need cocoa powder, clear packing tape, a makeup brush, and white paper."

"Coming up," Miss Lana said.

Two blinks later, I pressed my finger against the counter for our practice attempt. Harm dipped Miss Lana's makeup brush in cocoa powder, twirled it over the prints, and blew the residue away. He pressed tape over my print, peeled it up, and pressed it on the white paper. There I was—fingerprinted in cocoa powder.

"Cool," Dale whispered. Everyone looked at me, waiting.

The Colonel says a leader shows faith in her team. I slid my pendant to Harm.

He swirled the cocoa-tinged brush inside the locket and blew. "There's no print on the photo," he reported, "but I got a doozy opposite the photo. She may have held it still on this side, and dropped the photo in by its edges."

He reached for the tape, and I pushed his hand away. "Let me," I said. "It increases your chance of survival because if you mess this up, I might kill you." I held my breath and pressed the tape over the cocoa fingerprint. Gently, I peeled it away. Dale slid a sheet of typing paper to me and I stuck tape to paper.

The print's dark whorl stood out bold and perfect against the stark white paper.

I went dizzy as my heart spun along its swirls. "It's hers. I can feel her in my bones."

"We got a 911 situation," I told Grandmother Miss Lacy minutes later as she closed the darkroom door behind us. I handed her my open locket. "I want you to meet somebody."

"Oh my," she said, sliding her glasses to the tip of her nose. "Who is he?"

"That's what we want to find out," Harm said. "Only we need to make it larger."

"Of course," she murmured, and placed the locket next to her ancient enlarger—a crank-it-up praying mantis of a machine. "This photo's so tiny. Let's lift it out and see if we can make a negative. If we can, we'll use it to make a larger print."

"You probably have a special tool for that," I said.

"My eyebrow tweezers, dear," she said. "Back in a flash."

Her hand shook as she tweezed the photo out and placed it on the counter. I pressed close, staring at the mishmash of paper behind the photo. "Newspaper," I said.

She handed me the tweezers. I lifted the newspaper out and gently opened it. "Looks like part of an ad. An address. 67A South Ma . . ."

Harm frowned. "Every town has a South Main."

"Not us," Dale said. "We got First Street and Last Street. That's it."

I turned the photo over. There, in bold black ink, one word: **ALWAYS.** "Always Man," I said, turning the photo face-front. "Nice to meet you."

An hour later, I slipped our negative into the enlarger and cranked it up.

Always Man stood filling a car with gasoline, one hand on the gas nozzle, the other in his pocket. His face was wide and handsome, and his dark hair a little wild. Except for that, he was a detective's bad dream: average height, average weight. He wore dark pants and a lighter shirt, and a jacket left unbuttoned.

"Look at all those cars parked by the garage door," Harm said, leaning close.

"Maybe he did repairs too," Dale said. "Like Lavender."

"Wonder if we can run the plates," Harm said, and I cranked the enlarger again. The license plates went fuzzy, except the front plate on the car getting gas—a town plate. A sidewalk sign blocked most of the plate, but the last letters popped. ". . . TON, NC," I read.

"That could be a lot of places," Harm said. "Washington, Clayton, Wilmington . . . Check out that sidewalk sign. *Ann's Clothes.*"

Grandmother Miss Lacy adjusted her bifocals. "Fascinating. An everyday moment, trapped like a butterfly beneath glass."

Old-person thought. I moved on.

"So we're looking for a garage next to Ann's Clothes. On a South Main Street, in Somewhere-ton, NC," I muttered. "Unless that car stopped in from out of town."

I studied Always Man's face. He was smiling, and heading for a wink. "He has attitude. He's mugging for the camera."

"No, dear," Grandmother Miss Lacy said. "He's flirting."

"What do you know about flirting?" I asked. "You're old."

She laughed. "Maybe, but as I recall, this is flirting. He really liked the person taking this photograph."

"Yeah. He did," Harm said, his voice soft.

"And whoever took this photo had a very good eye,"

Grandmother Miss Lacy said, touching my hand. "Almost as good as yours."

"We got to go," Dale said a little later. "I forgot to tell you, Mama asked me to take Lavender's scarf to him. He left it at our house last night."

A visit with Lavender? Could the day get better?

It could have, but it didn't. Our trip to Lavender's fell apart as we pedaled by the Episcopal church. "What's that?" Harm asked, pointing.

I slammed on brakes. A thin beam of light flickered across the graveyard, wheeled up into the cedars and oaks, and back down.

Who would prowl a graveyard in the dark?

"Probably Jake and Jimmy Exum," I said, my throat going dry.

Dale shook his head. "They're dead scared of ghosts."

The light flickered, and voices rose and fell on the breeze.

"Let's check it out," Harm said, leaning his bike against a pine. He crouched and darted to the ivy-draped fence, Dale and me close behind.

I heard a man's voice, then another. "Did you bring a shovel?" the first man asked.

Dale gasped. "A shovel? In a graveyard?"

"We don't need a shovel—yet," a familiar voice responded.

"Gabriel Archer," I said as we peeked over the fence. The clouds shifted, moonlight tiptoeing along the tombstones as Gabriel hunched over his Ground Penetrating Radar.

Dale shook his head. "Gabriel's a Dead Peeping Tom."

"Or a grave robber," I said as the second man pointed to a cross-shaped headstone. "Surveillance mode," I whispered.

Gabriel muscled the GPR to the cross-shaped stone. On the other side of the cemetery, I could just make out his Jaguar and trailer.

"This is the last resting place that fits the bill," the stranger said. "If this isn't it, I flew a long way for not very much."

Resting place? I looked at the headstone and my heart dove to my sneakers.

"*Cross over resting,*" I whispered. "A *cross over* somebody's *resting* place." The men studied the radar's screen as Gabriel inched the machine along.

"And a river beside land," Harm whispered back. "*Loose beside still.*"

"I knew it. Gabriel has our clue. And if we don't do something fast, he'll have our treasure too." I grabbed a small stick, shoved it in my jacket pocket, and rose.

Harm grabbed my arm and pulled me down. "Wait, Mo. We don't have a plan."

"Yes we do. Ad-lib," I whispered, and stood. "Stop, thieves, you're under arrest!" I charged down the fence to the gate,

Harm a half step behind. As we tore through the gate, footsteps pounded toward the car. Gabriel stood alone in the moonlight, his hands in the air.

"Where's your accomplice?" I demanded.

He sneered, the razor-thin scar on his face made paler by moonlight. "My what?"

"Dale," Harm shouted. "Tell Starr's men to look for Gabriel's assistant. Male, six feet tall, thin with a little pot belly." Harm's good with details. Also with ad-libbing.

"Robert that," Dale said from behind the fence, and I heard him pedal off.

"He means Roger that," I said, walking behind Gabriel and jabbing my stick into his back. "Confess and I'll ask Starr to go easy on you."

"Confess to what? I'm just following up on a clue."

"A clue you stole—from us."

"Prove it," he said, his voice going cold and poison. "And if you've been robbed, I'd look at Tinks Williams if I were you. I wouldn't trust him as far as I can spit."

Please.

"A pathetic diversion," I told Harm. "I been knowing Tinks all my life."

We stood still as tombstones until, moments later, a siren warbled in the distance. Harm looked at me, his eyes wide.

Crud. Joe Starr's out of town. That's Dale, howling his coyote siren.

The howl grew closer. Grandmother Miss Lacy's Buick screeched to a halt at the curb—or where the curb would be if Last Street had curbs. Dale sang his siren winding down. He hurtled through the gate, Grandmother Miss Lacy hobbling behind on her cane.

"Really?" Gabriel said, his voice a velvet noose.

"Plundering our cemetery. The very idea." Grandmother Miss Lacy puffed, grabbing Harm's shoulder for support. "My mother rests here. My father too. Explain yourself."

"Miss Thornton, I'm so sorry these children disturbed you. I'm simply following up on a clue . . ."

"Under cover of darkness?" she snapped.

"Because I didn't want to upset anyone," Gabriel said promptly. "I checked your laws, Miss Thornton. They don't forbid bringing a GPR into a churchyard."

"They will by tomorrow noon," she fumed, and turned to me. "Have you checked the gravestones for damage?"

The Desperados fanned out. We searched grave by grave, Dale sticking to me like flypaper. Dale's not good with the dead.

"Nothing damaged," Harm reported. "Where's your friend, Archer?"

Gabriel's voice slid through the night like a snake. "No idea what you mean. Miss Thornton, are you calling an actual officer of the law? I need to get home."

"Come in here again, and I'll arrest you myself," she said.

"Then I wouldn't dare return," he said, and sauntered away.

He doesn't need to come back, I thought. He has our riddle and he took a darned good stab at solving it. He also checked every grave out here—and came up empty.

"We better solve that riddle before Gabriel does," I said as a small plane coughed across the sky. "If we don't, we can kiss the Treasure of Tupelo Landing good-bye."

Dear Upstream Mother,

We found the photo of Always Man! Lavender says he looks like a guy he'd like to know. Did you take it?

I'm good with a camera too.

On other fronts, Harm's cooking dinner for Kat soon. He's asked her twice, but so far she's busy. One day I will cook for you. I can do pb&j on whole wheat or white, hand-squished or fluffy.

Starr's back on Monday and I hope he arrests Gabriel Archer. This weekend we're working on the riddle and developing our crime scene photos from Harm's place. Starr will need them.

Mo

PS The fingerprints on our map were too smeared to lift. Crud.

Chapter Fourteen
The Cocoa Fingerprint

Monday morning Miss Lana and me taped a map of North Carolina on the wall by the jukebox and highlighted towns ending in TON. I freshened the stack of Ugly Trim flyers by the cash register and thumbtacked a photo of Always Man on the bulletin board.

By the time Starr blew in, we were ready for him too. Harm had already gone down his checklist: "Evidence from the break-in at my house, with photos—check. Notes on Gabriel in the graveyard—check. One cocoa fingerprint from Mo's pendant—check."

Starr strolled in, whistling. "Morning, everybody. Coffee please, Lana." He scooted onto a stool and placed his hat on the counter. "Nice weather for January."

Pleasant weather chitchat from Starr—a first.

"Welcome," I said, writing out a check for his coffee and ripping it from my pad. I held it up, crumpled it into a ball, and tossed it toward the trash. "Your coffee's on the Desperados this morning—a professional courtesy."

"You have to *be* a professional to offer a professional

courtesy, Mo," he said, placing two dollars by his cup as Miss Lana splashed it full. "So. What's new?"

"Let me, Mo," Harm said. "First, you missed a robbery. At my place."

"Gabriel broke in and stole our clue," Dale added.

"Your clue? Anything else disturbed?" Starr asked.

"Harm and Mr. Red," Dale said. "The dogs seemed fine."

Harm slid my crime scene photos to Starr. He thumbed through, frowning at the photo of the weird footprints. He kept thumbing. Somehow, he didn't seem surprised enough.

"Sorry I wasn't here, Harm. Any idea who would do this?"

"Gabriel Archer, like Dale said," I told him. "We found him in the graveyard, following up on our clue."

Starr clicked his pen. "He's not the only one after the treasure. There's Kat and Anna. The Exum boys are digging up half the town—I have a hat full of complaints. I hear your uncles are poking around, Dale. And I've had to invite a couple of strangers to leave town."

He studied the close-up of the handprint on Harm's windowsill.

"No fingerprints and that weird lifeline," Harm said. "I took a blood sample," he added, dropping our paint chip by Starr's cup.

"Nice job, Desperados," Starr said. "Mo—great photography."

Compliments? From Starr?

"I don't mean to pry," I lied. "But have you been away in

rehab? Because you seem like a changed person and Oprah says that can happen."

"Nope, but thanks for asking," he said, opening his notepad. "A few days off and a rosy future always cheers me up. Harm, I hear Kat dropped by the night you were robbed."

My Detective Senses went on red alert.

"How did you know?" I asked. "We didn't tell you which night Harm got robbed, and we didn't mention Kat's visit."

Starr clicked his pen. "Red left me a message the morning of the robbery. I called him this morning. I got his take on the breaking and entering, but I want your take too. As borderline professionals. So, Kat did stop in. Right?"

"She did, but she's not in this," Harm said.

Starr smoothed his eyebrow. "Right. I ran a background check on her."

Harm went six shades of red. "You didn't need to," he said, his voice sharp. "You could have asked me. Bad checks, a couple of eviction notices, unpaid parking tickets. It's hard to pay for everything when you're gigging for next to nothing and trying to feed a kid."

Starr nodded. "Right. So Kat comes to town with Gabriel and visits you for the first time in three years—on the day you find a treasure map. And that same night someone breaks in and takes your map and then runs off with your clue. Funny string of coincidences."

Not that funny, I thought, reading Harm's eyes.

"Did Kat see the map?" Starr asked.

"No," Harm said. "She was with us the whole time."

"Didn't leave to use the bathroom? Or stretch her legs, anything like that?"

"No," Harm said. "Besides, Kat has small feet. Those footprints are huge."

"Size twelve in a man's shoe," Dale said, sliding the cast to Starr. "Sal looked it up."

"Thanks. Anything else?"

Harm took out our cocoa fingerprint. "We're hoping you'll run this for us."

Starr picked it up. "Cocoa powder?" he asked, sniffing. "Good use of resources. I'll see what I can do." He swaggered to the door, and turned. Starr's nice-looking when he's not being a jerk. "One more thing. Did you see the map after Kat left?"

"Sure," Harm said. "I put it on the kitchen table."

"Did you lock your doors? Any sign of a break-in?"

"I locked up for sure. And no sign of a break-in."

"Interesting. Kat grew up in that house," Starr said. "Does she still have a key?"

Harm went pale.

Crud. The house key. Why didn't I think of that?

"We thought of that," I said. "While I can neither deny nor confirm Kat's key status, I can tell you we have the situation under investigation."

"Great. So do I. Let's stay in touch, Desperados," Starr said, and stalked out the door.

That afternoon after school, Harm paced the length of my narrow flat. "She has to have a key. Why didn't I see that?"

"Even if she does, that doesn't mean she used it," Dale said as Queen Elizabeth scratched at the door. He let her in. "Think about something else," Dale told Harm. "You're recessing."

"I'm *obsessing,*" Harm said, taking a deep breath. "And you're right."

He riffled through the old newspaper clippings Miss Lana and the Colonel collected, when I was a baby. "Did I mention I'm cooking dinner for Kat on Thursday night?" he asked. "At Miss Thornton's. You two are invited. And Sal."

"You told us twice," Dale said.

Harm studied a clipping. "You got a lot of publicity, Mo. You'd think somebody would have come for you. Only . . ." He scanned a photo of a flooded town, the roofs and chimneys peeking through the water. "Jeez, what a nightmare."

He opened my scrapbook, stopping on the articles on our first case. "No wonder we get so many letters," he said. "You guys were famous detectives before I ever came to town."

"True," I said, very modest. "Plus people write to see if I'm somebody they lost, or if I'm connected to their missing people. Miss Lana says it's natural."

"Really? What do you do with the letters?" Harm asked, turning another page.

I hesitated. "I archive them."

"No you don't," Dale said. "You throw them in your sock drawer. You probably have fifty letters in there." Harm lit up like Christmas.

"Fifty people looking for lost family members? Why didn't you tell me? We can send them a photo of Always Man. One of them might recognize him." He turned my album page, stopping on a scratchy old black-and-white. "Where's this? I recognize Miss Lana, but . . ."

"That's not Miss Lana," I said. "That's her mother. Outside Charleston."

Dale opened my sock drawer and pawed through for letters. "Harm's right, Mo. And Miss Lana looks like her mother, Harm looks like Mr. Red, I look like Daddy. Maybe you look like Upstream Mother did when she was a girl. We can send your school photo. Unless you want one where you actually comb your hair first."

Upstream Mother used to be a girl, like me. Somehow I never thought of that.

"Brilliant," Harm said, grinning. "We need a letter, Mo. A good one. And then all we need is postage and a little luck to carry you home."

The next afternoon, before the supper rush, I pulled the

Colonel and Miss Lana aside. "I got a surprise, and I hope it's a good one," I told them.

Tinks watched as we moved to a table by the Winter Tree. Miss Lana read the letter low and sweet, wrapped in the tree's neon halo.

> Dear Possible Family Member,
>
> Thanks for contacting the Desperado Detective Agency to see if I might be related to you or your missing loved one. Here's two photos I hope you'll take a look at. The first is a person of interest in the Mystery of My Life, and maybe yours too. Do you know him? Is he yours?
>
> The second is me, Miss Moses LoBeau, a sixth grader in her prime. Are you missing me or anybody similar? And if you are missing somebody similar and she might be my Upstream Mother, do you know where she is?
>
> I'm enclosing a stamped envelope addressed to my associate Harm Crenshaw for your reply. Or you can call the café at 252-555-CAFÉ.
>
> Sincerely—or, if we are related—love,
>
> Mo

The Colonel looked at the photo of Always Man, and then at my stack of envelopes, all addressed in Harm's neat hand and stamped with Grandmother Miss Lacy's stamps.

"What do you think?" I asked.

"I think I'm an arrogant fool," he said, looking at Miss Lana. "This was easy when we were looking for *her*. But now that we're looking for a *man,* I'm a queasy sack of what-ifs and let's-nots. I underestimated the collateral damage to your heart, Lana, and I am sorry."

I went rudderless in the moment's flow.

"You're not that arrogant, sir, no matter what people say."

He ruffled the envelopes. "You never completely understand what someone feels until you feel it yourself. Forgive me, Lana," he said, his eyes glistening. "I admire your courage."

"There's nothing to forgive, Colonel," she said. "You can't know before you know."

He stood and squared his shoulders. "Good letter, Soldier. Excellent planning deserves excellent follow-through. Hop in the Underbird, we'll mail them now."

I grabbed his elbow. "Wait, Colonel. I didn't know you'd be scared."

"Neither did I," he said. "But fear is a bully best met head-on."

Miss Lana snagged her 1940s swing jacket. "Tinks," she said, "I know you can't stand to touch meat and we cook up a lot of burgers, but can you handle the café until we get back? You can just do pb&j's, or soup . . . Is that too crazy?"

"Crazy ain't crazy if it works," he said, slipping to the business side of the counter.

She hooked her arm in mine and gave the Colonel a smile that would have melted a lesser man. "Let's get this show on the road," she said, and headed for the door.

That night I sat in bed, my 6x4 of Always Man propped on my bookcase, the *Piggly Wiggly Chronicles* on my lap. My phone jangled. Nine twenty-eight p.m.

I snagged it. "Desperado Detective Agency. Misdemeanors intrigue, felonies delight. How may we serve in the darkest hour of your life?"

Skeeter's voice came through calm and professional. "Mo? Skeeter. My staff's left but I thought I'd pick up the phone." Skeeter has staff like I got the measles. "The report on your sweater is in," she continued. "I called the café earlier, but Tinks said you were out on a case."

The sweater! My heart kicked into overdrive. "Is it hers?"

In the background, a knock at Skeeter's door. "Skeeter?" her mom called. "Lights out."

Skeeter sighed. "I'm sorry, Mo, I have a conference call coming through. Meet me at my satellite office tomorrow morning. All three of you."

"Skeeter! Now!" her mother shouted, and Skeeter hung up the phone.

Chapter Fifteen
Cover for Me

The next morning, I woke up ready for the biggest news of my life.

I dressed and shot into the café, which was already standing room only. "Miss Lana," I said, grabbing my order pad. "I got news. Big news. Skeeter called, and—"

"In a minute, sugar," she told me, grabbing an order. "I'm up to my eyebrows. Colonel, can you reload the coffeemaker? Dale, toast? Mo, jump in, sugar."

Miss Lana might be all smiles, but she ramrods a café crew good as the Colonel.

The town swirled in and out, keeping the cash register ringing.

"Good morning, fellow citizens," the mayor called, smoothing his tie over his round belly and beaming around the room. "Mother and I have returned from the Thorny Plant Convention!"

"You were gone?" an Azalea Woman asked.

"You're such a tease," he replied, tiptoeing to his usual

seat. "Mo, Mother and I would like an update on the treasure hunt this afternoon."

"That's bad," Dale whispered. "We don't have one."

"Dale means our report is complete, minus charts and statistics. We'll drop by this evening," I told him as the phone rang again.

"Café," I answered. "Mo speaking . . . Miss Retzyl! Dale and I were just saying how much we look forward to school today because . . . Gabriel Archer? Yes ma'am, please hold. GABRIEL! TELEPHONE."

Gabriel pushed through the crowd, jostling Tinks, and grabbed the phone. "Priscilla? I was just thinking of you," he said as Dale shot by with a tray of waters. "I hate to stand you up, but I must."

Dale skidded to a halt. "He's standing Miss Retzyl up," he said, frowning. "That's rude, only I'm glad. He'd be terrible for her."

"Another time," Gabriel said into the phone, smiling like an oil slick. "Ciao." He winked at the Azalea Women, who smiled at him like high school girls smile at quarterbacks.

Dale looked at him, shocked. "You had a date with Miss Retzyl."

Gabriel shrugged and strolled away.

"Nonsense," Miss Lana said, loading up on toast. "Pris wouldn't waste a minute on him."

I glanced at the clock. Skeeter was waiting. "Desperados," I called. "School!"

"But it's so early, sugar," Miss Lana said, frowning.

I turned my back to the Azalea Women, who may or may not read lips. "Miss Lana, we got a meeting with Skeeter. She called late last night, only you were asleep. My sweater's back. She might even have Upstream Mother's name—and her address."

She went fragile as first ice.

"Miss Lana?" I gasped, grabbing her arm. "Are you okay?"

The Colonel hurtled over and slipped an arm around her. He pointed to a stranger at the counter. "Out," he said, and helped her onto the stool.

Silence rippled across the café in soft, curious rings.

"I'm fine," Miss Lana said, the color finding her pretty face. "It's just . . . so sudden."

Sudden? How could it be sudden when I been waiting all my life?

"I wanted to tell you sooner, but we got so busy."

"I'm fine," she said again, blinking at me. "Wear your mittens, sugar. It's cold."

Mittens? I haven't worn mittens since second grade.

"Carry on, Soldier," the Colonel said. "I'm with Lana."

At the door, I turned to give her a smile. Even with the Colonel by her side, Miss Lana looked alone—like the still, forgotten place in the spin of a storm.

I swept back to give her a hug.

"Keep me posted, sugar," she said, smoothing my hair. "I usually love surprises—but not about this. I hate being an understudy in my own life story."

An understudy in her own life story? Sometimes trying to unscramble Miss Lana's words is like trying to unscramble eggs.

"Welcome, Desperados," Skeeter said moments later. "Take a seat."

We took a trio of teacher-quality chairs as Sal eased the office door closed. "Hey, Dale," Sal said, and Dale went bright red. Again.

Skeeter slid my Belk box to me. "I only have a minute, so I'll be brief."

I opened it. My sweater lay inside.

Thank heavens, I thought. It's come home.

Skeeter rattled a paper. "Mo, the DNA proves it. Your mom *did* wear this. Additionally, lab reports show the sweater's pure wool—hand spun, hand knit. And it was patched. Here," she said, turning the right sleeve toward me.

"I didn't see that before," I said. Somehow my voice sounded far away.

"Most people wouldn't. The lab tested the repair. It's a different yarn. There's more." She paused. "Sal's cousin ran your mom's DNA through the criminal database."

My breath bottlenecked somewhere near my heart.

Harm leaned forward. "And?"

"No match," Sal said, her voice soft. "I'm sorry she's not doing time, Mo. It would have been an easy I.D."

"I'm not sorry," Dale said. "Being in an outlaw family makes you a social leopard."

"A social *leper,* Dale," Sal said as Skeeter popped open her briefcase and shuffled some papers.

The first bell rang.

I scooped up my sweater box. "I got to make a phone call. Cover for me," I told Dale as they trooped toward class.

Skeeter nodded toward the phone on a neighboring desk. "I hate to mention it, but our internet search for Ann's Clothes came up empty too. I'm really sorry, Mo," she said, her voice soft. Beneath her hard-as-nails professional patina, she's really soft as Sal.

I dialed the café. "Miss Lana," I said, and my voice quavered away to soggy breathing. I hate it when I soggy breathe. I pressed the phone against my ear, trying to get closer.

"Was it hers?" she asked.

"Yes, but that's all I learned."

"I'm so sorry. But it's a good step, sugar. You'll find other clues. You have your whole life to find her."

"Yes ma'am. And Miss Lana," I said, finding the reins to my voice, "you can't be an understudy in our life. You're a star. In my life, and the Colonel's too. I got to go," I added before she could answer, and hung up the phone.

A heartbeat later, I slipped into the girls' room—a dingy dungeon of stalls—the box beneath my arm. I peeled off my jacket and tossed it over a stall door, dried a spot on the scratched countertop, and put the box down. I unfolded the sweater from the box.

I closed my eyes and slipped it on over my T-shirt and pendant.

The sweater still smelled faintly of river and rain. I smoothed it, and looked in the mirror. The shoulders sagged and the sleeves stretched long, but the color was perfect. Indigo—the color of water and skies. I scooched the sleeves to my elbows. It's like a hug knitted in wool, I thought as the tardy bell rang.

Did Upstream Mother knit this? Did someone knit it for her?

I touched the mend. *Did she tear it climbing a tree? Fighting a bully? Did she mend it herself? Where did she get the yarn?*

The yarn, I thought. A clue. Where did she get the yarn?

I glanced into the mirror. Me. Miss Moses LoBeau. Same height as when I woke up. Same eyes, same sturdy fire-hydrant shape, same unruly hair.

Only me in the sweater. Me times me.

Even in the bathroom's life-sucking fluorescent glow, I looked more like myself.

This sweater was my mother's, and now it's mine.

Some histories are written on paper, or stone. Mine's written in yarn.

Two blinks later, I pushed open the classroom door, hoping Dale had covered for me. He whipped toward me. "I can't believe it!" he cried as I strolled in. "It's a miracle!"

Thes and Sal applauded. "Thank heavens," Harm said, his eyes dancing. Miss Retzyl looked at me like a fish not taking a bait.

"It was close but here I am," I ad-libbed, sailing toward my seat.

"Good grief. She's not even limping," Attila said, oozing scorn.

Limping? Why did I ask Dale to cover for me?

I went into my signature limp.

"Lame sweater, Mo," Attila snipped. "It doesn't fit in the shoulders."

"Maybe not, but it's still a perfect fit," I said. "This belonged to Upstream Mother."

The class gasped. Attila looked like I'd clubbed her with a wet hen.

I folded into my desk and smiled at Miss Retzyl. "I am here despite the generic but grave peril described by Dale.

Because you are my role model, I try to be punctual. Because I am not you, I fail."

Miss Retzyl took a deep breath. Her gaze swept from Dale to me, to my sweater. Her eyes went soft. "It's lovely, Mo," she said.

"Excellent look, LoBeau," Harm said, giving me a wink.

The moment passed. Miss Retzyl snapped back into teacher form. "Take out a piece of paper," she said. "We'll get your math test out of the way."

We had a math test?

I hummed as I searched my messenger bag for paper. What did a math test mean to a kid wrapped in her lost mother's arms?

Chapter Sixteen
Dale's Secret

"I'm sorry, Dale," Sal said as we filed out for lunch. "I can't eat with you today. I'm finishing my appraisal of the things in the Littles' attic. I need the school's internet."

Dale went bright red as Sal sashayed away.

"When did Sal learn to sashay?" I asked.

"Last Tuesday," Dale said, his eyes following her.

Harm walked backwards, studying him. "Dale, what's changed? *Sal* used to blush. Now she's cool and you're . . . definitely not. What happened?"

Dale blushed deeper. "Nothing. I don't blush."

Denial, I thought, my heart plummeting. The first sign of everything bad.

We wound through the lunchroom, past the Popular Table, past the Last Person Standing Table, to the Detectives Table. Dale unwrapped his roast beef sandwich and brownies. Harm opened his orange Nabs and tilted his head, letting his hair fall over his eye. A good look. "*Hypothesis:* Dale blushes over Sal," he said.

Dale popped a brownie and looked at us, cheeks bulging.

"But why?" Harm muttered. An idea crept across his face. "You kissed Sal."

Dale went crimson, and shook his head.

"She kissed *you?*" I whispered.

Dale shook his head again. Harm crossed his arms and leaned away, studying Dale. "Ah-*ha,*" he said. "You're *going* to kiss Sal."

Dale sagged. "You're my best friends, so I might as well tell you. I *am* going to kiss Sal, just as soon as I figure out how. Only right now I'm so scared, I might throw up."

My world tilted. Dale? Kissing?

"Not retching is key," Harm said, very suave.

Dale slid his last brownie to Harm's place. A bribe. "Do you know how?"

"Well," Harm said, shooting me a look. "More or less. But . . . not exactly."

Dale slid the brownie toward me. "Mo?"

Me? "How would I know?"

His face fell. He slid the brownie back to his own place and leaned low to lick the crumbs off the waxed paper.

"You could ask Lavender," I said. "He's legendary."

Dale looked up. "Lavender! Why didn't I think of him? Rhetorical," he added.

"We'll stop by his new garage after school. I want to show him my sweater too," I said as Harm polished off his Nabs, leaving behind zero orange crumbs.

How does he do that? My entire life's set on auto-wrinkle. Harm looks creased even in clothes that have no creases.

The bell rang and we began the death march back to class.

Dale is pre-kissing?

Weird. I thought Harm would be the one to go first.

That afternoon as we stampeded for the door, Sal handed me a note. "My preliminary thoughts on your attic appraisal."

"Thanks," I said, and stuffed it in my messenger bag.

Five minutes later, we dropped our bikes outside Lavender's new fixer-upper garage—aka the old general store—and ran inside. Lavender had swept the pine floors until they shone, and cleared the cobwebs off the floor-to-ceiling shelves behind the old counter. He smiled and heaved an old crate of bolts onto the counter. "Hey Desperados. How's life?"

"Hey yourself," I shot back. "Dale's pre-kissing."

"With Sal?" he asked, looking at Dale.

Dale beamed. "She doesn't know yet. I need help. You know how."

"Rumor has it, little brother," Lavender said, heading to a cooler. He plucked out Pepsis, raked the ice down the cans, and handed them around. Lavender is a gentleman.

"Thanks," I said, hopping on the counter. "I hate to mention kissing again, but Dale's need-to-know."

Lavender looked at us the way he always does—like he's glad to see us and not surprised by what we say. "I need to think that over, little brother," he told Dale. "Doing's one thing. Teaching is something different."

"That's okay," Dale said. "I'm in hover mode until Valentine's Day."

"Meantime, I got something to show you," I said. I hopped down, walked into the middle of a dusty sunbeam, and tossed my jacket, revealing my sweater.

"Gorgeous," Lavender said. "Was it hers?"

"A DNA heirloom," Dale told him.

"It absolutely becomes you, Miss LoBeau," he said.

The sweater becomes me. That's what I'd been feeling, all day long.

"So far, we got this sweater, a locket with the initial *J,* the sign I rode into town on, and a photo of Always Man. I'm just not sure how to put it all together," I told him.

"You'll figure it out, Mo," he said, very easy. "You always do."

Lavender worked the tip of a screwdriver around a paint can's lid and popped it open. "So?" he said. "What do you think of the place?"

I looked around the former dump. If Tupelo Landing had a historic district, this old store would be its heartbeat. Outside, ancient bubble-headed gas pumps fronted the drive-under shelter. Lavender had popped two tin ads off the outside wall and propped them against the counter—Dr Pepper and Marita Bread, featuring the Lone Ranger.

"Very Tupelo cool," I told him. "And those shelves look great."

"They will when I get some paint on them."

"You keeping those old bubble-headed gas pumps?" I asked, studying the antique pumps. "Attila says they're worth a fortune and you should sell them."

"Sell them? They're history. And they don't work—a plus, since I don't want to pump gas," he said, grinning. "I'll keep everything old-fashioned except my services. Lana says it's a nice balance—yin and yang. I'll do repairs, restorations . . . And, I've found a barely used stock car over in Fuquay-Varina. I'll be racing again before you know it."

Lavender never downsizes his dream.

"You Desperados free? I could use some help."

Harm and Dale looked at me, their eyes saying yes. Lavender always helps us. Besides, we could brainstorm a report for the Littles, and try to solve Mary Ormond's riddle.

"Your windows are filthy, Lavender Shade Johnson," I said, grabbing a roll of paper towels. "Give me some Windex, and I'll do you proud."

"You always do me proud, Mo," he said. "Boys? Feel like slinging paint?"

"I'll whitewash creation if you tell me what I need to know about kissing," Dale said. "Really, all I need is a clue."

That's Dale. Give him a clue and he can do almost anything.

By day's end, Lavender's windows sparkled and his floor-to-ceiling shelves gleamed. We'd tried fitting Mary Ormond's riddle to everything we could think of while we worked.

Cross over resting—a bridge over the river (Lavender), a ferry (Harm), the church steeple watching over the sleeping town at night (me).

Loose beside still—water beside land (Lavender), wind beside stone (Harm), a bad trip to a dentist where the wrong tooth gets pulled (Dale).

"At least we know Gabriel and Kat haven't solved it either." I sighed.

"How?" Lavender asked.

"We haven't heard Attila bragging," I said, and described Gabriel and the stranger in the graveyard. "They struck out—on *our* riddle."

Lavender frowned. "I saw Kat with a strange man early this morning, at the inn. They were arguing. When I headed for them, he bolted."

Interesting.

"We got to go," I said, pulling one of our Ugly Trim flyers from my messenger bag. "Could I . . ."

"It would be an honor," he said. He taped the flyer to a front window, and then taped up a photo of Always Man with a note that said WANTED. He waited for Dale to finish dabbing the paint from his hair, and put a hand on his shoulder. "My top three thoughts about a first kiss, little brother. Ready?"

"I am," I said, and Harm slouched, trying to look cool.

Dale pulled his notepad from his pocket. "Shoot."

"First," Lavender said, "move slow so she has time to say no if she wants to."

"Slow?" Dale echoed. He moved his head forward a half inch at a time.

"Not like a chicken sneaking up on corn," I told him.

"Smooth," Lavender agreed.

"I thought so," Dale said, making a note. "Second?"

"Kiss light as a feather," Lavender said. "Sweet."

I looked over at Dale's notepad. No chicken to corn. Feather.

"Third, keep your hands to yourself," Lavender said.

Dale nodded. Pockets. "Noses?" he asked. "Noses are in the middle of everything. Which way do they go?"

Lavender studied Dale the way Miss Lana studies a recipe gone bad. "Let me do some research, and I'll get back to you."

We pushed our bikes to the edge of the blacktop and pedaled toward town. "Time to update the Littles," I said.

Harm went no-hands. "I've been thinking, Mo. Maybe we can give them enough to satisfy them without giving our clues away."

"The mayor does babble," Dale reminded me. Like I'd forgotten.

"I say we show them *Tupelo Mother* and keep the attic under lock and key," I said. "Don't mention the map or the missing riddle. Or the clothes—until we know if they're clues. The portrait should make them happy, and keep them off our backs until we find the treasure."

"Two stones with one bird," Dale said. "I like it."

"Sorry to keep you waiting, Desperados," the mayor said, bustling into his parlor. "Tinks and I were planting a cactus. Thorny issue." He chuckled. "I'm all ears."

Harm propped our draped portrait on the table across from the mayor and Mrs. Little.

"Is that treasure?" she asked, hunching forward.

"Depends on what you treasure," I said. "A picture's worth a thousand words, and so now—introducing *Tupelo Mother*." Harm whipped the tablecloth away like a magician.

Somehow, *Tupelo Mother* looked better in the attic's faint light.

Harm cleared his throat. "She looks really yellow in this light, but I think that's because the paint's old. A museum could probably restore the tones."

"I'm not sure about the nose," Dale added. "There's cosmetic surgery in Greenville if you have insurance, but I'm not sure they do art."

"She's gorgeous," Mrs. Little whispered, clasping her hands to her sunken chest.

"Sal's note," Dale whispered, nudging me. "Was it about the painting?"

Crud. I'd forgotten it. I rummaged through my messenger bag and scanned Sal's appraisal as Harm chatted, stalling for time. "Since we found it, it's half yours and half ours," he said. "Please enjoy it while we find the treasure. We actually think this is a portrait of—"

"Nobody!" I shouted.

Harm looked at me like I'd bit him.

"It's an anonymous model, and not a good one," I said. "A total unknown. Right, Dale?"

"Yes?" Dale guessed.

I passed Sal's note to Harm, who read it and gasped.

Mrs. Little's obsidian eyes glittered as she studied the portrait. "*Tupelo Mother.* We'll give her a place of honor, over the mantel." Her gaze whipped to us. "What else have you got?"

"Homework," I said, rising. "We'll be in touch."

"Wait!" she said, holding out her withered hand. "Let me see that sweater."

Crud. I wanted Mrs. Little touching my heirloom sweater like I wanted a plate of liver.

"She's a knitting authority," Harm whispered, shoving me forward. I shrugged out of the sweater, revealing my wrinkled T-shirt and locket. She laid the sweater on her lap and inspected the stitching.

"Handmade," she said. "And old. Very old."

"*Old* means a lot, coming from you," I said, wasting a smile.

"Irish," she replied. "Knitted before Hollywood gussied up the style—I'd say 1930, 1940. Some people say this double chain pattern represents a fisherman's line, and these diamonds mean riches." She ran her hand along the sweater's arm. "What's *this*?"

"A scar," I said.

"Scratchy wool," she muttered. "Pity. Mended, but not by its maker. Then, that's all of us. The mending yarn is hand-spun too, but it runs thick and thin." She frowned. "The original yarn's first-class, made by an artist. The mend's new yarn, bumbled up by a beginner."

"A beginner?" I said. "But . . . I mean, who makes sweater strings?"

I knew it was wrong, but you can't reel words back in and cast them out right.

"Sweater strings?" she shrieked. "You mean who spins *yarn!*" She hooked the sweater on her finger and handed it back, her eyes flashing. "Pearls before swine."

Did she just call me a pig? I counted to ten, just in case.

She reached out, pulled my locket close, and let it thunk back against my gravy stain. "I never cared for the letter *J*. Have that mosquito person look up hand-spinners on her contraption. There aren't that many of us and the mend is fairly new. Get cracking."

"Skeeter? On the internet?" I said, backing toward the door.

"Get out," she said, turning to smile at the portrait.

Outside, we grabbed our bikes. "Mo," Dale whispered, "why didn't you tell Mrs. Little that could be a portrait of Mary Ormond? She'd like that. Mary used to live in her house."

"Because," I muttered, mounting up. "I don't want the Littles to sell it."

"Sell it? Who would buy *that?*"

I looked around. Jake and Jimmy Exum were digging holes along an Azalea Woman's driveway. Other than that, the street was quiet. "According to Sal's note, if it's an eighteenth-century painting of someone nobody knows, it's worth thousands of dollars."

Dale whistled. "That's half of thousands to us."

"But if it's a portrait of Mary Ormond—the fourteenth wife of the most famous pirate ever—that painting's history, Dale. It's worth a fortune."

"Right," Harm said, his voice tight. "And that's half a fortune to us."

Chapter Seventeen
The Fix-It Yarn, Dinner & a Spy

The next day at school, Harm unraveled like a cheap ball of yarn. "Did I tell you I'm cooking for Kat at Miss Thornton's tonight? You're invited," he said at lunch, an orange crumb on his lip. Harm's lips never crumb.

"You told us plenty," I said. "We'll be there."

"Wow," Dale whispered as Harm left for the boys' room. "I haven't seen Harm this uncool since our first gig."

After school, it got worse.

"Mama, I'm home," Dale shouted as we pounded through the living room, to his boy pit of a room. He peeled off his jacket and dropped it on the floor.

"We're in the kitchen," Miss Rose called as Harm collapsed onto the beanbag chair.

Dale scratched Queen Elizabeth's head and hurried to his terrarium. "Hello, little newts," he said. "Dale's home. You remember Mo and Harm." They blinked. "Take it easy. Calm down, sweet amphibians."

Harm hopped up and paced, frowning. "Wear something

nice tonight, Mo. Not too dressy but . . . you know. Your usual cool."

"You already told her," Dale said. He grabbed his jar of freeze-dried bugs and sprinkled them at his newts' feet. "Newts are introverts. Newton's more outgoing, but Madame Curie's picking up social skills." Newton sat still as mud. "See?"

Sometimes I wonder how Dale and me can live in such different worlds and still be on the same planet.

"We need to refocus on our case before I start obsessing," Harm said, like we weren't a day too late on that one. He tugged his math test from his backpack and flipped it over to an obsessively neat list. "Okay, here's my report on the Always Man letters. So far, three people have written back."

My nerves stretched tight as fiddle strings. "And?"

"They were no's," he said, and my heartstrings sagged. "Which means we have forty-seven letters still out."

"We're closing in on her," Dale whispered to his newts.

"And then there's the sweater," Harm continued. "We know it's got two different kinds of wool, and two people wove it. We know it's old, and we know it's from Ireland."

Dale settled down by his bed, his arm around Queen Elizabeth. "You're from Ireland," he said, studying me. "Mo O'LoBeau. It has a nice ring." Liz leaned to lick his chin. She would die a thousand times for Dale, I thought, and him for her.

It's good to have people. And dogs.

Dale smiled at her. "Liz, play dead." She keeled over. "Good!" He scooped half a peanut butter sandwich from beneath his bed and tossed it to her. She thumped her tail.

Harm tapped his list. "You might be Irish, Mo, but I don't see how it helps us."

"Me either. *Yet,*" I said, scratching my arm where the mend hit. I stepped over Dale's guitar and walked over to the puppy portraits hung two feet off the floor. "I thought Grandmother Miss Lacy said to hang these at eye height," I said, straightening a photo.

"I did," Dale said. "Queen Elizabeth's eye height.

"Hey, Bill Glasgow works in a museum. He's a history guy. He might know about old-timey spinners. Of course," he mused, "Bill Glasgow and me are complicated. I made him godfather of Madame Curie. That *could* make Bill my godfather once removed, but I don't think he's a newt-in-law. I could be wrong. But even if he is, we could ask him about your sweater."

He shot to the kitchen, Harm and me on his heels.

"Hey, Desperados," Bill said, taking a pie out of the oven. Bill Glasgow visits Miss Rose most days after work. He's thin and wiry and moves like music owns his bones. He listens to Dale same as Lavender does, and he makes Miss Rose shine. "How was school?"

"School was need-to-know today and we didn't need to know it," I said.

"Sal and me are pre-kissing," Dale added, and Miss Rose looked up from her ledger. Miss Rose has dark hair and green eyes. She's look-again pretty and smiling more now that Dale's daddy ain't around. She's smart and warm, and moves easy as a wheat field in a breeze.

Dale took the plates out of the cabinet. "I'd love to have your top three tips on a first kiss when you have time," he told Bill.

Miss Rose's smile went horizontal. I jumped in, very sensitive. "This ain't a kiss-and-tell situation, Dale. I got a different question, Bill Glasgow. We know you're a history expert. It's about my sweater," I said, holding the mend toward Miss Rose as he cut his sweet potato pie.

"Beautiful work," she said. "Does that mend itch you, Mo? Some wools do."

"A little. Do you know anybody that makes old-timey yarn?" I asked Bill.

"You mean a re-enactor?" he asked. "Lots of historic sites use them. I can check for you." He hesitated. "You know, you can *buy* handspun yarn too."

My heart skipped like an engine with a bad spark plug.

"No. Mo's got rookie fix-it yarn," Dale said. "Not store quality."

Bill grinned, his smile lines deep as gorges. "Good focus, Dale. I'll make some calls, Mo. Meet tomorrow? Same place, new pie."

Harm hopped up. "Don't forget my dinner, Desperados. Come at seven. Mo, dress . . . dark. I'm making spaghetti. I know how you are."

Miss Rose laughed. "Mo knows how to dress," she said. It was a blind-faith statement, but I appreciated it. She tilted her head. "I remember your mom from high school, Harm," she said, her voice careful. "Tell her hello for me."

"Thanks, I will," Harm said, and headed down the hall. The front door slammed.

"And you two be careful around Kat Kline," she added.

"Careful about what?" I asked, picking up my fork.

"That's the thing about her," she said. "You never really know until it's too late."

The Colonel dropped me at Grandmother Miss Lacy's at seven, just as Lavender eased up. Dale and Sal hopped out of his truck, Sal carrying a garment bag. Dale slammed the door, opened it, and lifted the tail of Sal's skirt out. Lavender drove away.

The old house was lit party perfect. Dale smoothed Lavender's electric-blue tie over his black shirt, hitched up his black pants, and knocked.

"You look nice, Mo," Sal said, shifting the garment bag. "I

hope Harm won't mind, but Mama asked me to drop Kat's jacket off," she added.

Thanks to her seamstress mother, Sal's a middle school fashion icon. Her red plaid dress fit perfect, and her high-sheen patent leathers gleamed in the porch light.

I'd selected black spaghetti-proof cords and turtleneck, and my Upstream Mother sweater and locket. The signature plaid sneakers were a no-brainer.

The door swung open.

"You remembered," Harm said, his voice flooding with relief. "Kat called from the inn. She's running behind. You all look great," he said, but he was smiling at me.

I smiled and peeped in the dining room. He'd decked out the long table—tablecloth, real napkins, candles. "You look good too," I told him. True. He wore his usual black slacks and a white shirt, with the cuffs rolled up—a daring spaghetti choice.

"Listen," he whispered, and we stepped nearer. "Keep the conversation friendly, okay? Don't mention the treasure, or Gramps. Or the past. Or the future. Don't mention Gramps running out of money. Or the truck breaking down, or the pipes leaking, or . . ."

"We know how to act, Harm," Sal said. "We're your friends."

Harm closed his eyes. "Sorry. Hang on, I'll get us something to drink."

By the time Kat knocked twenty minutes later, we'd settled in the parlor, nursing iced teas. Grandmother Miss Lacy, in her navy dress, answered the door. "Kat! Come in, dear."

I peeked around the corner. Kat had dressed Nashville nice—slacks and sparkly black sweater, scarf but no jacket, like Harm. She looked nervous as Harm too. Grandmother Miss Lacy spoke low: "Kat, what's behind us is behind us. I forgive you. Welcome to my home."

"Thank you, Miss Thornton," Kat said as Grandmother Miss Lacy glanced my way. "Harm doesn't know and I—"

"*Do* come in," Grandmother Miss Lacy interrupted, frowning at me.

Harm doesn't know what?

Harm jumped up as Kat strolled in and gave her a quick hug. "Thanks for coming, everybody," he said. "Have a seat and I'll put the pasta on." He looked at me, his eyes a glassy shade of polite. "Mo, can you help me?"

"I'm a café kid," I said, heading for him. "I can dish up anything you got cooking."

By the time we sat down to eat, everything was just the way Harm likes it: Perfect.

Perfect salad, perfect spaghetti, perfect bread. Perfect chit-chat, perfect table, perfect candlelight. I draped my sweater over the back of my chair. My relationship with spaghetti is colorful and hard to wash out.

The conversation went fast and safe—school, Grandmother Miss Lacy's pansies, our search for Upstream Mother. Harm talked about our Always Man letters and photos: "Three no's, with forty-seven still out." The reminder kicked me like a mule.

Kat gave me a smile. "Three out of fifty? That's nothing," she said. "The odds against making it in Nashville are worse. Don't give up, Mo. We'll make it." She helped herself to more sauce. "Harm, this is delicious.

"You know, Mo, I'd love to sing at the café. Just to keep my voice in tune." She smiled at me, then turned to Harm. "How about it? We'd be great together. Please?"

Harm went tense as one of Mrs. Little's taxidermy projects.

Kat frowned. "I thought you'd love the idea, but if you don't want to sing with me . . ."

"It's not that," Harm said. "It's just that Dale and I have a group. I mean, we're a duo."

"On the Verge," Sal said. "They're very impressive."

The room went quiet, but the air felt like static. Kat broke the silence with a conversational curveball. "So, how's your treasure hunt going?"

Dale didn't blink. "Good except Gabriel stole our clue."

He looked at Sal and slumped. "I wasn't supposed to say that," he whispered, and she reached for his hand.

Still, true is true. I waited for Kat to deny it. She didn't.

"You mean that *Cross over resting,* blah-blah-blah?" she said. "Gabriel didn't steal that. Someone gave it to him. That's what he told me, anyway." She went stricken as Dale. "I feel terrible. Let me get it back for you."

"It's too late," I said. "He's already read it."

"You can't unread something even if you want to," Dale added. "I've tried."

"Let me make it up to you, then. Maybe I could update you from time to time," she said, and Grandmother Miss Lacy's eyebrows went sky-high. "No," she said quickly, "that wouldn't be right." She shrugged the idea away. "You're a very talented chef, Harm Crenshaw. I can't think of a thing that would improve that dinner."

"Dessert, maybe?" Harm said, beaming. Miss Lana says everybody looks better in candlelight. True. Harm looked golden. "I've made a—"

"Sorry. When you're in show business, you have to watch your figure. Besides, I'm expecting a call from my agent."

"At nine o'clock at night?" Sal asked, very soft.

Kat put her napkin on the table. "Let me know what day works for Lana, Mo. For Harm and me to sing, I mean. Harm, can I help you clean up, baby?"

"Thanks, but I've got it," Harm said. "And I'm not singing."

"Don't forget your jacket," Sal called as Grandmother Miss Lacy walked Kat out.

The door closed. I caught a flash of purple at the window, and Kat was gone.

"That was wonderful, Harm," Grandmother Miss Lacy said, straightening her dessert fork. "I couldn't be prouder if you were my own son."

"Me either," Dale said.

"And I say yes to Kat's offer," I added. "We could use a spy."

"No," Sal and Dale said, and Harm shook his head.

No? "But Harm," I said, "it would give you more time with Kat."

"No thanks, Mo," he said, very easy. "I'm good."

I looked at him, stunned. "How can you pass up time with your mom?"

He shrugged. "I'm willing to spend time with her, Mo. But Kat thinks whatever's good for her spins the universe. She'd be a terrible spy—we'd never be able to trust her information and we'd owe her on top of that. I'd rather just cook dinner for her now and then. If we can become friends, great. And if we can't . . ." He let his voice fall away.

"You'll let her go," I said, and jealousy swung through me so sharp, it sliced my breath in two. "How can you throw her away? She's your *mom,*" I said, my volume cranked up higher than expected. I looked into my friends' shocked faces.

"Moms are people," Sal said. "They aren't perfect. Not when you see them up close."

"Mine is," Dale said. "Mostly."

Harm rose, his white shirt still pristine. "I'm not throwing Kat away, Mo, but I'm not playing her game either. Dessert coming up," he said, and headed for the kitchen. "A new recipe special for tonight. And Mo, I think you're going to love it."

Chapter Eighteen
A Tip, a Lead, a Mistake

The next morning—Friday—Kat Kline waltzed into the café like she owned the place. She shrugged out of her jacket, its sapphire lining catching the Winter Tree's light. "Morning, everybody," she said, letting the door slap shut. "Our treasure hunt is slow getting started this morning. I'll take a cup of java, Mo," she said, grabbing a seat at the counter.

I slid silverware to her place as Miss Lana poured her coffee. "Lana, I'd love to perform here one night," she said. "For free, of course. It would be great for your business. Everybody likes a concert." She winked at me. "And Mo might convince Harm to join me."

Remember what Miss Rose said: Be careful, I thought.

"As a mother you naturally want to bond with Harm," I said, very casual. "But as his manager I can't recommend him to play. Him and Dale are cash only, and Tupelo Landing is our primary market. You can't give it away one day and charge the next."

She stirred sugar into her coffee. "We'll see. The offer's good even if he can't make it."

As a fellow performance artist, Miss Lana will snap her up, I thought. I was wrong.

"Thanks for offering," she said. "We'll be in touch."

Kat drank half her coffee and swaggered to the door. "Make sure you bus my place, Mo," she whispered. "I know how to tip, and how to even a score."

She did too. She'd left a ten-dollar bill. I grabbed the neat sheet of paper under it.

I unfolded it.

A photocopy of a map. She'd written across the top: *Gabriel's Treasure Map, sketched by a Pirate—hope we're even. Kat.* I turned just in time to see the flash of her purple jacket as she jumped into Gabriel's car and purred away.

"If that map's from Kat, it's a trap," Harm said at lunch. "She doesn't care about making things even. This deal's as phony as her promising to keep us together and then her going to Nashville without me." He breathed in like he could inhale calm. "Keep your eye on the ball, Mo. We're meeting with Bill Glasgow after school, to see what he learned about old-timey spinners. And we have to solve that *cross over resting* riddle. I even dreamt about it."

As I opened my lunch, Sal picked up the map. "It looks old. Did you find this in the archives?"

"In Mo's sock drawer?" Dale asked, frowning.

"No, Kat left it for me this morning," I said. "As a tip."

"Oh. Kat," she said like she'd found a dead bug, and looked at Harm.

He shrugged. "Okay, let's see it," he said, and we bent over the map.

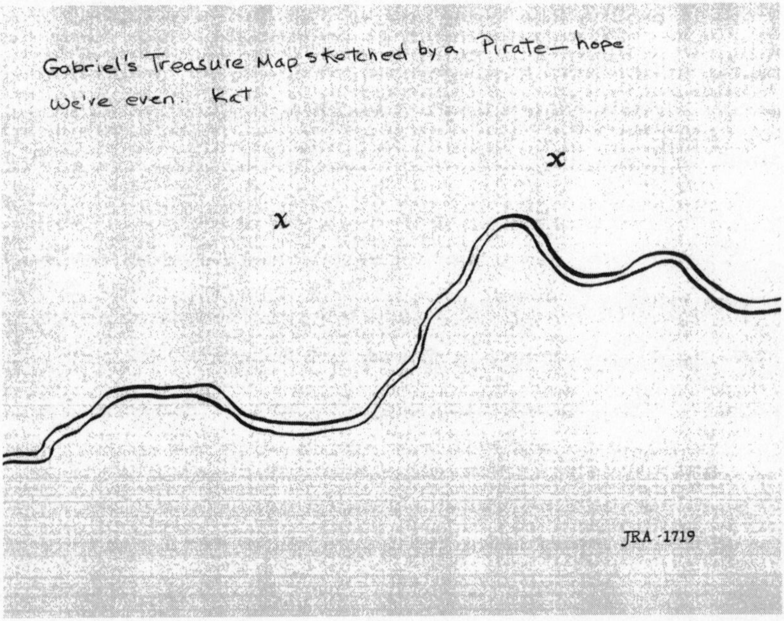
Gabriel's Treasure Map sketched by a Pirate—hope
we're even. Kat
x
x
JRA ·1719

"It's dated 1719," Sal said. "And signed: JRA. Who's that?"

"Beats me. It looks like one X is at the old marl pits, and one on Mr. Red's farm," Dale said. He frowned. "Is that why Kat came by Mr. Red's? Because of this X?"

"Come on, guys," Harm said. "If Kat gave us this, it helps her—not us. Either she's leading us in the wrong direction, or wants us to feel like we owe her. Forget the map. It's bogus," he said, and stalked away.

* * * * *

Harm was still grumpy that afternoon, when we found Bill Glasgow.

"Hey," Bill said as we blasted into Dale's room. "Didn't think you'd mind if I fed the newts." He closed the bug jar. "Several places use old-timey yarn-spinners, Mo. I made a list. Governor Brown's old home is closest—thirty miles or so up 264. I'd start there if it was me."

"Lavender loves a road trip," I said. "I'll ask him to take us."

"Good plan." Bill grabbed Dale's guitar and strummed it wrong. He's a mandolin player, not a guitar man. Dale moved Bill's pinkie and nodded. Bill strummed again.

I hopped up. "I better go see Lavender," I said, but I slipped down the hall to Miss Rose's office—the old oak desk in the corner of her bedroom. I knocked and peeked in. "Hey," I said, and she looked away from her work, her hair swept up and a pencil behind her ear. "I'd love to sit and chat, but Lavender's practically expecting me."

"He's at the garage, Mo," she said.

"Yes ma'am." I stepped in and closed the door. "Miss Rose, I was hoping we could talk woman to woman even if I am pre-puberty," I said. Her green eyes went wary. I settled on the edge of her bed. "You knew Kat Kline when she was a girl."

She nodded. "Back when she was plain old Rhonda Baker."

"What happened to make her leave? Grandmother Miss

Lacy forgave her at her front door last night, but why? Mr. Red dances around the subject like it's a Maypole. She makes Harm jumpy. In my experience as a café professional, only three things make people act that way. Bad love, bad money, bad-mouthing around town. Which is it?"

"It was a long time ago, Mo, but I'd guess a little of all three. Ask Miss Thornton." She gave me a time's-up smile.

"There's one more thing," I said, trying to sound casual. "They say jealousy's a green-eyed monster, but you have green eyes and you seem okay."

She turned to face me full-on and I felt the tears sting my eyes. "Jealousy? I've never known you to be jealous, Mo."

"Me either. But Kat's here and Harm barely wants her, and I can't find Upstream Mother and I've been wanting her forever. It's not fair," I said, my voice going raw. "I feel like I swallowed a cat and it's gnawing its way out of me. What can I do? And please don't say pray, because I'm in a hurry."

As a Baptist, Miss Rose prays about everything. "I can only tell you what I know. You can pray for Harm to have as much love in his life as you want in yours."

Crud. "How long before I hit the jackpot?"

"It's not a slot machine, honey, it's a prayer. You just keep praying until you can change." She hesitated. "Is Kat the kind of mother you'd want—if you could choose?"

"Kat? Gosh no," I said, very quick. "I'd want somebody

true and strong and talented and smart. Somebody I could trust. Somebody who wanted me in her life. Every day."

She smiled. "Close the door on the way out, Mo, and give Lavender my love."

I pedaled through town, and waved at Jake and Jimmy Exum, who were digging neat holes in Grandmother Miss Lacy's new rose garden, with her supervising from her window. I zipped past the school and over the bridge, and laid my bike into a skid at Lavender's garage.

His work boots stuck out from under an Azalea Woman's car. I told him about the fix-it yarn, and my need for a road trip. He slid out on his mechanic's board and looked up at me, his eyes ocean-blue, a perfect smudge of grease on his right cheek.

"Your Upstream Mother spins yarn? Must be hereditary. Nobody's spins a yarn better than you, Mo LoBeau."

"You're the first person I've asked about a ride. I'd like you to be there when I find her, and I think this could be it," I said, a blush sneaking up my neck.

He smiled. "I'm proud to be the first person you asked and the last one you *need* to ask. Tomorrow's good for me, Miss LoBeau. Pick you Desperados up at nine?"

"You're on. And Miss Rose sends her love," I said as he scooted back under the car.

Lavender never lets me down.

*****

Dear Upstream Mother,

I ain't saying it out loud to anybody but Lavender and Miss Lana, in case saying it throws its own curse, but get ready to meet me.

I will arrive tomorrow in Lavender's vintage pickup truck—a blue 1955 GMC, beautifully restored—around 10 o'clock.

Lavender will be the dashing race car driver behind the wheel. Harm's the tall passenger and Dale is short with blond hair.

I'll be the girl wearing your sweater, and your initial over my heart.

Mo

Chapter Nineteen
Bombshell

Saturday morning, Lavender wheeled into the parking lot, tooted the horn, and hopped out. I kissed Miss Lana's face. "Today is the day. I can feel it in my bones."

She smoothed her new red dress and patted her Marilyn Monroe wig into place. "I hope she's there too, sugar, but I don't want you to get hurt. Try to be realistic."

The breakfast crowd went quiet. *Realistic* ain't a word familiar to Miss Lana's lips.

"*You* bought a new dress to meet her in," I said, and she laughed. "Wish me luck!" I called, and I shot out and dove in next to Dale. Harm sat by the window, reviewing his checklist.

"Where to, Mo?" Lavender asked, settling beside me.

"Governor Brown's old home," I told him. "Skeeter set it up. It's free with guided tours. Miss Effy—who answers the phone—says they got sheep, and spin their own yarn."

"Do you think Miss Effy's your Upstream Mother?" Dale asked.

"She could be, but try to be realistic. Don't get your hopes up," I said. "Skeeter didn't ask her direct, but she says Miss Effy will let us ask all the questions we want."

"Miss Effy has no idea what she's in for," Lavender said.

We wound through the countryside, the distance between me and Upstream Mother melting away: thirty miles, twenty. My stomach launched butterflies. Ten miles, five. My hands went clammy. "How do I look?" I asked, trying to mash my hair flat.

"Beautiful," Lavender and Harm said together.

"The same as usual," Dale reported.

"I'm not sure what to say to her," I admitted. "Everything I practiced sounds lame."

Lavender tapped my hand, which I keep near the gear shift in case he needs it. "She's probably not there, Mo, but if she is, just be yourself. I know she'll love you, because we do."

As he put his blinker on, Dale leaned forward to study me. "Are you going to throw up? Because that's not a good first impression. We learned that Halloween of first grade, remember?"

We rumbled into the yard of a grand old farmhouse with grounds full of sprawling barns, paddocks, and outbuildings. A large woman in an old-timey dress strolled out to meet us.

"I'm Miss Effy," she said as we tumbled out. "You must be Mo."

I went voiceless—which is rare. Dale whipped out a hand-lettered business card. "She is. I'm Dale Earnhardt Johnson III. This is Harm Crenshaw and my brother, Lavender." He smiled, very polite. "Did you lose anything important about twelve years ago? During a hurricane?"

She blinked. "No, honey. Well, my porch furniture, maybe. My sister lost her roof and a husband, but I never liked him anyway. Why?"

"Anything else?" Dale asked, very casual. "A baby?"

"I'd remember that," she said, and winked at Lavender. Every woman alive winks at Lavender. He winked back. "Come on, I'll show you around," she said, heading for the house.

I grabbed her hand. "Wait. I'm looking a woman with the initial *J*. Tell her Mo's here."

"The letter *J*? Nobody comes to mind, honey," she said. "It's just me and the fellow that helps with the sheep, and he's hit-and-miss."

My heart tumbled like a baby bird falling from its nest.

An hour later, I had a clue pad of notes on wool—and a soul full of mud. How could I—Mo LoBeau, a top detective—have been so wrong about the mystery of my own life?

"Our sheep are Suffolks," Miss Effy said, strolling along a pasture fence. "Good wool. Come in and I'll show you how to spin yarn."

Within minutes, she sat pumping an old-timey spinning

wheel, her fingers teasing the yarn. "Being a re-enactor's a tough gig," she said. "You have to learn the skills and get the clothes right. Shoes are the hardest. I had these ugly old things made special, cost a fortune. Spinning's the easy part. See? Nothing to it."

"Can I try?" Dale asked.

Dale took to it like a bird to sky. Still, his yarn came out like the mending yarn in my sweater—like stretched-out teardrops, fat and skinny, plump and thin.

Lavender slipped close to me. "Show her your sweater," he whispered.

I took it off and handed it to her. "You ever seen this sweater before?"

"No. I'd remember it," she said, looking at the knitting.

I turned the mend toward her. "My mother left me this sweater and we're trying to find her. She might have done this mend. It's about the only clue I got. Do you know who did it? Her name maybe started with a *J*. I thought she'd be here, but she's not."

"Oh," she said, her face going soft. "Now I see. There's maybe eight or nine hundred hand-spinners in North Carolina. Old hippies, artists, try-it-oncers. I don't know them all, but I know this: Whoever mended this sweater used rug wool. Feel how scratchy it is? You can tell beginners not to do something and they'll do it anyway. Some people won't take advice, you know."

"Is that hereditary?" Dale asked. "Because Mo's like that."

"And I'm pretty sure she used natural indigo dye, which costs sky-high. Either she was rich and pig-headed, or she grabbed it on the cheap. She could have worked with an indigo demonstrator, maybe. Now, *those* are few and far between."

Dale pulled a photo of Always Man from his pocket. "Do you know him?"

"Wish I did," she said, and he tried our Ugly Trim flyer. "Now, that sign I *do* know," she said, and my heart jumped. "Can't say from where. Did they have Saturday dances, maybe? I never got to go, but my daddy used to drive us by that sign."

My hope lit up like the Fourth of July. "Where did he take you?"

"Mostly around home. He didn't have the gas money to take us very far. I grew up outside Patesville, if that helps." She walked us to the truck. "Wish I could help more, kiddos."

She winked at Lavender. "Leave a phone number?"

"You have our business card," Dale reminded her, and her face fell.

"Good luck, then," she said.

"We'll find her," Lavender said, hopping in the truck. "Mo's always been lucky."

Maybe. But I sure didn't feel lucky as we turned onto the blacktop and headed home.

"Come on, Mo. That was our first try. And we got a lot of leads," Harm said. "We know the sign was near Patesville. We know it's rug wool in the mend. And we've narrowed our suspect pool way down. When we drove up, we only knew Upstream Mother was in North Carolina the day you were born—with about ten million other people."

"And *ninety* million chickens," Dale said.

We went quiet except for the hum of tires.

"Thanks for that detail, Dale," Harm said. "But now we know fewer than a thousand people in North Carolina hand-spin yarn. And out of them, we want someone who's either rich enough to buy natural indigo dye, or demonstrates making it."

"A rich woman would buy the right yarn," Dale said.

"Great point," Harm said. "So that narrows it down too. Sets and subsets. Right?"

"Math," Dale said, spitting the word. "Only one person can problem solve on this level: Miss Retzyl." He looked at Lavender. "Can you go to her house with us? She likes you and it could mean extra credit for me."

"Sorry, little brother," Lavender said. "She's gone to Ocracoke, with Starr."

Ocracoke? Again? And she didn't tell me?

"We got the afternoon off, then," Dale said, settling against the seat. "Good, because I got a surprise. I know where the treasure is. Lunch first," he said. "Then I'll show you."

Miss Lana's gaze locked onto mine as I walked through the café door. I shook my head. "Next time, sugar," she said, giving me a hug. "Sit down, all of you. Lunch is on me."

"A failure? It must be the curse again." Attila sighed from the window table as Mrs. Simpson wheeled into the parking lot. "Pity," she said, heading outside.

"Pity yourself, Attila," I said as Queen Elizabeth zipped through the door.

As we polished off our burgers, Dale laid out his plan. "Queen Elizabeth and me had a dream last night," he said. "We were all in the woods, and Liz was chasing a rabbit and Harm had a rope and a shovel."

"A plan based on a dream, Dale? I don't know," Harm said.

"We have two maps," Dale said. "A pirate drew Gabriel's, and it has two Xs. Mary drew ours and it has one X. What do they have in common? An X near the old fish camp."

"So?" Harm said, leaning forward.

"So think like a pirate. *X Marks the Spot,*" Dale said. "The dream and the maps say it: The treasure's near the old marl pits and fish camp. Let's go."

"Hold on," Harm said. "Isn't *X marks the spot* a little . . . obvious?"

"Okay, we'll do your idea instead," Dale said, crossing his arms. Dale can be stubborn.

I sighed. My heart still felt like cement.

Lavender leaned to me and whispered, "Sometimes the best thing for a broken heart is to just keep moving."

Like I said, I love it when Lavender whispers. "I'm in," I said.

Harm shrugged. "Me too, I guess."

"We'll need a shovel and rope," Dale told Miss Lana as Liz shot to the door.

"In the toolshed, honey," she said.

I grabbed three dollars from my tip jar, slapped open the cash register drawer, and switched out my cash for rolls of pennies.

"What's that for?" Dale asked. "I didn't dream pennies."

"You're not the only Desperado with a plan," I said, and we walked innocent as lambs into the deadliest afternoon of our lives.

Chapter Twenty
Help! Somebody Help!

Lavender dropped us at the head of Fish Camp Road, and we took the rutted path into the forest, Queen Elizabeth sniffing for squirrels and rabbits.

We stopped at the fork leading to the old fish camp.

"Gabriel's camp lies to the right," Dale said, his voice low. He peered at the treetops. "The path to the marl pits goes left . . . Over there," he said, pointing to a dip in the canopy. "It's an old path, all growed over, but Daddy showed me once," he added. "Liz, slow down!"

I tugged a roll of pennies from my pocket and peeled the paper back. I hurled pennies into the trees and listened to them patter down like rain. "If they want to slow us down with a bogus map, we'll slow Attila's metal detector down," I said, and Harm laughed.

"Devious, LoBeau," he said, settling our rope over his shoulder.

We strolled deeper into the forest, Dale side-arming pennies in bursts, Harm spinning his into honeysuckle vines and up to the treetops.

Lavender was right. The sharp-cold air and crunch of leaves helped balance my teeter-totter heart.

"What's that?" Harm asked, heading for an odd-shaped oak. He yanked a curtain of pale vines off a crooked old sign nailed into the tree's trunk.

KEEP OUT! NO SWIMMING!

"Swimming?" he muttered. "Who'd be crazy enough to swim back here?"

"You, I imagine," Attila said, stepping from behind a privet, her metal detector in tow. "Isn't that what you people do? Find swimming holes because you can't afford a pool?"

Even in the cold she looked flushed and sweaty.

"I'm surprised you're out here," I replied. "I guess you got over your fear of snakes."

"Snakes hibernate in winter," she said, looking at the kaleidoscope of leaves at our feet. She swung the metal detector back and forth. *Beep!*

"That's the way we *professionals* do it," she said. She stooped and snagged her find. "What's a new penny doing out here?"

"Rhetorical," Dale whispered.

She swung the metal detector again, catching it in a screen of briars. "What *are* you people doing out here?" she demanded, yanking it free.

"You guessed it," Harm said, very easy. "Scouting

swimming holes. If you're still out here when it warms up, we'll invite you to go along."

"In your dreams," she muttered.

I frowned and looked around. "Why are you out here alone? Where's Gabriel and Kat?"

"At Gabriel's camp, reviewing his research and making new plans."

Because his map is totally useless, I thought as she thrashed off into the woods.

"Somehow she's even less appealing out in nature," Harm said.

Dale looked sharp right and left. "Where's Queen Elizabeth? Liz!" Liz yelped. "Come back," he shouted, heading toward her.

We pressed on, calling Liz and tossing pennies. Finally, the green pines gave way to bare-limbed maples. Ahead of us, a patch of bone-colored reeds stood still and quiet as ghosts along a cement-gray mudflat. The flat stretched to a pond, its water black and glistening, the sky clear and wintry up above.

I pushed through the reeds and started across. "Mo! Stop!" Dale shouted.

My feet dropped through the crust and the wet sand swallowed my shoes. "Help!" I gasped, windmilling my arms.

"Mo!" Harm shouted, his hand snaking out to grab mine. "Back up."

The muck gobbled me to my knees.

"I can't!" I said, surprised by the wail in my voice.

"Stay stiff and fall backwards," Dale said. He reached from behind to grab my other arm. "Fall like a tree," he instructed. "We got you."

I fell straight back, too scared to close my eyes, and slammed to the ground, my shoulders in briars. The boys' feet churned and slid beside me as they dragged me from the earth's slurping grasp. "Mo," Harm said, pushing my hair from my face. "Are you okay?"

Okay?

My heart pounded, my legs shook, I'd bit half through my tongue. Blood trickled down my neck from briars. "Fine," I said, blinking back the tears as I stared at my wet socks.

"The devil took your shoes," Dale said.

I tried to slow my galloping heart. "Thank you," I said. "Thank you for saving my life."

"So that's quicksand," Dale said, pushing the reeds aside and staring across the flat. "It looks so sweet."

He was right. The mudflat looked serene as the inside of an oyster shell. "That old pit's a great place for treasure. In fact . . ." He froze, his eyes taking the same distant look he gets when he's writing a new song. "What's Mary's riddle again?"

I rubbed warmth into my feet. *"Cross over resting, loose beside still . . ."*

"Quicksand," he said, very firm. "*That's* the answer. "That's why the Xs. Quicksand is loose sand beside still. And there's only one way to cross quicksand: by resting on top, like you're dreaming of flying. *Cross over resting*. The treasure's here. We just got to find a way to get it out."

The reeds stirred and Queen Elizabeth looked up at us, her brown eyes laughing. "There you are," Dale said, leaning down to smooth her ears.

Across the cement-colored flat, the grasses quivered. A rabbit peeked out.

Queen Elizabeth froze, her eyes locked on the rabbit. She tensed her muscles and shifted her weight. "Liz! No!" Dale shouted, grabbing for her collar.

Too late.

Queen Elizabeth sprang forward and stretched out on the air as the rabbit disappeared into the brush. She landed with a sickening *thwack* six feet from firm ground. She began to swim—and to sink. "Liz, stay still," Dale cried. She tossed her head and looked at us, her ears back, her eyes glassy with fear as she paddled, stirring the quicksand with her paws.

She sank one inch deeper, two inches, three inches.

The quicksand slurped up her ribs, to her shoulders. Her hips sank, her tail.

"No," Harm whispered, shrugging the rope off his shoulder and throwing it near her. "Not Liz." The rope splatted in the quicksand. She turned and paddled toward the rope, the quicksand grabbing the arch of her back and jerking her down.

She strained hard, holding her head up, her eyes rolling in terror as she looked back at Dale one last time.

"No!" Dale screamed. "You can't have her!"

And before I knew what he was thinking, he dove straight out from our solid place of safety, and sailed in behind her.

For one incredible heartbeat, Dale lay stretched out on the quicksand like Superboy flying across air. "Shhhhh, stop it, Liz," he said, his voice shaking, as he swam in slow motion, inching his way forward, the muck kissing his chin. "Shhhhh, we're okay, girl. Settle down."

Harm reeled the rope in. I grabbed it, and tied a loop in it.

Why are my hands so stupid? Why can't I move faster?

"Dale," I said, stepping back into briars. I felt thorns sink into my feet, but no pain. "I'm throwing the rope."

"Not yet," he said in the same gentle tone. "Liz, shhhh. I'm coming, puppy. Dale's coming."

Harm stood beside me. I listened for his breath and didn't hear it. Somehow his silence stopped my world.

Dale took a deep breath and sloshed onto his back, his left arm stroking back to grab Queen Elizabeth. He hauled her close, and rolled her onto her back, her thin legs frantically kicking at the air.

The move cost him. The quicksand found a new fingerhold.

Dale began to sink as Queen Elizabeth flailed at the air. She's going to kill him, I thought. Her fear is going to kill him. "Liz," I said, trying to sound like Dale. "Play dead. *Now.* Treat, Liz. Play dead."

Liz rolled her eyes so hard I could see the whites, but she stopped kicking.

"Good girl," I said, trying to smooth my voice.

I was shaking. When did I start shaking?

"Dale, I'm throwing the rope," I said, still trying to keep my voice calm.

"Don't try to catch it," Harm said. "If we miss you we'll try again until we hit you. Lie still, Dale. Don't move. You're right. Moving makes you sink."

Harm tied one end of the rope to a sapling. I coiled the rope and swung it, swung it, threw. The rope snaked out and landed too far to Dale's right.

Dale lay serene as a prayer. The quicksand rose to his ears, framing his face. His lips turned blue from the cold.

He's going under. It's not going to work.

"Help!" I screamed to no one. A flock of birds boiled into the sky.

"Dammit," Harm whispered, frantically reeling the rope to us. He coiled the rope, and let it fly again. It landed across Dale's chest. Dale didn't move.

"Dale, listen to me. Loop it around your free arm and hang on even if you go under," Harm said, his voice filling with tears as Dale slipped a breath lower in the muck. "We'll pull you out. If you can't hold on to Queen Elizabeth, you have to let her go. I know you don't want to, but it would be okay. She'll understand."

Dale pursed his lips as he looped the rope over his arm.

When did I start crying?

"Pull," I cried. Harm and me dug into the mud and pulled. We turned Dale slightly, and he sank a whisker deeper.

"Pull!" I shouted, and we plowed him through the quicksand, sliding him sideways toward shore. He weighed a ton with the greedy earth grabbing hold.

Dale closed his eyes and tightened his arm around Queen Elizabeth's chest.

He'll never let her go, I thought.

"PULL!" I screamed as he sank lower. He frowned that stubborn frown he gets when he knows he's right and people say he's wrong.

The quicksand licked the side of his face and slipped toward his nose.

"HELP US!" I shrieked. "Dale, hold on."

Dale took a deep breath and slipped beneath the surface.

Someone reached around me. "Now!" Attila said, digging her fancy hiking boots in by my sock feet and leaning against the rope. "PULL!"

We pulled like nobody this side of dead ever pulled. The rope inched along the surface like somebody had grabbed Dale and was dragging him down.

A bubble of air broke the surface.

"PULL!" Harm screamed, his voice shredding.

We pulled. The rope zigzagged nearer.

"Don't let go, don't let go, don't let go," I prayed.

Another air bubble.

Dale rose up at our feet and slung Queen Elizabeth onto solid ground. He rolled out coughing and gasping as we grabbed his jacket and hauled him in. I fell to my knees and raked the mud off his face as Queen Elizabeth scrambled away.

Harm whipped off his jacket and draped it over Dale's shoulders as he sat up, spitting and coughing and crying. Tears rolled down Dale's cheeks, leaving a clean trail through the mud.

I gazed at Dale as he gasped for breath. At the thin, freckled face I'd known all my life. The sand-flecked lashes. The eyes I trust, the eyes that trust mine.

Dale Earnhardt Johnson III. My best friend for life.

For one rare, tender moment, I thought I might kiss Dale, or write a poem. The moment passed. I socked him in the shoulder as hard as I could. "You idiot!" I bellowed, kicking at him. "You almost died! Don't you *ever* do that again!"

I pointed at Queen Elizabeth. "You either!"

I looked at Harm and Attila, who stared at me wide-eyed. "Leave me alone, all of you," I shouted, and burst into tears.

* * * * *

Dear Upstream Mother,

Do you believe in curses? I never did but when Dale disappeared beneath that quicksand, I felt cursed to my soul. Surge of blood, snap of bone, loss of mortal breath.

Attila helped us to Gabriel's camp. Kat drove us home.

The Colonel says going face-to-face with death can break you, or make you strong. Fingers crossed Dale and Liz ain't broke.

Liz looks shaky, but I think Dale may be okay, because he asked Gabriel for his top three tips for a first kiss.

Gabriel said, "Don't ask, move fast, think like a movie star." Then he tossed his car keys to Kat, and we climbed in the Jag.

About our search for you: We got a no at Miss Effy's place and now also no's on twelve Always Man letters. But after a lifetime of no's, that ain't nothing to a girl like me.

Mo

PS The quicksand stole my shoes!

Chapter Twenty-one
Dale Has Another Plan

Word of our near-death experience hit different people different ways.

Miss Rose checked on Dale every ten minutes to make sure he was still breathing. Queen Elizabeth went clingy. On Sunday afternoon, Miss Lana and the Colonel offered a free CPR class at the café and twenty people showed up.

Afterward, Harm and me studied the NC map on the café wall, and plotted our next move. "Miss Effy grew up here, in Patesville," Harm said, sticking a pin in the map. "If she saw the Ugly Trim when she was little, let's guess the sign was within fifty miles of Patesville." He drew a circle around the tiny town. "Our rivers flow toward the ocean, to our east. That means Upstream Mother lived somewhere between the western edge of this circle, and Tupelo Landing."

He crossed his arms and studied the map. "I say we focus there. It's got just two historic sites with yarn-spinners. I'll call them, and see what I can learn."

"And I'll ask Skeeter to check for sheep farms in that area."

The phone rang and Miss Lana grabbed it. I heard her

murmur, and hang up. "Mo, Miss Thornton wants you to stop by in the morning. She has something for you."

Excellent, I thought. A perfect chance to follow up on Kat Kline.

The next day, a Monday, I knocked on Grandmother Miss Lacy's door. "Hey, I hope you're doing good. I'm possibly cursed and wobbly from almost losing Dale and Queen Elizabeth, but otherwise well," I said, stepping inside.

She hugged me tight. "You're not cursed and you know it. These are for you," she said, handing me a shoe box. Inside lay a pair of red plaid sneakers, laced in my signature weave. I followed her into the parlor, kicked off last year's toe-biters, and slipped the new shoes on.

"Thanks. They're perfect."

I glanced at a photo on her end table—an image of a sour-faced girl with a ski-slope nose.

"I don't think you've seen that one," she said. "I put it out yesterday. Myrt Little was fourteen when I took it. She was at the height of her beauty, I'd say."

I grinned and picked up an old photo of Tinks. "Grandmother Miss Lacy, I heard you forgive Kat before Harm's dinner, but why? What happened? I can't figure her out."

"Oh, a high school prank. Kat and a friend of hers broke in here," she said, like it was nothing. "I caught her friend red-handed. Kat got away—and let him take the blame. Red and Kat were already at odds over her music, but they never saw eye to eye after that."

"And Harm doesn't know? Why didn't you tell me before?" I asked.

"You didn't ask me before, dear."

True.

I picked up another photo. Grandmother Miss Lacy's mom, leaning against a long, lean roadster. "The Azalea Women say your mother's birthday is this Sunday."

She nodded. "I'm putting flowers in the church, in her honor."

"I'd like to honor her too," I said. "I could photograph you putting flowers in the church—for your photo albums. If you want me to."

She smiled like sunrise. "I'd love that, Mo. Can we settle on a price?"

A price? For Grandmother Miss Lacy?

I wiggled my toes in my new shoes. "Your money ain't worth nothing to me," I said, and kissed her good-bye. "Thanks for the shoes. And the information. Grandmother Miss Lacy, who was the boy Kat broke in with? You didn't say."

"My goodness, look at the time," she said, and closed the door.

I headed for my bike. Good information, new shoes, and a photography gig. Already I felt my swagger coming back.

*****

As I stood at the classroom window an hour later, pretending to sharpen my pencil, a shiny black van pulled up and Tinks hopped out cradling pink gladiolas.

My heart jack-knifed into my belly.

Gladiolas: Tupelo Landing's funeral flower of choice. "Somebody died," I announced.

The Exum boys rummaged through their desks for their caps and held them over their hearts as the rest of the class rushed to the window. "Please sit down," Miss Retzyl said. "People send flowers for all kinds of occasions. Birthdays, Christmas . . ."

Attila headed for her seat. "Mother gets flowers every Mother's Day *and* every National Dental Hygiene Day. Father is a dentist," she said, like we didn't know.

"What do you send for Dental Hygiene Day?" Harm asked. "Floss-me-nots?"

Tinks rapped at our door. "Flowers for Priscilla Retzyl from a secret admirer." He placed the glads in her arms and fled.

A secret admirer? Starr would never send flowers. "It was sweet of Starr to send flowers," I said. "You're lucky. Boyfriends who love flowers and shoot are rare."

Dale whispered: "I'm ninety-four percent sure those aren't from Starr. Only twelve percent of me thinks they are."

"Dale," Miss Retzyl said, "do you have something to share with the class?"

"No," he said. "I just hope nobody's trying to steal your heart."

"Hearts can't be stolen," she said. "Which reminds me, Valentine's Day is just weeks away. This year, I thought we'd give a Valentine's gift to the entire community."

We went still and blank as bowling pins. Even Dale knew not to move.

In Teacher Speak, "gift for family" means lame art. "Gift for friends" equals an Orange and Grapefruit Sale, which last year the entire town got gum ulcers from Vitamin C overdose. Gift to *Community* can mean only one thing: Performance Art.

I raised my hand. "I think I speak for the entire class when I say it can't be Performance Art, which is cruel and unusual. I'm guessing a trip to the NASCAR Hall of Fame. Lavender will drive the activity bus if we borrow one. Three cheers for Miss Retzyl! Hip, hip . . ."

"Be quiet," Miss Retzyl said.

Attila raised her hand. "I'd love to hear *your* idea, Miss Retzyl."

"Thank you," Miss Retzyl said. "This year, we'll offer a concert of romantic tunes." If we'd gasped any harder, the windows would have shattered on the floor. "Dale and Harm, you'll be center stage."

Is she mad?

Jake raised his hand. "Jimmy and me tap-dance. Mama home-schooled it into us," he said. "We'll perform. Come on, Jimmy. Let's show them."

"Sit down, boys," Miss Retzyl said. "You can audition later."

Dale put his head on his desk. "Help us," he whispered.

I smiled at Miss Retzyl the way Miss Lana smiles at a salesman who's selling what she ain't buying. "It breaks my heart to RSVP you this way, but Regrets. The Desperados got two cases going plus we're dedicated to sixth grade." She's not buying it, I thought. "And Dale and Harm are already booked at the café's Valentine's Extravaganza," I added.

"We are?" Dale whispered, looking hopeful. Dale kills me.

"I don't believe I've heard that around town," Miss Retzyl said. "And if Lana tells me . . ." The bell gobbled up the rest of her words.

It was still echoing in the hall as I skidded into Skeeter's office and dialed the café. "Miss Lana? Harm and Dale are playing the café's Valentine's Extravaganza. We been planning it for a while in case Miss Retzyl asks you."

"Wonderful," she said, and I could hear her smile. "I'll start planning the decorations."

One disaster sidestepped, I thought. But we had another waiting at the café.

*****

"Somebody sent Pris flowers?" Starr said as we dumped our books and shot to Miss Lana's red velvet cake. "Why? Is it her birthday?"

"No, it's not," Miss Lana said, cutting the cake. "But if you didn't send them, who did?"

"Gabriel Archer," Dale said. "He already stood her up once."

Miss Lana frowned. "I don't think so, Dale. Of course, Gabriel's handsome. And he's a treasure hunter—which is romantic."

"That reminds me," Dale said, taking his clue pad out and looking at Joe Starr. "I'd love to have your top three thoughts on a first kiss. You too, Colonel."

Starr ignored him. So did the Colonel, who was working on the jukebox. Starr picked up his hat and headed for the door. "I nearly forgot, Mo. I ran your cocoa powder fingerprint. I didn't get a match, but I'd guess it's a man's print, based on the size. There's a scar across the tip, if that helps any. Sorry I couldn't do better for you."

"Thanks," I muttered, trying not to look crushed.

"Maybe that's Always Man's print, then," Harm said.

Starr took out his clue pad and flipped it open. "And the blood evidence from Harm's windowsill was pig's blood, which is flat-out strange. Nobody's missing any pigs."

Harm scowled. "Why would somebody . . ."

"To scare us off the case," I said. "Just like with the curse. And the strange boot prints."

Starr turned at the door. "Three tips on a first kiss, Dale. Be respectful, be honest, try not to bump noses." As he drove away, Dale turned to me.

"If Starr didn't send those flowers, Gabriel did. He already stood Miss Retzyl up once. He called her here, to tell her. Remember? If Gabriel steals Miss Retzyl's heart, he'll take her away. Which means we'll get a substitute. Maybe Mrs. Little—for the rest of our lives."

"Mrs. Little? Yeeow," Harm muttered. "But Dale . . ."

"I want Miss Retzyl here until we finish middle school," Dale said. "Miss Lana, I got to propose Starr to Miss Retzyl. They can live at her place. What's the rules of love?"

"The rules of love?" she said as the Colonel shoved the jukebox into place. "Well, flowers. Poems. Candy . . . But Dale, I don't think Priscilla even likes Gabriel Archer. And when it comes to romance, Joe Starr's hopeless."

What Dale said next made every hair on my body stand up like it wanted to run. "Don't worry about Starr romancing Miss Retzyl," he said. "I've got a plan."

Chapter Twenty-two
Another Robbery!

The next morning, Harm and Dale practiced songs for the Valentine's Extravaganza as we rolled silverware for the breakfast rush. They sounded good. Really good.

"I can suggest love songs," Miss Lana said.

"Thanks, but we're going with the classics," I said.

"That means songs we already know," Dale explained as Detective Joe Starr's Impala blazed past the café, blue light swirling and siren blaring.

"What on earth?" Miss Lana gasped as we blasted out the door.

We'd just made the edge of town when we saw a red light swirling too. "That's Grandmother Miss Lacy's neighborhood," I said, panic spinning through me. I stood on my pedals and flew past the Piggly Wiggly.

"It's the Littles' house," Harm said. "And that's an ambulance!"

"Desperados, thank heavens!" the mayor cried as we shot inside.

"What's happened? Where's Mrs. Little?"

"We've been robbed," he cried, bobbing from foot to foot like a little kid. "Mother twisted her knee trying to catch the culprit. Heavy man, slippery as all get out." He blinked back tears. "Starr's here and so are the medics."

We stepped into the parlor. "Jeez," Harm said, looking around.

Understatement.

The table drawers gaped open, books sprawled helter-skelter on the floor. Candlesticks, lamps, Mrs. Little's black rocking chair . . . all of it topsy-turvy.

I looked at the mantel. "*Tupelo Mother* is gone!"

"Who?" Starr said behind me.

"Our portrait. It was on the mantel. It's gone. And it's worth thousands."

Please let our other clues be here, I thought. As if he could read my mind, Harm bounded out of the room and down the hall. I heard the attic door slam.

"Gabriel Archer did this, same as he stole our riddle," I told Starr.

Starr stood in the center of the carnage, his face still and open as he surveyed the scene. "Something's odd here."

Dale saw it first. "Everything's tossed but not broke. What are the chances of *that*?"

"Zero," Starr said. "Somebody was looking for something.

He was quiet. If Mrs. Little hadn't come down for milk, he could have stayed here for hours," he said as the mayor padded in. "Mr. Mayor, do you have anything of value in here?"

"I hope so," the mayor said, scurrying to his safe. He tapped the hidden panel and the safe swung open. I lifted my camera. The safe was empty! *Click click click.*

The attic door slammed again and Harm shot in. "Attic's safe," he whispered.

"My oldest coins are gone," the mayor said, his voice shaking. "I had a few doubloons and pieces of eight . . . And they stole our cash and Mother's rings!"

"What are they worth?" Starr asked, making a note.

"A lot." He shook his head. "Mother will simply be beside herself."

"Is Myrt all right? What's happened?" Grandmother Miss Lacy demanded, rushing in. "I hear the ambulance was here."

"Mother's in her room. She twisted her knee, but she sent the medic away, which I take as a hopeful sign," the mayor said.

"Thank heavens," Grandmother Miss Lacy said, closing her eyes. "There's nothing like an enemy to make you feel like yourself again." She set a hideous vase upright. "Who did this?" she asked. "Was it Gabriel? I'm sorry I ever invited that scoundrel to town."

"I'll check," Starr said. "The thief will probably hold on to the stolen goods awhile."

Dale nodded. "They're too hot to fence. He might pass them to a friend, or put them in the freezer under the frozen vegetables until later."

It's amazing, the things Dale knows.

"Thanks Dale," Starr said. "Mr. Mayor, I'll need a description of your coins and rings."

"And I have photographs of the portrait," I told him. "And Sal's appraisal."

Starr nodded, very crisp.

"How can I help?" Grandmother Miss Lacy asked, her eyes on the mayor.

"Could you speak with Mother? This insult to our home has hurt her sweet heart. I'm afraid . . ." The mayor's face crumpled like a little kid's. "I'm afraid my mother's crying."

Minutes later we skidded through the classroom door. "Joe sends his greetings," I said. "If we're late, which I hope we're not, it's because we assisted Joe on a case."

Her eyes went chilly. "You assisted *whom?*"

"Detective Joe Starr, *whom* wrote you a note," I said, forking it over. "By the way, I admire your flair for lower education. Have you ever considered offering middle school at night, when nothing important's happening anyway? That would be better for us."

"Take your seats," she replied, tucking Starr's note in her pocket. "How are your book reports coming along?"

Book reports? She was serious about those?

"Good," I said, reminding myself to check out a book.

"Mine's done," Harm reported, unwinding his scarf.

"I've practically started," Dale said. "Sal's helping me."

We settled into our desks. Crud.

It's hard being an ace detective trapped in middle school.

Surprisingly, the school day wasn't a total bust.

Sal gave her Extra Credit Pirate Report, *Fashion on the High Seas*. "The charming sociopath Anne Bonney was the most fashionable pirate. According to some sources, she targeted trade ships to take their cargoes of silk.

"Fashion counted, even on the high seas. Blackbeard's ship the *Queen Anne's Revenge* may have had a tailor on board. Artifacts found on his ship include handmade, brass straight pins. They were made in England."

Like the straight pins in Mary Ormond's calico dress, I thought, remembering Sal pricking her finger in the Littles' attic.

"Straight pins were big bucks in the colonies. So was fashion. Rich women wore silk dresses, linen underthings from Denmark, and shoes imported from England. Blackbeard was a flashy dresser, like his friend the governor."

As we applauded Sal to her seat, Thes marched to the

front of the room and announced his title. *"Swearing Like a Pirate."* Even Jake and Jimmy sat at attention.

Thes went red-faced, handed his paper in without a word, and shuffled back to his seat.

But it was Hannah Greene's report on the Spanish treasure ships that got my blood singing. "During a single hurricane in 1715, eleven Spanish treasure ships sank off the coast of Florida, and pirates later claimed millions of dollars' worth of the coins, jewels, and silver destined for Spain. Did Blackbeard help himself to part of that treasure?" She winked at me. "I hope so, and I hope the Desperados find it, because everybody who gives a report gets a cut, including me. Thank you."

"Extra credit for all three of you," Miss Retzyl said, and Attila huffed.

"Useless information," Attila said as the bell rang.

"You're hooked up with a thief, Attila," I told her. "Enemy to enemy, I'll tell you this: Whatever you think Gabriel's going to do for you, he ain't."

Dear Upstream Mother,

We got 18 no's to our Always Man letter. But like Miss Lana says, the no's don't matter. We only need one yes to take me home to you.

Mo

Chapter Twenty-three
Sunday Shockers

Sunday morning Grandmother Miss Lacy wheeled across the café parking lot at eight sharp. "Thank you for letting me and Liz come on your photo shoot," Dale said, scooting to the edge of the backseat. "Liz is still feeling puny from the quicksand. A day with flowers will do us good."

"Certainly," she said as I clicked my first photo. "This will be a day to remember."

It was, too. But not for the reasons we expected.

As we puttered to the florist's shop, we filled Grandmother Miss Lacy in on our cases. "Harm's called the historic sites in our search area, but so far we got nothing. It almost feels like the clues are pushing us away instead of pulling us closer," I said.

"Not all of them," Dale said. "We got a yes on our Always Man letters."

A yes? The entire universe held its breath.

I whipped around. "When? Who?"

Dale looked into Queen Elizabeth's eyes. "That was supposed to be a surprise." He sighed. "Harm called last night.

He got a yes. But *he* wants to tell you, Mo. So stop giving me your Truth Serum Stare. And don't tell him I told you."

We got a yes!

By the time we got back to the Episcopal church with a carload of purple irises, Dale had shifted into hyper-chat and I was fighting to keep my feet on the ground. "I got to find a way to get Starr to propose to Miss Retzyl. Which reminds me, Sal and me are pre-kissing," he told Grandmother Miss Lacy, arming up a bunch of irises and following her to the church's tiny kitchen. "My problem is the nose. Which way . . ."

"Dale," I said. "Photo for Sal." He burned a look through the irises in his arms. *Click.*

Grandmother Miss Lacy grabbed my camera. "I want one of you too, dear." *Click.*

As I shot more photos, music played soft and sweet from the steeple. "Mother's favorite hymns," Grandmother Miss Lacy told us. While they arranged flowers, I slipped into the sanctuary, with its tall praying windows.

I backed up to catch the windows' crosspiece shadows on the old stone floor. The stone beneath my foot wobbled and I lurched, snapping a blur. Crud. I scuffed the stone—the same one I stumbled on the morning Elvis sang in the steeple.

It seemed like forever ago, I thought, lining up another photo.

"Here we are, dear," Grandmother Miss Lacy called, placing a vase by the altar. "Irises were Mother's favorites." *Click, click, click.*

"This stone's off," I told her, taking one last photo.

"A tad," she said. "We could fix it, but it hardly seems worth it. When will you develop your photographs, Mo?"

"Now, if you want," I told her.

"Wonderful. The darkroom's yours, and there's turkey in the fridge. Invite Harm too." She led the way to the door. "Red and I are going to church, and to lunch. Mother was . . . You would have loved her—both of you. And she would have loved you too."

Her eyes filled with tears and I gave her a hug.

Odd, I thought, to miss your mother after all these years.

An hour later, as Grandmother Miss Lacy left with Mr. Red, Harm took her front steps two at a time. "We got a yes, Mo," he called, tugging a letter out of his jacket pocket. "From a woman in Salisbury, North Carolina. She thinks Always Man is her lost cousin. Here's her number if you want to call."

If I want to call? I started for the phone and he grabbed my arm. "Mo, Gramps says you should ask Miss Lana to call with you."

"You could even think what to say before you dial," Dale added.

"Yeah," Harm said, his eyes laughing. "It's novel, but it could work."

"Right," I said, my heart doing handsprings. "I'll ask Miss Lana soon as I get home."

A lead on Always Man, I thought, heading for the darkroom. A lead to follow up on.

At lunch a couple hours later, I dealt my new photos around Grandmother Miss Lacy's table. "These are great," Harm said, biting into a turkey sandwich. He studied the image I'd snapped as I stumbled on the loose stone. "Is this a face?"

I studied the photo's wild arc—a blurred face with a streak of dark hair? "Maybe," I said, shuffling my photos and stopping on the windows' crisscrossed shadows on the stone floor.

"What, Mo?" Dale asked. "You look like you swallowed a firefly."

I spun the photo toward him. "Our riddle. Shadows *cross* over a *resting* stone. And a *loose* stone beside a *still* one. *Cross over resting, loose beside still.*"

"Seems like a long shot," Harm said. "But let's check it out. If you're right, Tupelo Landing's been walking on Blackbeard's treasure for three hundred years."

"Fix the church floor for free?" Grandmother Miss Lacy said that afternoon, sitting by Mr. Red. You'd never think Mr.

Red would look at home in her parlor, but he does. "Why?"

"Because we're generous," I said.

She looked from me to Dale. "No, really," she said. "Why?"

"We want to look under it. It's a clue," Dale said. "We'll fix it back."

"I'll set it up if I can," she said. She slipped closer to Mr. Red and opened our gift.

"We mixed your old photos with today's," I said as she turned the album's pages. Photos of her parents, her as a baby, their family through the years. Then photos from today: the florist, the church, Dale bringing in flowers. She sniffled.

"Why is she crying?" Dale whispered. "I thought she'd like it."

"You have a lot to learn about women," Mr. Red told him, handing her his handkerchief.

"I know," Dale said. "What are your top three tips on a first—"

"Hush Dale," Grandmother Miss Lacy said, blushing. "I love this, Mo. Thank you so much, all of you."

"You and your mother were perfect together," I said, looking on as she turned the page.

Mr. Red laughed.

"Perfect?" she said, looking shocked. "Good glory, no. Mother and I were half too different, and half too much alike. But we loved each other dearly," she said, running her finger across a photo of her mother's face. "And I miss her every day I open my eyes."

That night, in the quiet of our home, Miss Lana and me made The Call. I sat close as she dialed. The Colonel sat on his leather chair, stone-faced as a sphynx.

"Hello?" Miss Lana said, and I jumped. "Mrs. Duncan? My name's Lana. I'm calling for my daughter, Mo LoBeau. I'm following up on a letter she sent . . . That's right, the photo of Mo, and the good-looking man pumping gas."

She smiled as she listened to the woman's story. "Anthony? What a handsome name. And you last heard from him when?" Her smile wavered. "Oh my, that's a long time ago."

She looked at me and shook her head so slight, I barely caught it.

"Thank you so much. I'll call you if we find him." She hung up and sighed. "Anthony is old enough to be your great-grandfather, sugar. Somebody else will write. You'll see."

The Colonel stood and stretched his arms over his head. "Courage, Soldier," he said. "That's the first step in everything that matters."

"Yes sir," I said, rising. My heart felt like a bad ride at the county fair—spinning, falling, no way to get off. "Excuse me," I said. "I may or may not have homework."

I went into my flat and closed the door. I hate it when I cry.

Dear Upstream Mother,

My lead on Always Man fizzled.

On the treasure case, we will lift the wobbly stone in the church floor if we can get permission from the Floor Committee. We also checked for footprints outside the church window, where a blurry-faced person maybe spied on us while I was shooting photos this morning.

The footprints had been swept clean, same as my heart. I miss you every day I open my eyes.

Mo

Chapter Twenty-four
A Long Shot Pays Off

Monday, Attila announced she had found an old coin for Gabriel Archer.

Harm looked at me, his eyebrows high. Was it the mayor's? I made a note to call Starr.

Tuesday, Miss Retzyl discussed sets and subsets, and I asked to be excused with a possible future nosebleed. No luck. And still no word from the church's Floor Committee.

Wednesday, Tinks tapped at our classroom door. He stepped inside, cradling dented roses. "Delivery for Priscilla Retzyl."

"Tinks got those roses thrown back at him during a delivery-gone-bad," Dale whispered. "I told you I had a plan to marry up her and Starr."

Tinks fished a paper from his pocket and read:

POEM FOR MISS PRISCILLA RETZYL BY JOE STARR
Glads look flashy and cheap,
roses are good, not for creeps.
To avoid soon divorcement

choose Joe in law enforcement,
he'll lock up your heart for keeps.

"Oh my," Miss Retzyl said in the tone she used the day the Exum boys brought a flat highway frog for science.

"Poem, check. Flowers, check," Dale murmured as Tinks fled. "Starr and Miss Retzyl are halfway down the aisle."

Before I could reply, Skeeter clicked the intercom on. "Attention Desperados," she said. "You have a meeting with the Church Floor Committee after school."

"Good luck with that," Attila said, smirking.

"Our luck's changed, Mo," Dale said. "I can feel it in your bones."

But if we'd gone lucky, we didn't stay lucky long.

After school the chair of the Floor Committee—mean, beige Mrs. Simpson—tapped her foot against the church floor and shook her head. "No," she said.

"But this stone's dangerous," I said. "A clumsy person could fall."

"Mo's clumsy," Dale added. "She nearly fell. Twice."

"I ain't suing you because I haven't thought of it yet," I added.

Mrs. Simpson scowled. Cul-de-sac people fear lawsuits like Miss Lana fears snakes. "This floor is *history*. *Some* families haven't been here long enough to appreciate that," she said as Grandmother Miss Lacy strolled in.

"I'll vouch for the Desperados, Betsy," she said, "and pay for the repairs if they fail. Thank you so much for humoring me."

Pre-emptive gratitude. Brilliant, I thought as Mrs. Simpson hissed and clacked out.

"I'd love to join you," Grandmother Miss Lacy whispered, "but I have a meeting with Gabriel. Someone scattered pennies in the woods, and it's driving Anna's metal detector mad," she said, her eyes twinkling. "And he says he has a new clue—one he says will let him search the inn grounds." She headed for the door. "Take plenty of photos. Betsy Simpson is right: This floor is part of our history."

An hour later, with the fill removed, Harm pried the stone up.

Dale zipped his flashlight beam across its former resting place.

"There!" I cried as something glinted. I spit on my finger and rubbed the glimmer. "It looks like copper," I said. "It's jagged and . . ." Harm slipped the pry bar beneath it and we lifted out a copper plate.

"What's a copper plate doing there?" I said.

Dale raked the soil it had rested on. "A ring!" he whispered. He wiped it on the knee of his jeans and held it to the light—a heavy gold ring with a flat, engraved face.

"A skeleton stabbing a bleeding heart! Blackbeard's seal!"

"Desperados!" a voice roared.

We jumped and someone screamed. Possibly me. Gabriel Archer strolled toward us, cape flowing. I slid the copper plate under my shirt and Harm shoved the ring in his pocket, and we all stood to face him. His stare crawled over us like a searchlight.

"Play defense," Dale whispered. Brilliant.

The Colonel says the best defense is a good offense.

"Grandmother Miss Lacy's waiting for you at her place. And you're *late*. What have you got to say for yourself?"

"Miss Thornton will keep," he said like she was a piece of meat. "What's that?" he demanded, staring at the gap in the floor.

"Dirt," Dale said. Dale has a way with the obvious.

Harm stepped up beside me, the pry bar still in his hand. "Mo's right. Miss Thornton's waiting. And you don't have permission to be here. This is a construction site."

"Standing up for your little girlfriend," Gabriel said. "Cute, Crenshaw. But don't push me unless you want your mom singing in cheap honky-tonks the rest of her unremarkable life."

"Don't talk bad about Harm's mother," Dale said, and Gabriel turned to loom over him.

A lifetime of standing up to his daddy paid off. Dale stared Gabriel down easy as a playground bully. "All life's remarkable," Dale said as Gabriel broke his stare. "It's sad you can't feel that, especially in a church."

Gabriel tossed Harm one last sneer. "Stay out of my way, Crenshaw."

"Here's a better idea," I said. "You stay out of ours."

The door slammed shut behind him, and I slipped the plate from beneath my shirt. "Good going, Desperado," I told Dale. "Let's fix this floor and get out of here."

Dale nodded. "He'll come back, and when he does, we should be someplace different."

Later, at my flat, Dale tugged our copper plate from my bag and wiped it clean. "I hoped for more treasures under that stone, but . . . hey!" he said. "It's a Jolly Roger! I'd know him anywhere. Even with his crossbones nipped off on one side, he's still smiling. There's squiggles engraved on here too."

I stepped over yesterday's jeans, which lay in a strategic holding pattern by my bed, dropped to my knees, and pulled our plaster map from beneath my bed. Dale turned the copper piece and fit it into the shark-bite-shaped space in the map's corner. "Perfect," he breathed.

We carried it to my bathroom mirror and pushed aside my Elvis toothbrush holder. With the last piece of Mary's puzzle in place, our map followed the river from below the fish camp—its X marking the spot where we nearly

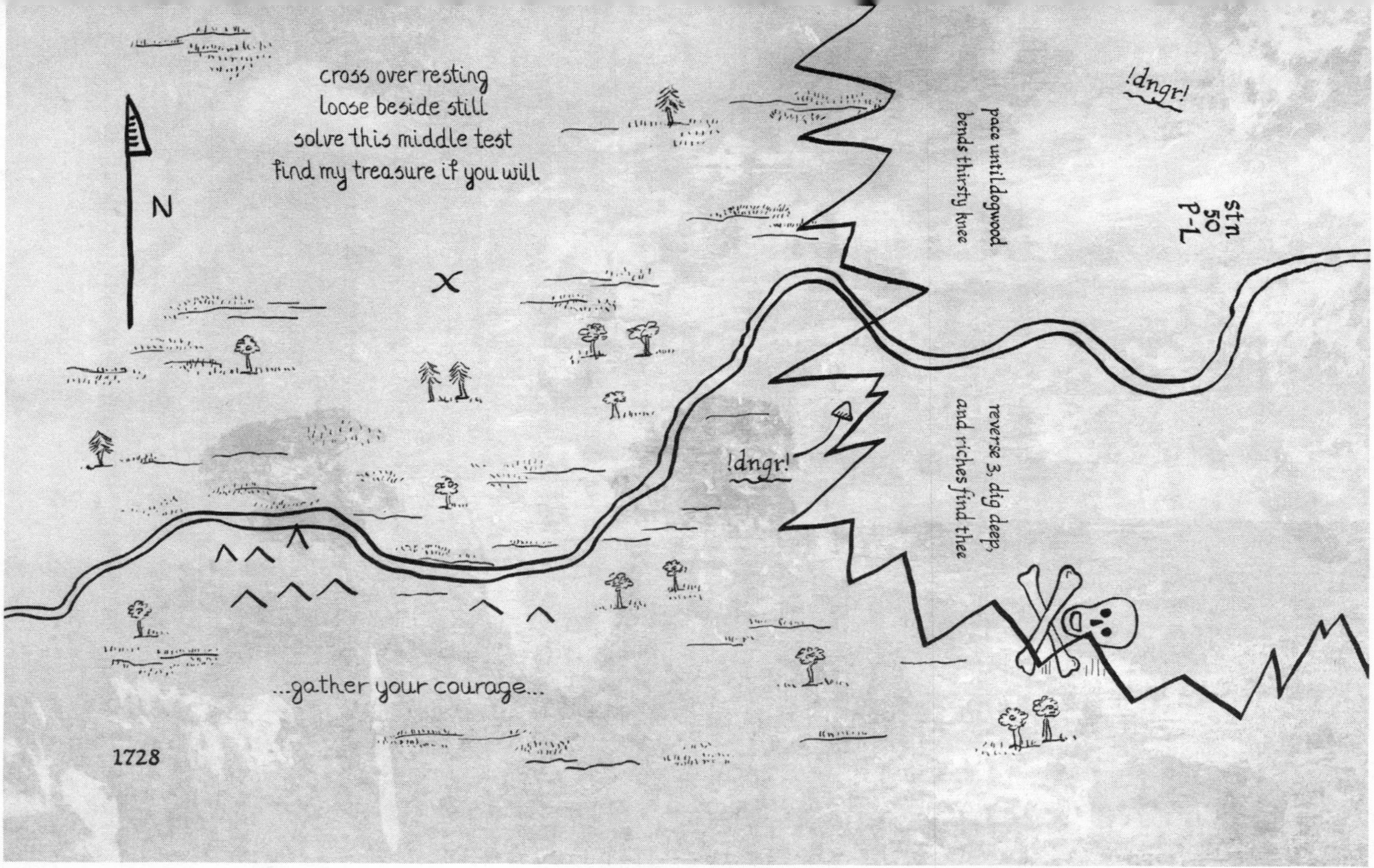
cross over resting
loose beside still
solve this middle test
find my treasure if you will
N
X
!dngr!
pace until dogwood
bends thirsty knee
stn
50
P-L
!dngr!
reverse 3, dig deep,
and riches find thee
...gather your courage...
1728

died—up, through Mr. Red's land, to the inn. "The lines on Mary's map fit Roger's bones," Harm said. "That makes this one giant treasure map."

"And here's the letters *stn,* the numeral fifty, and *P-L,*" I said, squinting.

"*P-L.* It's Peg-Leg," Dale said, his eyes shining.

"*Stn*? That could mean stone," I said. "But Tupelo Landing's all dirt except on the cul-de-sac, where they import status boulders. I never spent much time past the springs, though." I tilted my head. "Here's another riddle," I said. "*Pace until dogwood bends thirsty knee, reverse three, dig deep . . . and riches find thee.*"

Harm picked up my phone. "I'm sick of riddles," he said. "But this map should get us permission to search the inn grounds. We're *this* close to treasure. We just got to get there before Gabriel does. Maybe luck will smile on us this time."

Luck not only smiled on us, she kissed us on both cheeks. First, we got the go-ahead to search the grounds around the inn in nothing flat. Second, Miss Retzyl called the café after supper: "The school heater's out. No school tomorrow while Tinks works on it."

Yes! A day to search for treasure!

Early the next morning, we pedaled up the inn's curving, cedar-lined drive and bounced across the neat grounds.

We zipped past Lavender's pickup to the old springhouse, which sat covered in vines.

"Peg-Leg says *fifty* paces from a *stone*," Harm said. Wind-twisted pines fringed the low, blue-and-orange clay cliff overlooking the river. "But you're right, Mo. No boulder."

The trees rustled. "Hey, good-looking," Kat said, stepping into the clearing. "Thought you kids might like an update from your favorite spy."

"You're not our spy," Harm said. "And you're not supposed to be here."

"I thought you'd be glad to see me," she said, and Harm blushed.

She's not a friend, I reminded myself. "Where are your partners in crime?" I asked.

"Attila's shopping in Raleigh with her *charming* mother," she said. "The GPR blinked out and Gabriel says repairs will take forever." She went full-blown mother. "Look, Harm. Gabriel says you were rude to him in the church and I'm embarrassed. I'd like to know why you did that."

"Harm wasn't rude, I was," Dale said, calm as glass.

"And if Gabriel's your friend, he sure doesn't act like it," I added.

"Funny you're poking around up here," she said. "Gabriel thinks the treasure's here too." She kissed Harm's face, and she was gone.

"She drives me crazy, popping up all over my life," Harm muttered.

Sad, I thought. I'd give anything for Upstream Mother to pop up in mine.

An hour later Dale poked his head through a tangle of vines. Dale's not allergic to poison ivy. Harm and me are. "Found the stone!" Dale called. "Iron ore, but wide and blobby. Red and brown with yellow spots . . . Like a giant sun-dried toad or a huge chunk of space vomit."

"You're a poet," Harm teased, pulling twine from his backpack. "I thought about this last night. We'll use the stone for the center, and mark fifty paces out as far around as we can go. Our spot should be somewhere on that arc."

Dale stood on the stone holding the end of the string. Harm tossed me a roll of green tape and marched off, counting his steps. ". . . forty-eight, forty-nine, fifty," he said, and broke the string. I marked it. He came back and took a different angle through the trees. I popped green tape on another tree, two trees, three. We soon had a nice arc to search—if you knew to look for the green tape among the pines.

Smart. "You're not just another pretty face," I said.

"Thanks, LoBeau," he said, grinning. "Neither are you. We're fifty paces from the stone in all directions, but now what?"

Dale's belly rumbled. "We could eat," Dale said.

"Lunch at my house and we can figure out what to do next," Harm offered. "It's closest and it's *my* turn to treat."

By the time we bounced into Mr. Red's yard, my stomach was rumbling too. Harm laid his bike into a skid by his front steps.

"Kat again," he said, looking across the yard. "What's she doing here?"

Mr. Red and Kat stood toe to toe by the dog pen. Same thrown-back shoulders, same glare. "We'll see about that," she shouted, and jumped in Gabriel's car.

She slid to a halt beside us and rolled her window down. "Hey, baby, Trent and I are coming to your Valentine's gig," she said, breathing so hard, she pinched her nostrils thin.

"You are? Why? Who's Trent?"

"My agent. I want him to hear you sing. I want you to move to Nashville, with me," she said, making her eyes soft. "Please? You'll love it."

"He can't go," I said. "He's busy."

"We'll work up a mother-son act," she continued, watching Harm. "It's a great plan. It helps Pops—he's nearly broke. We can spend time together like I always wanted. We'll be rich. You'd like that, wouldn't you? Sure you would. Otherwise, why search for a treasure?"

"Harm can't go," Dale said. "He's half of me and him, and a third of me and Mo and him. Fractions," he added, like she'd miss that.

Harm took a deep breath. "Thanks, Kat, but my life's here. I'll pass."

"I'm your mother," she snapped, her voice losing its smile. "Your life is where I say it is." She looked around the homestead, at the whitewash the three of us had slapped on the house. At the front steps Harm and Mr. Red built, at Grandmother Miss Lacy's curtains hanging in the windows. "Believe me, this is exactly the kind of place you want to be *from,*" she said, and Harm looked like she'd kicked him.

My temper jumped. "This ain't Harm's *from,* it's his *home.* And it's great."

"If you don't like running water and a bank account," she said, and spun out of the yard.

Harm slapped our sandwiches together like he could barely see the bread and spooned up the pudding like he didn't know the bowls. Outside, Mr. Red shoveled a trench by the dog pens. He moved like a machine, working Kat out of his system.

I went to the door. "Mr. Red! Lunch!"

He let the door slam behind him. "Smells good."

"It's just balogna, Gramps."

We slipped into our seats. Mr. Red bowed his head. "Bless these sandwiches and the boy that made them. Keep us close. Amen." He opened his sandwich and peppered it hard. He slid the pepper to Harm, who did the exact same thing, the exact same way.

Kat sat between them clear as if she'd walked through the door.

Mr. Red closed his sandwich. "I like having you here, Harm," he said. "You deserve good as you give, and you give a lot—to everybody at this table. Lacy loves you too. What little I have is yours if you want it. I hope you'll stay." He switched courses like a PBS gazelle with a cheetah on its heels. "I've almost got that last leaky pipe dug out and I could use some help. It's going to freeze hard tonight, and if that pipe freezes and busts we'll be in a mess."

"Right," Harm said. "Only we're close to the treasure. Once I find it, we can hire the best plumber in the state."

"*If* you find it," Mr. Red said. "I need help now."

I reached for the pepper, and time to think. "Lavender's covering the inn's desk for Miss Lana today—we saw his truck. He can make sure Kat doesn't go back up to our search site. Gabriel's repairing his GPR, and Attila's in Raleigh."

"Plus we don't know what to do next," Dale said, diving into his pudding. "We need some ideas, and ideas are like chickens. Hard to chase down. But if you leave the hen-house door open, they naturally come home."

Dale looked at me, his eyes questioning. I gave him a thumbs-up.

"We can help, Mr. Red," Dale said, and the worry left Harm's face. He always seems surprised when we help—even though we help him every time.

By midafternoon, we'd dug out the old pipe and replaced the leaky section. My ideas had flown the coop. Harm's had too. "You're trying too hard," Dale said.

Harm glanced at the dowsing rod at Mr. Red's feet. "I can't believe you found all those leaks with a stick. I mean, it's crazy, but it's kind of brilliant too."

"Crazy ain't crazy if it works," Dale said. "People been dowsing forever. Willow and dogwood work good, but some people like sycamore. Daddy uses wire."

"It's not so much the kind of wood as the person using it," Mr. Red said, checking the pipe. "I have a feel for water. My mother did too."

"Think I can do it?" Harm asked.

A quick lesson later, he crossed the yard, holding the forked branch in front of him. "Keep it strong," Mr. Red coached. "Wrists up. Water strikes like a fish. You'll feel it."

"All I feel is stupid," Harm muttered. "Somebody else try."

I hopped up. "I will." The wood felt alive in my hands. I glided. It bobbed, like a nibble on a fishing line. Another step. It dipped, and pulled straight down over the pipe.

"See?" Mr. Red said. "Some people just got a feel for water."

*****

Dear Upstream Mother,

Do you have a feel for water? I do.

Thanks to Blackbeard's ex, we've found the treasure site up near the springhouse. We just got to figure out where to dig. Also we found the ring Blackbeard used to seal his terrifying notes. It's in a box under my bed.

As far as our search for you, stay brave. We're zeroing in. 22 no's on Always Man, but our yes is out there.

Yours in courage,

Mo

PS: Thes says we'll be ten degrees tomorrow morning. That never happened in Tupelo Landing. I can't wait to feel it.

Chapter Twenty-five
Murder

Thes nailed the forecast. Friday morning woke up crystal cold and sparkling. The river went pale with ice, and the café regulars steamed in bundled to their eyebrows.

Lavender came in sporting denim, a dark green scarf, and a shake-me-down shiver.

Gabriel, on the other hand, swirled in like cold couldn't touch him. "Cheese biscuit, to go," he said. "I hear you're searching by the inn, Mo. Waste of time."

Kat *is* a spy, I thought. His.

Miss Lana shoved a two-dollar biscuit in a takeout bag and slid it to me. "Four dollars," I said. I rang it up and stuck two dollars in my tip jar as Gabriel drove away.

Lavender grabbed his own takeout. "Bacon and egg sandwich," I said, ringing him up. "Would you like a side of Marry Me with that?"

He handed me a five and a smile. "Marry you? You're a baby. Want a ride to school, Mo? It's too cold for bikes this morning. I'm picking Dale up too."

Lavender never has to ask me twice.

We rumbled out of the parking lot, my bike in back. "How's life?" he said.

Rhetorical, I thought, but my mouth was already in gear. "Kat wants to take Harm away and I don't want him to go."

He frowned. Even frowning, he's fall-apart gorgeous. "Why? What's in it for her?"

That's Kat in five words, I thought. *What's in it for her?*

"She wants a mother-son act. She's bringing her agent to hear Harm sing Valentine's Day," I added as the pines blinked past. "What can we do? I can't imagine Tupelo Landing without Harm in it, and I got a world-class imagination."

"You do," Lavender said. He smiled, but his eyes had gone tired. "Kat's going to do what she's going to do, and we may not be able to stop her. All we can do for sure is tell Harm how we feel, and be a friend."

That's *it?* That's all he's got for me?

He turned on his blinker and muscled the truck into Miss Rose's drive. We bounced across the yard, scattering chickens, as Dale ran to us and slung his bike in the back of the truck.

"Move over, Mo," Dale said, diving in beside me. He looked at his brother. "Can you help me find a movie for me and Sal? Nothing too baby but nothing scary or—you know," he said, and pulled out a calendar.

Dale? With a calendar? The earth wobbled.

"Since when do you carry a calendar?" I asked.

"Bill says it might help keep time in a straight line. Lavender, Harm and me are singing at the café Valentine's and you're invited. I can reserve for you."

Lavender gave a quick nod. "Table for two."

"Sal and me can movie date on February twelfth," Dale said, studying the calendar. "On the thirteenth I help Harm with harmonies, and I'll kiss Sal on Valentine's Day. If I don't stroke out."

"You won't, little brother," Lavender said. "And I'll keep an eye on the movies."

"Arctic dip," Thes shouted as we unloaded our bikes at school. "Deadly cold," he called as we pushed our bikes to the bike rack. "Enjoy it while you can."

Jake looked side to side, leaned down, and licked the metal bike rack. He pulled. His tongue stretched. "Elp!" he bellowed, flapping his arms. "Elp!"

Harm slipped his bike into the rack. "Why did he do that?" he asked Jimmy.

"Thes said it would stick, but it seemed wrong," Jimmy said, his round face worried. "Will Jake die?"

"Maybe," I said, and did a double take as Attila hopped off the school bus. Attila never rides the bus. She Cadillacs everywhere. She minced over, her chlorine-colored snow coat dull in the morning light. "Oh, for goodness' sake," she said, thumping Jake's ear. "How can I park my bicycle when your stupid head is stuck to the rack?"

"You didn't ride your bike," I said. Attila only rides her show bike in parades.

"Well, I could have," she said. She hesitated. "But maybe you're right, Mo. Let me know if I can help you today. We treasure hunters have to stick together."

"Stick with Attila? I don't think so," Dale muttered as Sal strolled over, sipping hot chocolate. She dribbled a little on Jake's tongue.

"Pull," she said, and dribbled a little more. Jake ripped free, blinking back tears.

"I owe you, Sal," Jake said.

Sal winked. "Let's stay in touch," she said, and she and Dale walked inside.

I looked at Harm, who'd worn a jacket for once. "Harm . . ." He blew into his hands and looked at me. He has long lashes, like Lavender.

"We got to figure out where to dig," I said, "before Gabriel beats us to that treasure."

After settling into my desk, I propped my math book open and slipped my brain in neutral, like Miss Lana meditating in the living room. I breathed deep, pinched the air, and floated our clue through the cosmos: *Pace until dogwood bends thirsty knee . . .*

I unlocked my mind and let the images flutter through: Lavender driving, Miss Lana styling a wig, the Colonel flipping a burger, Harm winking, Dale singing, Mr. Red dowsing.

Nothing.

I invited the images again. Nothing.

Again. *Bam!*

"I got it!" I shouted, slamming my palm against my desk.

The class turned. Miss Retzyl frowned. A blush crept up my neck.

So, I thought. This is what it feels like to be Dale.

"Leg cramp," I said, hobbling to Dale.

"I got it," I whispered to him. "I know where to dig."

Before he could answer, the intercom crackled on. "Attention," Skeeter boomed. "The school's heater's broken again. School's dismissed."

Miss Retzyl cheered. Interesting.

As every kid in school bolted outside, Attila shouted from the door: "Desperados, wait!"

"Fly like the wind, Desperados," I said. We hunched over our handlebars and flew.

At the bluff, I cut a dogwood branch. "*Pace until dogwood bends thirsty knee*," I said. "Dowsing's hundreds of years old. Mary knew about it—she could maybe even do it." I walked the arc we'd traced earlier, holding the dowsing rod like Mr. Red showed me.

It swayed and bobbled, like minnows nibbling a fishing line.

I walked a few steps more: Nothing. *Could I have been wrong?*

The rod bent sharp to the ground. "Here," I said. "We dig here."

"I don't know," Harm said. "We're looking for treasure, Mo. Not water."

"*Pace until dogwood bends thirsty knee.* Reverse three, *dig deep, riches find thee,*" Dale said. "Back up, Mo."

I took three steps back, to the place the dowsing rod stayed absolutely still, and dropped it as a *haalloo* drifted to us. Attila trudged up, puffing. "Didn't you hear me call you after school? I need your help."

"We're busy," I said. "And you ain't allowed here."

She looked at Dale. "*I* didn't ignore *your* cries for help when you were in quicksand."

"Touchy," Dale said. "How can we help?"

"He means touché," I told Attila, and sighed. Dale always pays his debts.

"I had Mother drop me by Gabriel's camp early this morning so I could use the Ground Penetrating Radar," she said. "*That's* why I caught the school bus this morning. Hideous. Anyway, the GPR slid down the bank, to the water. I need people like you to drag it back up."

"People like us?" I said.

She looked around like the trees might hear. "*Detectives.* The GPR tipped because I jumped, and I jumped because of the image on the screen." She edged closer. "I found three graves," she whispered. "Only I don't know if they're old graves, or the graves of somebody . . . new."

Four of us sprinted for three bikes. Harm pedaled away. I looked through Attila like she was water. Dale sighed. "You can ride on my handlebars. Hop on."

Attila frowned. "How?"

Several ugly minutes later, we stood on the riverbank, looking down a four-foot drop to the river's edge. The GPR lay on its side, its computer screen muddy, two wheels in the water.

"What happened?" Dale panted, clutching his side.

"It fell, obviously," Attila said, and then looked sheepish. "I woke up last night thinking we hadn't searched that little bit of land. And what a nice surprise for Gabriel if I found the treasure. He's flown to Williamsburg, to do some research, but he'll be back soon."

Dale put his hands on his knees and took a deep breath. "That was sweet of you."

She scuffed her shoe. "Not really. Mother invested in Gabriel's dig. I get a bigger percentage if I find the treasure."

Finally. Attila the Intern made sense.

"Where are the graves?" I asked.

"Up on the bank. Help me and I'll show you." We heaved the GPR upright. Attila and I scampered up the bank to pull as the boys shoved. With the GPR in place, Attila flipped a switch and the screen blinked on. A sketchy outline filled the screen. "That's definitely a body—and a pistol," Harm said.

We pushed. The screen blinked again.

"Grave number two," Attila said. "With a pistol, metal buttons, musket balls . . . And here's grave number three."

We stared at a tiny form over the body's shoulder. A roundish blob with an outstretched . . . arm? A wing?

Dale gasped. "No! They killed a chicken!"

We waited. Dale edged closer. "It's a parrot," he announced, his voice sad. "These are pirate graves, then. But who killed them?"

"Blackbeard, obviously," Gabriel boomed, swooping in behind us. "Do you think he'd let the men who buried his treasure live to tell about it? Step away from my GPR, thieves."

"We're not thieves," Harm said. "Anna asked us to help. Tell him, Anna."

Attila smiled at Gabriel. "I found these pirate graves for you, Gabriel." She looked at me and curled her lip. "Go find your own clues, Desperados."

Chapter Twenty-six
Only One Way to Find Out

"What a double-crossing weasel," Harm fumed as we grabbed shovels from the inn's storeroom. "But why were the graves back *there* if the treasure's up *here?* Maybe Gabriel's map is right. Maybe the treasure isn't up here at all."

"There's only one way to find out," I said. "Start digging."

A half hour later, we were two feet down. "We should have hit clay a foot ago—only this dirt's mixed up," Dale said, eyes glowing. "Somebody's dug here before."

I tipped my shovel in and pounced. It scraped something hard.

Dale chopped along the side of the pit, fell to his knees, and dug with his hands. "A copper sheet, like the one Mary left for us in the church. Only huge. And up-and-down."

"Vertical, like a wall?" Harm said. "Hold on." He headed for his backpack. "Check this out," he said, grabbing a book. "There's a chapter about a pit on Oak Island, Canada, that may hold some of Blackbeard's treasure. Six people have died there, and they've dug over a hundred feet deep. It had a lot of built-in stuff. Floors, shafts, copper wires. This is some kind of pirate technology, maybe . . ."

"Six people died?" Dale asked.

"Booby-trapped," Harm said, turning a page.

I studied the lay of the land—and considered the springs flowing into our springhouse, just downhill. "This isn't a wall, it's a dam. To keep Mary and Peg-Leg safe while they worked—and to keep us safe while we strike it rich."

"The Canada pit was booby-trapped?" Dale muttered again, picking up a shovel. "Mama's going to kill me."

At sundown, I dragged into the café, muscles screaming like bobcats. Tinks sat at the counter, talking with the Colonel. Miss Lana polished the cash register, the Winter Tree's colors softening the scene. "It's like a neon Norman Rockwell painting, isn't it, sugar?" she said. "Any luck?"

I collapsed into a chair. "We found the right spot. This time tomorrow, we'll be rich."

Miss Lana froze. "Really?"

"Harm's standing sentry. I got guard duty tomorrow night," I said as the Colonel plunked my supper plate down. "Want to go, Colonel? It's warmed up. We could camp out, build a fire, talk with the stars."

He poured my milk. "You're on, Soldier. Who's with Harm?"

"Nobody. We found a treasure shaft. It's got a wall to hold the water back. We already dug it elbow deep."

"Who else has been there?" the Colonel asked, frowning.

"Kat and Attila. Gabriel knows about it too."

The Colonel picked up the phone and dialed. "Red? Harm's camping up by the old springhouse tonight, and I thought you might like to join him. . . . Right-o," he said, and hung up shaking his head. "Red's sick as a dog."

He looked at Miss Lana. "I don't want Harm out there alone if Gabriel shows up. Or Kat, for that matter. I'll grab the sleeping bags."

"And I'll pack some food," she said, grabbing a takeout bag.

Tinks hopped up as she tossed in a bag of marshmallows. "I got a backhoe on my tractor, Mo, if you want to use it. It digs real deep real fast. I'd love to see you kids strike it rich." He stretched. "Like me to pick up supplies for you tomorrow, Colonel? I could use the work."

The Colonel needs help picking up supplies like Miss Lana needs help ordering costumes. Still, he nodded. "We're having pork chops tomorrow. I've already called the order in," he said, and hurried out to get his camp gear together, and to keep Harm safe.

The Colonel ain't a people person, but if every Tupelite he ever helped stepped forward at the same time, the town would slide off the map.

* * * * *

The next morning—Saturday—the Colonel and Harm rolled in smelling like smoke. Dale flew in next, his hair still damp from his shower. "Who's standing watch while we help at the café?" Dale asked, heading for the ice machine.

I looked at Miss Lana. "Take the weekend off, sugar," she said. "The Colonel and I can manage. You kids eat breakfast and go get rich."

"It might take longer than a weekend," Harm said.

She frowned. "You can't take many days off without failing sixth grade."

"Yes ma'am," I said. "Repeating sixth would be a double dip of doom, but this is a once-in-a-lifetime opportunity. And if we leave our dig unguarded, Gabriel will be on it like white on snow."

The Colonel frowned, but I saw a smile teasing his thin lips. "We *could* ask Myrt Little to tutor them, Lana. Just to catch them up if it takes longer than the weekend."

Dale went pale, but I stuck out my hand. "Deal."

Miss Lana laughed. "Three days, Mo, counting today. No more than that. And you'll need adult supervision if you dig over nose deep."

"I'm in," Lavender said, swaying toward the cash register. "I can be there by lunch."

"Count me in too," Tinks added, from the other end of the counter. "Lana, are you sure this bacon's done?"

"You should be a vegetarian," the Colonel muttered, but he carried the bacon back to the kitchen.

Harm grabbed the phone. "I'll call Gramps and tell him we're going to be rich."

By lunchtime we'd dug chin deep. Dale heaved a shovel of dirt up and out, and closed his eyes as a small avalanche rained back down on him.

"My turn," I said. "Climb out."

Dale looked up at me. "How?"

"Good question," Lavender said, strolling up.

Lavender! For Adult Supervision, he'd gone Garage Chic—perfectly yet truly ripped jeans, boots, red wool shirt, denim jacket.

"Welcome to our excavation," I said, very sophisticated.

"Thanks, Mo. It's a doozy." He beamed at Dale. "I've seen men paint themselves into a corner, little brother. But this is the first time I've seen a boy dig himself into a pit."

Dale looked up, his face smudged. "Get me out."

Lavender held a hand down to Dale. "You need a ladder," he said as Dale scrambled up.

"On it," Harm said, walking up with Miss Lana's new ladder over his shoulder. "Rope and buckets too."

"I'm next," I said. I sat on the side of the pit and avalanched in, landing loud.

"Graceful." Harm grinned, sliding the ladder into place.

Dale had dug us down neat as a tabletop. I started digging, and filling Harm's buckets. Moments later, I tapped the shovel in, and jumped on it. *Cloinggggggg.* The impact sang through me like middle C through a tuning fork.

"The treasure chest!" Dale cried, dropping beside me light as a kitten.

We worked like maniacs for a couple hours—me and Dale digging, Harm and Lavender hauling up dirt until we reached a rough wood floor about eight feet down.

"Just like the Canada pit," Harm said. It had a wooden floor every eight feet—and the timbers were thick. "We need a chainsaw."

Lavender glanced at his watch. "I have a customer in thirty minutes, and I can't afford a no-show reputation. You all take a break. Tinks has a chainsaw. I'll call."

I made an Executive Decision. "Ask him to bring his tractor with its digging claw too."

Tinks and his chainsaw made fast work of the heavy timbers in our floor. "They're thick—just like in the pit in Canada," Harm called up, pulling our chain to the first timber.

"What's under them?" I asked.

"Dirt," Tinks said, scurrying up the ladder. "Somebody filled in the pit, to keep us out." He jumped onto his old green tractor, which he'd parked between the pit and the edge of the woods. He fired the tractor up, jammed the clutch to the floor, and edged the back wheel closer to the pit's edge.

Harm hooked the chain. "Go," he shouted.

The engine whined as Tinks lifted the jagged metal claw, the timber dangling from the chain.

We lifted the timbers one by one, and slung them aside. "Ready to dig?" Tinks called.

"Don't hit the copper wall!" I shouted.

He nodded and turned backwards on his tractor seat, lining up the claw. He swooped it down, swiping out a trench maybe two feet wide. Tinks lifted the claw, and dumped the soil next to the pit.

A half hour later, with our formerly neat pit a small crater, he hit the second floor.

"Chainsaw," Harm called, lowering the ladder, ready to clean the earth off the pit's floor and copper wall. "I'll cut this time."

"Nope," Tinks said, hopping off the tractor and grabbing the saw. "But give me a hand."

"It's my turn to help," I said. "And Mo LoBeau always takes her turn."

Cleaning the pine floor took time and muscle. The copper seam along the floor leaked slightly as Tinks grabbed the saw. It whined through the thick planks, spewing bright red sawdust. I swept the chips aside with each cut, clearing the path to the next cut.

"Chain!" I shouted. Dale dropped our heavy chain down to haul up the boards as Tinks and me stepped onto the last, uncut timber.

I looked up at Harm—his crooked smile, smudged face, bright eyes.

A sharp crack at my feet set my world spinning as the timber tilted beneath us.

Tinks and me danced like marionettes. As our end of the plank dropped, the other end sliced up through the copper wall like a little kid's seesaw.

The pent-up water behind the wall roared free, slamming me into Tinks, spinning me down, down, down and into a pool of ice-cold water—helpless as a twig.

Even underwater, my lungs caught fire.

Help me, I prayed, twisting and kicking, bumped by timbers and Tinks's flailing arms and legs.

Miss Lana's voice came to me from nowhere. "Slow and steady, sugar, think it through."

I opened my eyes. Pitch-dark. Swim up.

Which way is up?

I cupped my hands inches from my face and opened my eyes wide. Slowly I exhaled maybe my last breath, feeling the bubbles cross my chin and the insides of my wrists, my neck . . .

Bubbles always rise. I'm upside down!

My lungs screamed. I kicked against a timber and turned a desperate flip. I felt for the bubbles and kicked for my life. Up, up, past Tinks's frantic hands, up.

The water went lighter, and I looked up into a kaleidoscope of daylight.

I broke the surface, gulping in air, and staring into Dale's terrified face. "Mo!" he screamed, pushing the chain to me.

I grabbed and pulled myself up, hand over hand.

Dale, on a tiny jut of timber over the water, pulled me near and hoisted me upward, his arms shaking. Harm reached down and grabbed the back of my jacket, hauling me up.

I rolled into the grass and stared into the pit. Tinks sputtered to the surface. Dale leaned over the water, pushing the chain to him. Tinks clung to it with one arm, the other arm trapped beneath the water.

He looked up at me, his face demon-wild.

"Tinks! Climb!" I shouted.

"Can't," he said, fighting to keep his head above water.

I flew to the tractor and vaulted into the seat. I turned the key and the tractor roared.

"Now!" Harm yelled, arms waving. "Go, go, go!"

I closed my eyes, picturing Tinks on the tractor. His hand on the gearshift, his foot on the clutch . . . *The clutch!* I jammed the metal pedal to the floor. The tractor bumped into gear and lunged into the edge of the woods. The chain snapped tight behind me.

I ducked my head as I crunched into the forest. Briars grabbed my hair. The tractor bucked forward, bumping my face against the metal steering wheel. I looked back. One huge wheel gnawed its way up a tree stump, tipping me over, over . . .

"Jump," Harm screamed, running toward me. "JUMP!"

I jumped as the tractor teetered, crashed, and choked off. We looked back. Tinks sat on the ground, crying. Dale sat beside him, his face white as death.

Suddenly the cold leaned through me, freezing me to my bones.

Harm grabbed my hand. "That was close, Mo. That was so close." He swiped the tears off his face. "What made us think we could outsmart a pirate?"

"I quit," Dale said an hour later as Harm stoked the inn's big fireplace. We'd collapsed into the parlor's heavy chairs. "Rich ain't worth spit if you're dead."

"We can't quit," I said. "We've *found* it. We just have to be smarter."

Dale draped a blanket over Tinks's thin shoulders.

Tinks winced and pulled away. "Just wrenched it out of joint," he said. "It'll pop back in. Dale's right. There's nothing in that pit worth dying for."

I caught my reflection in the window. A scared, shivering girl with a fat lip. I turned my head. Still, when I warmed up and got rid of the scared, the lip would look tough-kid good.

Dale drew a shaky breath. "I don't believe in curses, but look at us. *Surge of blood,*" he said, pointing to my lip. "*Snap of bone,*" he said, pointing to Tinks's shoulder. "*Loss of mortal breath,*" he said, his eyes filling with tears. "Give the treasure to Gabriel. He can have it—and the curse."

Harm looked at me. "Dale's right. It's too dangerous, Mo. Let's cut Gabriel in, and let him bring up the treasure."

Tinks coughed. "I wouldn't go back even if I could swim."

"No. It's *ours,*" I said. "We just got to find a way to get it home."

Sadly, Detective Joe Starr thought different.

"I'm closing you people down," he said late that afternoon, long after Tinks had left to fix the school's heater. Starr kicked dirt into our flooded pit and watched it dissolve away.

"You can't close us down," I said. "We're borderline professionals on a break-through case, and this is private property."

"Watch me." He tied his yellow crime scene tape to the nearest tree, and unwound it.

"Why are you using crime scene tape?" I demanded. "We didn't do a crime."

"Because they don't make stupid scene tape," he snapped. "We're lucky not to be planning two funerals right now. You're lucky an adult called me about this."

"Who?" I demanded, my heart going dark.

"Tinks Williams," Starr said, looping his tape around the next tree. "Stay out of here. All of you. I mean it," he said as Dale handed him his clue pad.

"Could you write our eviction notice? In cursive? And sign it?" Dale asked.

An eviction notice? Has he lost his mind? Dale doesn't even read cursive.

Starr scribbled a note and signed it. "Go," he said. "Now."

We headed toward the inn, me seething, Harm brooding, Dale humming.

"Is Kat still coming to our Valentine's Extravaganza?" Dale asked, and Harm nodded.

Apparently almost drowning in a booby-trapped pirate pit shoots honesty straight to your lips. "I *really* like you, Harm," I said. "I hope you don't go."

He gave me a crooked smile. "I like you too, Mo. A lot," he said, and glanced at Dale. "You too, but not the same way. I want to stay. But Miss Thornton's attorney says I might have to go. If Kat wants me . . . I'm hers."

"She only wants you because you sing," I muttered.

Dale hopped on his bike, very serene. "Exactly," he said.

"Mo, Harm and me got to practice. Don't interrupt us. And I need two good marriage proposals Tuesday morning."

"Marriage proposals? On Valentine's Day? Why?"

"I'm the big-picture man," he said. "You handle details. Don't let me down."

That night, I tapped on Miss Lana's door. "Mo?" she said, closing her *Old Hollywood Magazine*. "What is it?"

"Valentine's question. If you were proposing to the Colonel, what would you say?"

"What a sweet question," she said, and yawned. "I'd say, 'Life's a miracle, dear Colonel. There's no one I'd rather share it with than you. Marry me.'"

"Thanks," I said, and closed her door.

I found the Colonel in the café kitchen, mixing up his special slaw recipe for tomorrow's lunch. "Hey," I said, hopping up on a stool.

"Soldier." He shoved the cabbage into a neat pile and grabbed his knife. The Colonel chops cabbage like a machine gun fires. Rat-a-tat-tat-tat.

I waited for him to reload.

"Colonel, if you proposed to Miss Lana, what would you say?"

He said the words like he'd thought them a thousand times before. "Marry me, Lana. I love you like the ocean loves the taste of salt."

⋆⋆⋆⋆⋆

Dear Upstream Mother,

I should drape my entire life in stupid scene tape.

I can't find you, Harm's getting stolen, Starr closed down our treasure hunt, and Valentine's Day's hurtling toward me like a heat-seeking missile.

Book reports are due Monday. I got A General History of the Pyrates. It's 733 pages. If I felt better about life, I'd retch.

Mo

My phone jangled and I scooped it up. "Desperado Detective Agency. Your tragedy is our bread and butter. How may we help?"

"Mo? It's Effy Stevens, from the historic site. Remember me? Plump, cheery, able to spin wool into yarn? How are you, baby? Have you found your mom?"

I sat bolt upright. "No. Have you?"

"No, but I thought of something," she said. "Actually, Matilda at circle meeting thought of it, but I'll take the credit since I'm picking up the phone. If you don't act on an idea, what good is it? Like I said the other day—"

"Yes, ma'am," I said. "I hate to hurry you, but I got a book report on a book I haven't read and it's 733 pages long."

"Just read the index, honey. That's what I did and they graduated me. It's about the fix-it wool in your sweater. I can't promise, but it *could* have been from a Jacob sheep. Long, scratchy fibers—just like your fix-it wool."

"Where do we find Jacobs?" I asked, my pulse leaping.

"A farm near Contectnea raised Jacobs until the hurricane. They taught folks to spin and dye wool too. I forgot all about them the other day."

My heart surged like she'd hooked me up to jumper cables. "Where? Who?" I asked.

"Near Contectnea is all I know," she said. "Listen. Tell that driver of yours—what's his name? Oregano? Tarragon?"

"Lavender," I said.

"Lavender. Take my phone number down for him, honey. And tell him Effy says hey."

Chapter Twenty-seven
The Worst Mistake of My Life So Far

Skeeter called early Sunday morning, soft steeple music playing in the background. "Sorry Mo, there's no Contectnea Sheep Ranch online. Gotta run."

I tried Lavender, who was working the inn desk for Miss Lana.

"Hello?" he said. I love it when he says hello.

"Hey," I said, "I got a lead on Upstream Mother and the Colonel's gone in the Underbird and I know you love a road trip. I hear you're not driving Dale and Sal to a movie date since there's no middle grade movies out now, and Harm and Dale are practicing, so it's just me. I can be ready in ten."

"Sorry, Mo. I'm working. I'm free tomorrow, but you have school . . . Next weekend?"

Next weekend felt a lifetime away.

I took a deep breath and made the worst mistake of my life so far. "Miss Lana gave me one more day to hunt treasure, and Upstream Mother's a treasure to me. I'll meet you at your garage at eight tomorrow morning."

"If you're sure Lana says it's okay," he said, and hung up the phone.

Monday morning I pedaled past the school, to Lavender's garage. "Miss Effy says a farm near Contectnea raised sheep with my kind of fix-it wool," I told Lavender as I hopped in the truck. "It's a long shot, but I *got* to try."

All day, we crisscrossed little Contectnea and the surrounding countryside, showing Always Man's photo in every crossroads store we could find. We stopped once to buy valentines and eat lunch. Beyond that, we fielded a day full of no's.

My heart sank with the sun.

"One more try." I pointed to a stooped man by a mailbox. "Hey," I said, hopping out. "I'm the well-known detective Mo LoBeau of Tupelo Landing."

He looked at my plaid sneakers. "I heard of you. I thought you'd be taller."

"You're very wise. I'm taller than I look," I replied. "Was there a sheep farm around here twelve years ago?"

"Sure," he said, like it was nothing. "Contectnea Wool. Had a herb garden, made their own dyes, spun wool. Bunch of weirdos. Hurricane closed them down twelve years ago."

"Are they still around?" I asked, my heart thundering.

"Nope. Went to Asheville after the flood, maybe. Or Chapel Hill."

"Do you know this man?" I asked, showing Always Man's photo.

"Maybe, maybe not. Good luck, Mo," he said, and slumped away.

I hurled myself into the truck. "Contectnea Wool! They made their own dye, and they might have moved to Asheville or Chapel Hill. And he might have seen Always Man."

I grinned like the grille of a '57 Chevy all the way home. But my smile crumpled the instant I walked through the café door. Tinks looked up from the cash register.

"I sniffed the air. No bread baking, no coffee brewing. "Where's Miss Lana and the Colonel? Why are you in charge? Tinks, what's wrong?"

He looked away from my eyes. "Lana's at home. You better ask her yourself."

Sometimes no answer's the most terrifying answer of all. Fear slung me around the building and catapulted me through the door. "Miss Lana!"

"Mo!" she cried as I hurled myself into her arms. "*Where* have you been?"

"With Lavender. Where's the Colonel? What's wrong?"

She squeezed me tight and then held me away, her eyes going permafrost. "*He's* out looking for *you*. Where were you? You didn't go to school—Harm and Dale are worried sick, and so is Priscilla. I've called half the town. Miss Thornton is scared to death you went back to that treasure pit and drowned. And *I* am at my wits' end, Moses LoBeau. Explain yourself. Now!"

I took a breath, giving her time to count to ten—which it didn't look like she was counting. "I can explain," I said, giving her more time. "Maybe I should have double-checked this, but I had one day left on my excused absence and an out-of-town clue to follow up on. Dale and Harm are rehearsing for the Extravaganza. And I didn't want to disturb you and the Colonel." So far so good. "I won't say I'm selfless, but—"

"Selfless?" she said, her voice shredding the air like a cat shreds tissue. "You had a *clue* worth worrying us to death? Clues worth repeating sixth grade?"

My temper exploded. "You gave me three days to hunt treasure and today makes three. And I *was* treasure hunting. Upstream Mother is a treasure to me. And I don't care if I *do* fail sixth, I'm searching every clue I can get every day until I find her."

"You certainly are not. You're going to school. Every day. End of discussion."

"That's not fair," I wailed. "I was *excused*. By you. And I was with Lavender. And you can't tell me what to do." My temper went off like fireworks. "You're not my m—"

The silence glistened between us, cruel as hooks.

She quartered to the window and crossed her arms over her heart. I saw her lips move, and I knew she was counting.

"Miss Lana, I'm sorry," I said, my voice wobbling like a bent wheel.

"Be quiet, Mo," she said, her voice dead. "Just. Be. Quiet."

Then she whirled like a tornado and hugged me so tight, her arms shook. "Miss Lana, I don't know how those words got inside me or why they came out. It's like a dam breaks . . ."

She gave me one last squeeze. "I know, sugar. This is hard for all of us. Go to bed. I'll tell everybody you're home." She picked up the phone. "And Mo? We'll talk later."

In my room, I slipped into my karate pants and T-shirt, and turned out my light. I listened to her dial, and murmur. I heard the Colonel stomp in and I thought I heard her cry.

When the house went quiet, I grabbed my jacket and slipped to the side yard. I plunked down by the sawed-off stump and leaned against it, staring into a brushstroke of stars.

"Soldier?" the Colonel said, behind me. "Are you okay?"

"No sir," I said. My feelings swirled like gritty smoke in my chest.

He settled beside me like a shamble of angle iron, and covered us with Miss Lana's throw. It smelled like perfume and popcorn. "I'm sorry, sir. I don't know what's wrong with me. Treasure hunting's making me greedy for things and people I don't know, and making me hurt the people I know and love." I looked at him. "Dale's right. It's not worth it."

"Maybe not." He leaned back to stare into the night. "Tell me what you see, Soldier."

"Oceans of stars," I said, going calmer. "And an ache where the moon ought to be."

We sat together, breathing. "That's starlight, some from stars that died millions of years ago," he said. "I admire its courage. And yours. And Lana's."

"I'm not brave, I'm scared," I said. "Scared I'll never find Upstream Mother, scared I will and she won't want me, scared of hurting Miss Lana."

"Lana's scared too," he said. "Scared of losing you."

I sat up. "She can't lose me, sir. She claimed me off the river. I'm hers."

Just like Mr. Red claimed Harm, I thought.

I leaned against him, feeling his bony chest rise and fall and rise again. "Thank you for keeping that ugly sign for me, sir. And the rest."

"Thank Lana for that," he said. "I wanted to burn it for trash. She made me put the sign under the house. She packed the other things too, for the day you were ready."

Miss Lana? Who's afraid of losing me?

He pulled me to my feet. "You have school tomorrow. And apologies to make."

I looked at our home, which slept in the crook of our river.

"Life's full of surprises, Soldier. Tonight I'm molding a hundred heart-shaped meatloaves for tomorrow's Valentine's Extravaganza." He smiled into my eyes. "Love takes many shapes and wears a thousand disguises. The trick is to welcome it with a cheerful heart—even when it puts you elbow deep in ground beef. Remember that."

"Yes sir," I said. I slipped my hand in his, and we headed home.

Chapter Twenty-eight
Valentine's Day

Miss Lana tiptoed by my door just before dawn, her red stilettos dangling from her fingertips. "Miss Lana?" She turned, her crimson sequins glowing in the lamplight.

I handed her a red envelope, and handed the Colonel his as he slipped up behind her.

She slid out her card. "Will you be mine?" she read, and opened her arms. "Sugar, I've been yours since the moment I laid eyes on you, and I'll be yours as long as I live. Longer, if I'm right about reincarnation."

The Colonel read his card, his dark eyes dancing. "Me too, Soldier."

I placed a paper on our coffee table. "I made us something."

OFFICIAL PAPER

We are an Official Family-of-Choice forever, never to be torn apart by People or Fate, always to honor and share. The three of us together, always true to each other, true to our stars.

Signed,
Miss Lana
The Colonel
Miss Moses LoBeau
PS: Anybody tries to tear us apart has to deal with me. Mo

Miss Lana signed. The Colonel signed and underlined his name.

"Miss Lana, if you want me to stop looking for Upstream Mother, I will."

"Don't you dare stop," she said. "Always follow your heart." She glanced at the clock and jumped up. "Mercy, look at the time. We have breakfast and lunch, plus the Extravaganza tonight. Dale and Harm are sold out. This is a big day."

It was, too. Miss Lana found the Colonel's valentine by the cash register; he found his in the coffee can. They'd hid mine in my order pad. At 7:17, Lavender gave me a red rose, and I gave him a panda card with a marriage proposal penciled in.

But Cupid got the jitters the instant I hit the playground.

Dale paced by the school steps. "Hey Desperado," I said, heading over. "I'm sorry, about yesterday. I should have—"

"Not now, Mo," he interrupted. "Today I kiss Sal. Lavender helped me make a plan. I'll give Sal her Valentine's gifts. I'll walk her home from school. Today I kiss Sal," he said again, and stumbled over his own feet.

"Are you okay?" Harm asked, grabbing his arm.

"Breathe deep," I said. "You'll be fine, Desperado. Remember your notes."

He bent double and wheezed. "Move slow," he mumbled. "Hands in pockets. Don't bump noses."

"Here she comes," Harm whispered. "Try to stand up."

Sal sailed over as Dale went upright.

"Hey, Dale." She stepped close, tilted her head, and kissed him square on the lips. "Happy Valentine's Day," she said, and hurried inside.

Dale looked at me, his eyes round as hubcaps. "I did it," he whispered. "I kissed Sal." And he walked away like a boy dreaming.

As Harm and I trotted up the steps, Attila flounced by. "I hear you're leaving Tupelo Landing, Harm," she said. "Don't let the door hit you on your way out."

"We'll see," Harm said, very even.

I hate Attila Celeste Simpson.

News of Dale and Sal's kiss shot through the sixth grade like a flaming arrow through rat cheese. "We're a power couple, Dale," Sal whispered as we walked into the classroom. She smiled and headed to her seat.

Dale turned to me. "Did you bring the marriage proposals?

We got to move fast. I saw Miss Retzyl in the office, but she won't be there long," he said, snagging a handwritten note from Miss Retzyl's desk and stuffing it in a large manila envelope. I dropped in Miss Lana's and the Colonel's proposals. He tossed in Starr's note evicting us from the treasure pit, and grabbed Jake's sleeve.

"Jake, I need a favor," Dale said, holding out the envelope.

"No. It's Valentine's Day," Jake said, smiling at Hannah Greene. "Jimmy and me want to fall in love."

"It would mean a lot to me," Dale continued. "I could trade you for it. I could let you and Jimmy tap-dance at the Extravaganza tonight. Hannah will be there. Her sisters too."

Jake hesitated. "I would, but I already owe Sal. She might want a favor at the same time."

Sal smiled. "Dale's favor would make us even too."

"Done," Jake said, snatching the envelope and hurrying to his brother.

As Dale followed Sal to her seat, I looked over to see Harm drop a red envelope on my desk. Despite my lifelong future romance with Lavender, Harm's valentine set my heart wobbly.

Was it a cute baby card, or a real one? I'd bought him one of each. But which one to give him?

Dale handed Sal a box of candy, a daffodil, and a card. She opened the card: "This flower's not red and the candy's not blue, but I think I love you so please love me too."

"Candy, poem, flower—check," Dale whispered to himself.

Harm gave me a wink. I winked back.

"Dale," I said. "What kind of valentine did Harm get me?"

He peeped over at my desk. "Red?"

Why do I even try? I reached in my messenger bag, my fingers darting between a borderline sophisticated card and my Fallback Panda—both signed and ready to go.

"Hi, Mo," Harm said, swaggering over. He gave me a smile—all dimples firing.

I opened my mouth. My brain threw a fuse.

"Mo?" Dale said. "It's your turn to talk. Harm said hi."

My face went red. I forked over my Fallback Panda.

"Thanks," Harm said, opening it. "This is really . . . cute."

Cute. The only thing worse than cute is tacky. I fled to my desk and stuffed Harm's valentine in my bag as Dale slipped into his seat.

"That was terrible," he said.

"I don't care," I snapped. "I'm going out with Lavender in just seven more years. He gave me a rose."

"Lavender gives roses to all the women in his life. Queen Elizabeth ate hers," Dale said.

"Happy Valentine's Day, Dale," I said, handing his panda card to him. "And I'm really sorry about yesterday. I didn't mean to scare you."

He sighed. "I know. You're self-centered is all," he said. "You might grow out of it but Bill says a pup's personality is set in the first few weeks. With humans it takes longer, but by now we're pretty much who we are. I love you anyway but not like Sal. With you, it's futonic."

"You mean platonic, Dale. A futon is a couch."

"Right. I sleep on your couch sometimes," he said as he plundered his backpack. He dragged out the valentine I gave him last year, marked out my name, and wrote his. He handed it over as Harm slumped in his seat.

"Mo," Dale said as the bell rang, "Kat's picking her agent up at the airport this afternoon. They're coming tonight." My hope circled the drain like dirty dishwater. "We've been practicing, only—"

"Good morning, class," Miss Retzyl interrupted, sailing in. "Happy Valentine's Day." She started down the aisle with a box of cartoon-style valentines. I pulled myself together.

"The Desperados have a situation," I told her as she handed me a detective card. "We'll be in the office."

"No," she said, handing Dale a puppy valentine.

"Thank you," Dale said, handing her a card. "Queen Elizabeth sends her love." She fished out a second puppy valentine and signed it for Liz.

I grabbed her sleeve. "Harm may be contagious. I need to quarantine him ASAP."

She slid her glasses to the tip of her nose and studied Harm. He'd slumped in his desk, his long legs crossed at the ankles, his handsome face pale. "Harm, are you sick?"

"Sick of my idiot life," he muttered, and she headed down the aisle.

Crud.

Harm's leaving, I thought. And he still doesn't know how I feel.

At day's end, Jake dropped Dale's big manila envelope on his desk as Harm headed out the door. "The best forgeries in the county," Jake said, hooking his thumbs in his belt loops. "See you tonight. We'll bring our tap shoes."

They really do dance, I thought. My life is a nightmare.

Dale reached into the manila envelope, pulled out a red envelope, and dropped it on Miss Retzyl's desk. Across the front in Joe Starr's blocky handwriting: MISS PRISCILLA RETZYL.

"Now all we got to do is find Joe Starr," Dale said.

"We're never going to find Joe Starr," Dale said an hour later as we dropped our bikes at the café door.

Tinks sat inside, wolfing down chili. "How's the treasure hunt going?" he asked.

"It's not, thanks to you, traitor," I said.

His shoulders sagged. "I knew you'd be mad. Is Starr guarding the treasure pit? He should be."

"No," Dale said, dialing the phone. "We just looked." He snapped to attention. "Hello? 911? This is a stranger at the café. We need Detective Joe Starr. It's an emergency. . . . No, this isn't Dale and yes he did kiss." He hung up and looked at Tinks. "Can we trust you?"

"Try me," Tinks said, and Dale slid a red envelope to him. Across the front of the envelope, in Miss Retzyl's neat handwriting: Detective Joe Starr.

As me and Dale settled in with the last of the Neapolitan ice cream, Starr skidded into the parking lot, siren blaring. He zipped through the door. For some reason, he zeroed in on me. "Faking a 911 call is illegal," he said.

Tinks slid the red envelope his way. "This has your name on it."

He smiled. "That's Priscilla's handwriting." He opened the card as Miss Lana cruised in with the glittery red hearts for the Winter Tree.

Not Miss Lana! Not now.

Starr read his card out. "*Life's a miracle, dear Detective Joe Starr, and there's no one I'd rather share it with than you. Marry me. Miss Priscilla Retzyl.*"

Miss Lana gasped. "But that's my proposal for . . ." I put my finger over my lips.

"*Marry* her?" Starr said. "Has she lost her mind?" And he sped away, siren blaring. Weird.

"Mo, how did *my* words wind up in Joe's card?" Miss Lana demanded as the phone rang. She snagged it. "Café. Lana speaking."

"Go," I whispered, and Dale and me tiptoed to the door.

"Freeze, you two," Miss Lana snapped. We froze. "Oh, Priscilla," she said. "No, Joe just left. He what? . . . Read that again," she said as the Colonel strolled in with new Neapolitan. "Mercy, I didn't know Joe was such a poet." She closed her eyes: "*Marry me, Miss Priscilla Retzyl. I love you like the ocean loves the taste of salt. Detective Joe Starr.*"

The Colonel whirled to me. I smiled my best smile, the one I'll use if I'm ever hauled before a firing squad. Because who wants to die unattractive?

Miss Lana clattered the phone into its cradle. "Priscilla just proposed to Joe Starr, using the words *I* gave *you,*" she said, putting her hands on her hips and glaring at me.

"And that was *my* love song to Lana," the Colonel said.

Miss Lana studied me like I was new. "You used *our* words to propose to Joe and Priscilla? Why didn't *I* think of that?"

She glanced at the 7 Up clock.

"Three hours to curtain time. Run home and change," she told Dale, and he sped out the door.

I sighed. Three hours before Harm leaves Tupelo Landing—maybe for good.

At 6:25 I hung the last red glittery heart on the Winter Tree and gave the café a final inspection—white tablecloths, candles, microphones. Outside, the parking lot was packed.

Dale and Sal tapped at the door. "Good news," Sal said as Jake and Jimmy clacked in behind them. "The school heater's out again. No school tomorrow."

Jake and Jimmy peeled off their jackets and plopped on the floor, stretching their stubby legs and bumping their heads to their knees.

"Harm's working off nerves in the kitchen," Miss Lana told Dale as he set his guitar by the mics.

"He's throwing up again, isn't he?" Dale asked. "He hates doing anything not perfect."

Miss Lana ignored his question—which meant yes to throwing up. "Leave him alone—all of you," she said. She smoothed her tuck-waisted 1950s suit over her hips and patted her Ava Gardner wig into place.

"Action!" she cried, and flipped our closed sign to open.

Car doors flew wide and the crowd surged toward us. "Good evening, don't push," I said. "I'm Mo, and I'll be taking care of you. Tonight we're serving the Colonel's heart-shaped Meatloaf of Love, which comes individual on the plate and dressed in a delicate ketchup sauce. For sides we got Cupid's Collard Casserole and Mashed Potatoes of Desire, all for fourteen ninety-nine cash, including tea and entertainment. Don't push."

We filled every table in three minutes flat. Mayor Little and Mrs. Little. Miss Rose and Bill Glasgow. The entire sixth grade. Miss Retzyl and Joe Starr. Mr. Red took his seat and Harm bounded over, his dimples green but determined.

"Is she here?" he asked. Anxiety rolled off him like heat off August sand.

"No, and with luck she won't be," Mr. Red told him.

"Listen, I'm not leaving, Gramps," he said, lowering his voice. "I just hope you won't be ashamed of the way I've found to stay. Where's Miss Thornton?"

"Went to get Gabriel. She doesn't trust him around your treasure," he said as Lavender strolled in with a twin.

Supper came and went. At eight, Grandmother Miss Lacy's seat still sat empty.

So did Kat's.

"Ready?" I whispered as Dale tuned his guitar. I pointed to Sal. She killed the overheads and Skeeter flipped on the spotlight. I stepped up to the microphone. "Good evening, and welcome to our first-ever Valentine's Extravaganza. Tonight, we present Tupelo Landing's Duo of Doo-wop and Crooners of Country Tunes. You know them, you love them—Dale and Harm—On the Verge! With Special Guest Dancers Jake and Jimmy Exum!"

The café roared. Sal whistled.

As Harm headed for his mic, I gathered my courage and grabbed his arm. "Everybody's going to love you tonight, Harm. I know they will. Because I do."

For one instant, Harm looked like I'd handed him bad wiring and flipped the switch. Then he grinned wide as his face and swaggered for the spotlight.

Dale stepped up to his mic, easy as coming home. "Hey, everybody, and thanks for clapping. It's Valentine's Day, so we'll open with a love song by Hank Williams, Senior. Let's sing it pretty, Harm. This one's for Sal."

The door swung open. Harm's grin collapsed.

Kat Kline swayed in wearing fringe head-to-toe, a slicked-back catfish of a man on her arm. "Sorry we're late, everybody," she said. "You know how Raleigh traffic is."

Dale covered his mic as I rushed up. "Harm," Dale whispered, "we got to use Plan B."

"You got a Plan B? What is it?" I asked.

"Sing it the way we practiced—rough and wrong," Dale told Harm. "Keep your eyes on Mo. She's tone deaf. She won't mind."

Dale's a genius! That's why they've been practicing songs they already know. To learn them wrong.

I looked at Harm. He'd gone green again. Dale's right,

I thought. Harm loves perfect, even when not perfect's better.

Dale uncovered the mic and looked at Harm. "Ready, Harm? You got the lead." Harm locked eyes with me. "Just like we practiced. And one, two, three, and . . ."

Harm glanced at Kat and froze. Dale kept strumming, very smooth, waiting.

The crowd rustled. Mrs. Little booed.

"Sorry," Dale said, and stopped strumming. "I messed that up a little. I guess I'm nervous. Ready, Harm?"

"Stop," Harm said, bumping his mic and making it squeal. "I'm sorry, Dale. Mom, I'm sorry. I can't do it. Maybe you can solo, Dale. I feel sick."

The crowd rumbled. Attila, in the front row, snickered.

"Hold it, baby." Kat swaggered up. She put her hand over his mic and whispered in Harm's ear. He shot me a look so sharp, it sliced my soul in two. "It's a good deal, Harm," she said as I started for him. "Take it."

"What's going on?" I asked. "I'm Harm's business manager. What deal?"

She smiled razor-quick. "Good news," she said, her voice low. "I found the clue of your lifetime, Mo. The clue that will lead you straight into your Upstream Mother's arms. So, here's the deal. Harm sings like an angel, my agent loves him, and Harm moves to Nashville with me. And you get the clue." Attila—eavesdropping from the front row—gasped. "Win, win."

"Harm belongs here, with us," Dale said. "So lose, lose. Right, Mo?"

My heart wobbled like a kid walking a fence. On one side, the clue I've been looking for all my life. On the other side, Harm—here, with Dale and me.

I looked across the room at Miss Lana and took a deep breath. Miss Lana would go brave, I thought. She'd follow her heart.

I ain't Miss Lana's kid for nothing.

"Forget it, Kat," I said. "I'd never trade Harm for a flipping clue, or anything else. That's not a deal a real mother would even offer."

"Oh really? Well, let's let Harm decide," Kat said.

She stepped up to Dale's mic and shouldered him aside, knocking his hand away from the microphone. "Thanks for that intro," she said, taking his guitar. She smiled past me, into the crowd. "Lots of things in life you can't start over, but a song isn't one of them." She winked at Harm. "Ready, good-looking?"

Harm squared his shoulders and looked at me. He's made up his mind, I thought.

"Please," Dale whispered. "Sing it bad."

"You got the lead, Harm," Kat said, and counted it down. "And one, two, three and . . ."

Harm closed his eyes, and his voice rolled out strong and clear and true. *"Hey, good-looking, what you got cooking? How's about—"*

The café door slammed against the wall, stopping him mid-line as my heart cracked in two. Skeeter jerked the spotlight around. "Help," Grandmother Miss Lacy gasped, staggering in. "Gabriel's trapped in the treasure pit, and he's running out of air. Help!"

Chapter Twenty-nine
Good-byes with a Hello

Harm, Dale, and me dove into the backseat of Starr's Impala. Grandmother Miss Lacy sat in front, flushed and rattled.

"How long has he been down there?" Starr asked, turning on his blue light.

"I don't know," she said, her voice shaking. "He said he was having car problems, so I went to pick him up. His air tanks were gone—and so was he. I found his spare tank by the pit, with his safety rope tied off . . . I can't pull him up. How could he be so stupid? You *have* to save him," she said, tears crowding her voice.

Starr flipped his siren on. "I'll do everything I can."

My heart sank. "I'll do everything I can" isn't the same as "I'll save him." Not the same by a long shot.

We sped across the bridge. The edge of Starr's whirling blue light danced across the water and outlined an odd craft in the middle of the river.

Harm and me whipped around to stare out the back windshield. "What the heck?" he muttered, and it was gone.

Starr skidded into the inn's drive and across the lawn, to our dig. We tumbled out, his flashlight beam flitting across the water flooding our pit, and the pit's hodge-podge of broken timbers.

I tugged the rope Gabriel had tied to Tinks's tractor, so he could find his way up. It was caught tight on something down below. "How much air in those tanks?" I called.

"For a man his size? An hour if he's calm," Starr said. "Less if he's fighting for his life."

"Bring those cars closer," the Colonel shouted to the crowd as he scrambled out of the Underbird. "Shine your headlights over here. Don't worry about the landscaping, get over here!"

"Get those timbers out of the way," Starr said. Dale and me dragged the heavy chain to the pit's edge, and Lavender hopped on the tractor. He lifted the claw time and again. One by one, the timbers rose.

Time after time, Gabriel didn't.

Grandmother Miss Lacy looked like a short, sad statue ready to crumble.

"You ain't breaking Grandmother Miss Lacy's heart, slimeball," I shouted at Gabriel, yanking his safety rope again. Nothing.

"Forget it, Mo," Starr said, reaching for the rope.

I turned away and jerked the rope to the left, hard. It popped free!

"Pull him up!" I shouted, and the Colonel jumped in beside me. We pulled Gabriel up, but there wasn't an ounce of fight on the line.

Deadweight, I thought.

Grandmother Miss Lacy burst into tears as Starr hoisted Gabriel to land, his arms limp, his wet suit gleaming.

"He's not breathing," Starr said, rolling Gabriel onto his back. "Call an ambulance. Now!" he shouted, and Miss Retzyl ran for the Impala and its radio. "Get that regulator out of his mouth," Starr said.

I knelt in the thick shadows and slipped scuba gear from his mouth. Starr pumped his chest, Gabriel's chin bouncing in time to the curt, steady pressure. "Breathe, you arrogant buzzard," Starr muttered. "*Breathe!*"

Dale fell to his knees beside me. "Doesn't seem right for him to meet his Maker hiding behind a mask." He stripped the dive mask away.

Someone moved and a shaft of light fell across Gabriel's face. My world stopped spinning. "That ain't Gabriel Archer," I said, my heart tumbling like dice.

"That's Tinks Williams. What's *he* doing here?"

The Colonel shouldered Starr aside, raised his fist, and slammed it against Tinks's chest. "Get up, Tinks!" he shouted. "Lana needs you to drive. You're late." He hit him again.

Tinks sputtered and Starr shoved him to his side. Tinks

coughed up an ugly river of water and chili, and flopped onto his back, gulping in air. "Am I dead?"

Somebody laughed high and hysterical.

"Stop it, Mo," Dale said. "It's not funny."

"You ought to be dead, Tinks Williams," I shouted. "You can't dive. You can't even swim! And no, you ain't dead. Do I look like a flipping angel to you?"

Tinks closed his eyes and smiled. "Mo," he said, very soft.

"Tinks, I hope I'm wrong, but it looks like you were robbing us," Dale said.

"Dale," Tinks murmured. He looked at us. "I had the treasure in my hand. Then something hit my head . . ." His voice faded as a distant siren wailed.

Dale took Tinks's hand in his. Gently he pried Tinks's pruney fingers open. Dale twisted a brass handle from Tinks's hand and looked at me. "The handle from our treasure chest," he said.

"I did it for you kids," Tinks said, his eyelids fluttering.

Skeeter wedged in. "You were acting on behalf of the Desperados?" Tinks nodded and spit up a little more chili. "Congrats," Skeeter said, looking at me. "The treasure's yours. Claim it. Fast," she added as Attila tore through the crowd.

I grabbed a shovel and scaled a mound of backfill in the crisscross of the crowd's headlights—center stage. Dale scrambled up beside me. "Thanks to our consultant

Tinks, Dale and me claim this treasure for the Desperados Detective Agency," I shouted, and Dale stabbed the shovel into the earth like a flag.

"You're all invited to the Treasure Grand Opening at the café a week from Saturday," I said, and the crowd cheered.

"Where's Harm?" I whispered. "He should be up here getting rich with us."

We shielded our eyes to look through the lights' glare. Attila had pulled Grandmother Miss Lacy aside. Odd.

"There," Dale said, pointing. Harm and Kat stood toe to toe, her agent checking his watch, Mr. Red standing with his arms crossed. "It doesn't look good," Dale said. "Run."

Dale and me skidded to a halt next to Harm. "Harm's future's in Nashville," Kat said, glaring at Mr. Red. "Where he can *be* somebody."

"He already is somebody," Mr. Red said, very steady.

Feelings danced across Harm's face like sheet lightning.

Dale smiled at Kat's agent. "Harm didn't get a good chance to audition for you," Dale said. "Give us another try. We can sing Acapulco for you right here and right now."

"He means acapella," I said. "Kat's probably too proud to beg for another audition, but I'm not. Let Harm and Dale audition now, please? Harm sings great—at least until his voice changes, which could be any minute," I added. "Sadly, puberty doesn't have a backup gear."

"Nice try, Mo, but he heard enough," Kat said, pushing me aside. "Come on, Harm."

"Hold it," her agent said. "Go ahead and sing, sons. But hurry. I have a plane to catch."

This is it, I thought. Harm's last-chance audition. Please sing it wrong.

Dale took the lead. Harm closed his eyes, took a deep breath—and came in late. His voice rose pitchy and rough, flat as rusty tin. They sang their song through, and their voices wibble-wobbled to the stars.

A coyote yowled somewhere distant.

Excellent, I thought. It couldn't have been worse if I'd sung it myself.

I smiled at Kat's agent. "See? Harm's gold. As his business manager, I'd like to review the contract."

He looked at Kat. "Really? You brought me here for this?"

"He was faking," she said. "Only a genius can be consistently a quarter-tone flat. He's good," she shouted as he walked away. She snatched Harm close. "You're taking my last chance from me? After everything I've done for you? You must really hate me."

"Might be easier if he did," Mr. Red said.

Harm sighed. "I don't hate you, Kat, but if I went, you'd get tired of me again. The truth is, you can make me go, but you can't make me sing. So really, what's in it for you?"

Harm, I thought, watching her. He's the treasure in this hunt.

"We could have been amazing. And rich," she said. She looked at me. "Tough luck on your clue, kid."

Grandmother Miss Lacy walked up and slipped her arm in Kat's. "I'll walk you to your car, dear," she murmured, and they strolled away.

"Heck of an audition, son," Bill Glasgow said, clapping Harm's shoulder. He smiled at Dale. "Smart move, those terrible harmonies."

"Thanks," Dale said. "We'll go back to singing good for our next gig. We could use a mandolin player."

Bill nodded. "At home, sure. In public, it's you two."

At home. He said it just like that. Bill Glasgow and Miss Rose together make Dale at home in his own house, maybe for the first time. "Yes sir, heck of an audition," Bill said.

"Heck of a life," Harm said, letting his hand bump mine.

Minutes later, Grandmother Miss Lacy meandered up and placed a battered Christmas card box in my hands. "Kat asked me to give you this," she said. "Because you love photography."

I opened the box. An old photo of Tinks topped the pile of Polaroids. "That's a terrible band uniform," Dale said, looking with me.

"No dear, Tinks was a history geek. That's a Revolutionary War uniform," she said, and we stood together, watching Kat's taillights fade away.

Dale smiled. "A treasure found and a friend kept. Can this night get any better?"

"It can," I said, scanning the crowd. If we're lucky, Gabriel's still away from his camp, I thought. Kat's definitely gone. Attila's busy running her mouth.

I looked for Lavender. "It can get much better. But only if we don't get caught."

A half hour later, Lavender dropped us Desperados at the Old Fish Camp Road. We slipped through the forest, the air sharp with the scent of pines, Gabriel's camp dead ahead. "Grandmother Miss Lacy said Gabriel's gone," I whispered. "If *Tupelo Mother*'s here, this is our chance to get her back."

An owl hoooed and we ducked. Something clunked on the river.

We dropped low and slunk forward to peek from behind a privet hedge at the edge of the camp. The ramshackle house sat still and dark, its porch listing. In the side yard, the GPR and three camp chairs huddled near a cold fire pit.

I peered down the rickety dock. The clouds shifted and moonlight glinted against a small airplane at dock's end, its cargo door gaping open.

"That's what I saw when we crossed the bridge," Harm whispered.

"It must have those little canoes on its wheels," Dale whispered.

"Pontoons," I said as a tall, thin man jumped from the plane, onto the end of the dock. He snatched a canvas covering several boxes, and looked around like a wild animal.

We ducked, and he went back to work.

"Gabriel's buddy," Harm whispered. "From the graveyard."

I thought back to the graveyard, to the tall, thin man spying on the dead as he and Gabriel tried to solve our riddle. "That's him."

The man grunted softly as he picked up the first box and heaved it into the airplane.

We crept nearer as he loaded a smaller box and turned for the third—a thin, rectangular package. "That's *Tupelo Mother*!" I whispered.

"Stop, thief!" I shouted. He turned to run to his plane as Dale spurted past me and dove for his ankles. The thief spun, sending *Tupelo Mother* spinning into the air.

Harm sprang like a cat. He batted the painting into the air and shot crazily down the dock, grabbing at the portrait.

Dale wrapped his arms around the man's leg and closed his eyes, stubborn as a cocklebur. "Get off me," the thief shouted, kicking.

I lowered my shoulder and charged, crunching his ribs. He grabbed my arm and spun me around, shooting his arm across my throat and cutting off my air. I ducked, turning my head, and bit him. Hard.

He screamed and body-slammed me onto Dale.

The man jumped into the airplane. Its engine coughed as Harm ran up, *Tupelo Mother* tucked beneath his arm, and helped us to our feet. He pointed to the numbers on the tail of the plane as the plane pulled away from the dock. "Remember those numbers," he shouted. "Dale, get the letters. Mo, the last three numbers. I got the middle."

The little craft sped down the river. "Whatever he just took, *Tupelo Mother* ain't it," I said as the plane lumbered into the sky.

Dear Upstream Mother,

Good news! Harm stays in Tupelo Landing, plus I told him I love him and I didn't die from it! He didn't say it back but he bumped hands with me, which is similar for middle school.

More good news: Tonight we staged our Valentine's Extravaganza, which I think people will talk about for years to come. Then I helped save Tinks's life, bit a thief, recovered a stolen painting, and called in our airplane numbers to Starr.

The Colonel's holding Tupelo Mother until we need her.

That's the good news. Now this: I had to turn down a clue to you to help Harm stay. Also we got just one more Always Man Letter out. I ain't holding my breath and I don't want you holding yours either.

Please don't lose heart. I know for sure there's another clue somewhere, and I won't stop looking until I find it. I promise.

Mo

PS: We found the treasure. I am stupid rich!

I'd almost drifted off when I remembered Kat's photos. I smiled. Grandmother Miss Lacy must have made her leave those behind, I thought, because Kat ain't in a mood to be sweet to me. I snapped on my lamp and opened the box of black-and-whites.

I lifted a photo. Tinks in his hideous uniform.

Harm as a little boy, wearing shorts and eating a cracker. Cute.

A photo of Kat standing before an old restaurant, costume sharp, hat tipped back the way Harm tips his back. She smiled twenty years younger, twenty years less used up. I flipped it over. "Cowboy Cadillac Crabhouse Café. Langston, NC. Knocked 'em dead. Kat."

Cows, cars, crabs . . . My heart jumped.

She didn't give me a photo of her. She gave me her clue—a photo of my sign.

"Miss Lana, Colonel!" I shouted, dialing Harm's number. "Wake up! I found a way back home!"

Chapter Thirty
A Heart Full of Maybes

The next morning at the café, Half-Drowned Tinks and Treasure were the Topics du Jour. But not for long.

At eight a.m., I stepped up on my Pepsi crate. "Attention!"

"Own the stage, sugar," Miss Lana whispered. "Be one with the moment. Project."

I projected. "The Desperados will open Blackbeard's treasure a week from Saturday. But today, I want to talk about a different treasure. A treasure of the heart."

Dale raised his hand. "Why do we have to wait so long to open Blackbeard's treasure?"

"Good question!" Mrs. Little shouted.

Dale kills me. Because we don't know *how* to raise a treasure? Because if nothing's down there, we need a Plan B? Because I got something more important to do?

"Because we got school," I said as Gabriel strolled in.

"Sorry to stand you up for last night's little show, Miss Thornton," he said, veering toward her. "I took in a movie instead. Perhaps I should have called."

Her glare stopped him in his tracks.

"You should have," she said. "But then I'd never have gone to get you, or noticed your missing dive gear. And in *that* case, Tinks would be dead."

"And *we* wouldn't have Blackbeard's treasure," I added.

Gabriel looked like a little kid who'd just dropped his ice cream. "You found the treasure?" His face went red. "Ridiculous. *I'm* the professional, and you're . . ."

"Rich," Dale said, taking Sal's hand.

"Gabriel, do sit down," Grandmother Miss Lacy snapped, and he collapsed next to Attila, his face going soft and pale as raw dumplings.

Miss Lana says always savor the moment. I savored.

"Today," I said, "we got a lead on a treasure I been hunting all my life. Harm?"

Harm stifled a yawn. "Sorry," he said. "We've been working on this all night."

He strode to our North Carolina map, by the jukebox. "We're here," he said, pointing to Tupelo Landing. "Thanks to Kat, we now know Mo's birth sign came from Langston—here. And we know the floodwaters generally moved west to east the night Mo was born." He drew a line a little west of Langston. "So this is the edge of our search zone.

"We think Mo's Upstream Mother got the scratchy fix-it wool for her sweater from Contectnea Wool, here," he said. "She may have even worked there. Sal?"

Sal hopped up and took Harm's Sharpie. "The average

commute in our area is about twelve miles. So if she worked at Contectnea Wool, she probably lived somewhere in here," she said, drawing a circle. "Dale?"

Dale rose, holding a photo. "Here's Always Man pumping gas on a Main Street. Because of a license plate, we think he maybe lived or worked in a town ending in TON."

Harm drew lines under several little towns on our new search map, each ending in TON. He drew circles twelve miles out from each town, with several circles overlapping. "Always Man could have lived in one of these areas."

Mrs. Little scowled. "Your map looks like an ugly flower."

"Thank you," I replied. "Always Man knew Upstream Mother, whose name starts with a *J*. We'll show his photo, and describe her sweater and pendant."

Mrs. Simpson sniffed. "You don't have much to go on."

"You're right," I said. "I got a heart full of maybes and a mind full of probably-nots. I'm following my heart." Miss Lana nodded.

"That would make a good country song," Dale muttered, but again he rose and faced the crowd. "Now we need serpentdipity, and you all," he said.

"He means serendipity," I added. "Where life flows together like two rivers."

Miss Lana put her hand on my shoulder. "My friends, we leave this morning at ten, to go door-to-door. Priscilla says school will be out until a new heater part comes in, so you young people are welcome. We'll caravan. It's a lot of doors and we'd appreciate your help. But if you can't help, we'll understand."

"I won't," the Colonel said. Like me, he holds grudges.

"Count us in," Miss Rose said, and Bill nodded.

"Me too," Lavender said, strolling in. "Whatever it is."

"Us too!" the Azalea Women called.

"Joe and I can help until the school's heat comes on," Miss Retzyl said.

The *I'll help*'s and *me too*'s whirled around the room—to Attila's table. Even Attila's going to say yes, I thought, watching her face. But when mean, beige Mrs. Simpson shook her head, Attila went the other way.

"I might wash my hair today," Attila mumbled.

If I do have past lives, which so far one feels like more than I can handle, I've despised Anna Celeste Simpson in every last one of them.

We looked at Gabriel. "I'm sure Kat's busy, but I wouldn't miss this little search for the world," he said, and Mrs. Simpson's mouth fell open.

"I'll go if I can ride with Gabriel," Attila said. She looked into her mother's scowl. "I look good in a Jaguar." She flounced her hair.

Excellent, I thought. We can keep an eye on both of you.

"Thank you," I said as the Colonel snapped the coffeemaker closed. "Breakfast is on the house except for Mrs. Simpson," I added, and the café cheered.

At ten o'clock the Underbird led the way, our cars and trucks strung along the winding country roads like pearls. At the search zone, we fanned out, each vehicle with its own map, its houses marked.

"Knock three times," Harm shouted. "Give them time to answer."

"Stage fright, sugar?" Miss Lana asked. "Just take a deep breath and walk out there. It gets easier each time."

She fluffed her Marilyn Monroe wig, but to me her smile looked fragile as old glass.

As car and truck doors flew open up and down the road, she and the Colonel headed for a small brick house, and I trotted across a toy-strewn lawn. I straightened my pendant and knocked. A cigarette-smoking woman opened the door. "Hey," I said. "I'm Mo LoBeau of Tupelo Landing, and I'm looking for my long-lost mother. Are you she—or, is she you, as you prefer?"

She exhaled a cloud of smoke. "Nope."

"Secondhand smoke kills," I said, whipping out Always Man. "Do you recognize this man? He lived around here maybe twelve years ago. Or this sweater? My mother wore it. Her name started with a *J*. Maybe you met her?"

"Nope."

I handed her my card. "Call me at the café if anything comes to mind."

"Right," she said, closing the door.

A total strike-out. I squared my shoulders like the Colonel, and marched on.

Miss Lana was right. It got easier. I knocked, I smiled, I chatted.

The doors closed one after another: No. No. No.

We surged up and down roads, across lawns, up steps. Once I saw Grandmother Miss Lacy jump a ditch. By noon, the Azalea Women's hair had wilted. By suppertime, most folks had gone home. "Tomorrow, sugar," Miss Lana said as we walked to the Underbird.

"Courage, Soldier," the Colonel said.

The next day only my core people showed: Miss Rose, Bill Glasgow, and Dale; Harm, Mr. Red, and Grandmother Miss Lacy, whose feet were swelling; Lavender; Miss Lana, the Colonel, and me. We wound our way to tiny Taylor, NC, and a day full of no's.

As the sun set, a thin, sharp-smelling old man answered my knock and squinted at the photo of Always Man. "Looks familiar," he said.

My heart jumped.

"The service station was on South Main," I said. "Well,

the photo cut it off at 'South Ma.' Thanks to my legendary powers of deduction, we know it's South Main."

"No Main Street in this town," he said. "We got county names. Mecklenburg Street, Lenoir, Martin . . ."

"South Martin, then," I said.

"Martin? Now that you mention it, there was a station on South Martin. Don't remember much about it."

I used Miss Lana's trick for awakening memories: "What did it smell like? I know one mechanic that smells like Ivory soap."

"Ivory soap?" He laughed. "Well, it was down from the bakery. Smelled like fresh-baked bread and gas fumes." His belly rumbled. "You know, I *do* remember this fellow. Replaced a fan belt for me, got a nasty cut on his finger. Still cleaned a right good windshield."

He looked out at Miss Lana as she traipsed back to the Underbird. "Is she with you? Does she know her hair doesn't look real?"

"Yes sir, she knows. Is this man still here? Does he have people? A name?"

He tilted his head. His toupee slipped. "What's that sign say? 'Ann's Clothes'? I used to buy shoes there. Closed after the flood. Government bought most folks out on this side of the river. Ann left. This fellow probably did too. Sorry."

He pushed the door to. I jammed my foot in its way. "I

have to find my mother. Her name started with a *J* and she knew how to knit and she liked to wear this sweater," I said, opening my jacket. "The man in the photo knew her. He's even flirting."

"Sorry, young lady."

"Mo," I said. "Mo LoBeau. A possible orphan."

"Orphan or not, I can't tell you what I don't know, and I don't know his name," he snapped, but he eased the door off my foot. "Maybe it had to do with earth. Because I used to roll down my window and say, 'How on *earth* are you?' and he'd laugh. What *was* his name? Clay? Sandy? No . . . Sanders, maybe. That's it. Sanders. He's not around here or I'd know him. Try the other side of the river," he said, stronger. "If he stayed, that's where he is."

I made an Executive Decision. I hurled myself against the door, ricocheted into him, and hugged him so hard, his toupee went crooked. I pounded to the Underbird. "His name is Sanders from the Probably Side of the River."

"Sanders," Miss Lana said, rubbing her feet. "What a handsome name."

The Colonel smiled in the rearview mirror. "We'll start again tomorrow. But Soldier—never let your hopes rise higher than you can stand for them to fall."

"Yes sir," I said as the first star of the evening blinked against a friendly sky.

The next day started slim. Harm, Dale, and Lavender in the truck. Me, Miss Lana, and the Colonel in the Underbird. To my surprise, Attila and Gabriel cruised up in Gabriel's Jaguar. "Miss Thornton asked us to take her place," Attila said. "Her feet hurt, and we're glad to help."

Dale looked at her, his eyes steady. "How much did she pay you?"

Attila flipped her hair. "We might have come anyway."

Mercenaries. Still. Eight seekers.

Skeeter's internet search for Sanders had come up empty, but we hadn't let that slow us down. Harm had drawn new search maps of the Probably Side of the River. He passed them out. "We're closing in on Always Man," he said. "Knock three times and give people plenty of time to answer. Don't mark the house no unless an actual human tells you no. At the end of the day we'll double back to houses where nobody answers."

"Got it," Lavender said, and we fanned out. We knocked. We smiled. We knocked again. The more we knocked, the lower my hopes fell. By sundown, we'd doubled back on the houses where no one had answered and knocked again.

No, no, no. No more clues, no more houses, no more hope.

And that was that.

"I'm sorry, Soldier," the Colonel said. He looked at me,

his brown eyes soft. "Mustering the courage to try is always a win. I'm proud of you."

Miss Lana slipped in the backseat, beside me. "We'll find new clues one day, sugar."

I went to bed without eating a bite, or saying a word.

I had hoped too high, and fallen too low. I picked up my pen and Volume 7.

Dear Upstream Mother,

To almost find you is harder than thinking I will never find you at all. My heart feels like a red balloon, drifting away.

Mo

Chapter Thirty-one
The Unthinkable Happens

"I'm sorry," Dale said the next morning, sitting down at my table.

"You're the umpteenth person to say that today," I said as Harm joined us.

"Mo," Harm said, "this case isn't over unless you say it is."

I drummed up a smile. "We'll find another clue one day. The good news is you'll be here to help us search."

"And we're almost treasure barons," Dale added, handing Queen Elizabeth my toast. "Gabriel called last night and offered to raise the treasure for us—for free."

"A professional courtesy? From Gabriel? *Why?*"

"No idea," Harm said. "But we could use his help."

I looked at Dale. "When can he start?" I asked.

"In about fifteen minutes ago," he said, glancing at the 7 Up clock. "I made an Executive Decision. You want to watch? It might make you feel better. Grandmother Miss Lacy's over there. And Joe Starr," he added, nibbling my bacon. "And Lavender."

"Lavender might need me," I admitted as the phone rang.

"Soldier, it's for you," the Colonel called. "Anna Celeste."

Harm scowled. "What does she want? Overtime?"

"Tell her I'm not here," I shouted.

The Colonel put the phone back to his ear. "Did you hear that? Ten-four," he said, and hung up. "She'll catch up with you later."

"Not if I see her coming," I muttered, and my energy surged.

Grandmother Miss Lacy was right: There's nothing like an enemy to make you feel more like yourself again. "Miss Lana, I'm going out," I said as she waltzed up with two extra breakfast plates. "I already ate and . . ."

She put the plates down. "You've pushed your eggs around and given your toast and bacon to Dale," she said, sliding Dale's toast and bacon to me. "Breakfast is the most important meal of the day, sugar. Eat. Then you can go."

"Hey, Desperados," Lavender said as we coasted up. "I was hoping you'd come by. I could use some help at the garage later today, if you have time. Sometimes the best thing for a broken heart . . ."

". . . is to keep moving," I said. "Count me in."

I waved to Grandmother Miss Lacy, who sat swinging her legs on Lavender's tailgate. Tinks's tractor sat by the pit, the heavy chain hooked on its claw. The claw nosed the dark water, sending the chain deep. Bubbles broke the water's surface.

"Gabriel's attaching the chain," Starr said, sauntering over. "We'll raise whatever's there, load it in Lavender's truck, and take it to an undisclosed location."

"My house," Dale whispered.

"Gabriel's being surprisingly helpful," Starr added. "I'd keep an eye on him, if I were you." He smoothed his eyebrow. "Listen, I meant to thank you kids for sending those valentines to Priscilla and me. They were sweet."

Please. The old say-thanks-and-see-who-says-you're-welcome trick. Does he think we're rookies?

Harm and me went bland as vanilla pudding.

Dale jammed his hands in his pockets and smiled. "You're welcome. How did you know it was us?"

"You just told me," Starr said, and Dale's smile wilted. "But why did you send us marriage proposals, Dale?"

"Pull her up!" Gabriel shouted, hoisting himself out of the water, and we ran toward him, leaving Starr looking baffled.

Lavender sprang to the tractor. He eased the claw higher, higher. A copper-wrapped cube broke the surface. He lifted it and swung it to the ground.

The treasure, I thought. At last.

Dale looked at me, his face flushed. "We could open it now."

"Smart boy," Gabriel said, kicking off his dive fins. "I'll help you."

"We'll open it Saturday," I said, very firm. "That's what we promised the town."

And by then, I thought, maybe I'll find my heart.

An hour later, at Lavender's garage, the Unthinkable: Attila careened up on her show bike, handlebar streamers limp. "She never rides that bike," I muttered, watching her try to find the kickstand. "What's she up to?"

"Who cares?" Dale said, lining up a trash-can free throw from the foul line he'd drawn with his sneaker. Dale will go varsity if we ever get a team.

Attila knocked. "It's a store," I shouted. "You don't knock."

She pushed in and stood studying the glistening white shelves lined with car parts and pyramids of oil cans, at the handsome old tin advertisements on the walls, the gleaming floor. "This is surprisingly nice," she said. "I've been looking for you, Mo."

She took a deep breath. "It's . . . Well, Gabriel and I helped search."

"I know," I said, very quick. "Thanks."

"Don't thank me. Not yet," she said as an Azalea Woman tooled up and leaned on her horn. "When we gave our search map back yesterday, we . . . That is, *Gabriel* wasn't truthful. He lied." She took a deep breath. "And I *let* him. Which is as good as telling a lie myself."

"Lied about what?" Harm asked.

"Gabriel told you we went back until we got a no at every house on our map, but we didn't. One house looked trashy—not our kind of people." She shrugged. "We didn't go back. At another house, dogs nipped our tires. Gabriel's not good with dogs and I don't like them either. They're so . . . excitable."

"Dogs have opinions," Dale said, smoothing Liz's ears. "But they're honest."

"Anyway, I'm sorry," she said as Lavender bustled in. "I should have told you then."

I stared at her, my soul reeling. "There's another house?"

Attila frowned. "Don't you people ever pay attention? *Two* houses, about a mile apart."

Two possible Upstream Mother houses?

"Lavender," I said as he slapped open his old cash register and stuffed a handful of cash in the drawer. "We have to go back. There's two more houses."

"Sorry, Mo. I can't right now. I got a repair in forty-five minutes. That's only enough time to get there and back."

"I'll put our bikes in the back of the truck," Harm said. "You can drop us off."

"Put mine in too," Attila said. I stared at her. She curled her lip. "I'm the only one who knows where the houses are, Mo-Ron."

"Right," Harm said as Dale grabbed two bags of Doritos.

"I'll be right there," I shouted, snagging the phone. "I got to call Miss Lana."

Lavender dropped us at the first house. "Be careful," he said, helping us unload our bikes. "I'll pick you up at five, right here. Stay together. I mean it. If anything happens to you all, Lana will kill me."

My heart pounded as we walked our bikes up the first house's dirt drive. Ten minutes later, we walked back down the same drive, another no echoing in my heart.

"That was just our warm-up shot," Dale said. "We still got one house to go."

"This way," Attila said, setting her jaw. She leaned down to hand-push her pedal into the Mount Position, stepped on it, and wobbled into place. "Follow me," she shouted, and hunched over her handlebars.

Harm, Dale, and me pedaled behind, down a winding two-lane, through pines and sleeping fields. "I hope nobody thinks Attila's our leader," I said. "She's pitiful."

Dale studied her. "She needs shorter legs."

"Or a higher seat," Harm said, taking his hands off his handlebars. "Listen, Anna's not good with dogs or a bike, but she's trying. Mo, Dale and I will handle the dogs. You take Attila with you."

My stomach clenched, but I nodded.

Attila rolled to a shaky halt at the head of a path and toppled sideways onto her feet. We coasted up beside her smooth as sunrise. "This is it," she said, her face flushed. "The last one."

The dogs met us halfway up the rutted path: a long-legged hound with a booming voice, and a terrifying ball of red fur with scissor-fast teeth clicking. "Don't act scared," I told Attila.

"Here, doggies," Dale called, hopping off of his bike. "Dale and Harm are here. Sit for treats. Doritos, your favorites," he sang. "Be sweet," he added as Harm hopped off beside him.

The terrier sat, quivering, as the hound grumbled up, tail wagging.

Harm gave me his crooked smile. "Good luck, Mo. We'll find you."

I pedaled up the path at Attila speed, leading the way around ruts and deep sand, zigzagging to a neat little yard back in the woods. I ignored Attila's awkward dismount and moist panting as I studied the black-roofed house with its bright red door.

Pecan trees stood to one side, their bare limbs clicking in the breeze. A rusty car sat by a shed. Beyond, a row of cedar trees stood tall-to-short along the back edge of the yard. Old Christmas trees, taken root.

"I'll wait here," Attila said, heading for a metal yard swing.

I dropped my bike, my heart pounding half out of my chest. This was it.

My last-chance house.

I headed up the wooden steps and across the narrow porch. I peeled off my jacket, straightened my sweater, and pointed my locket *J*-side out. Just three knocks, I told myself. Like at every other house on our map.

I gathered my courage and knocked. Silence. I knocked again. Silence.

I raised my fist. She's not here, I thought. One more knock and I go away empty. One more knock, and she slips away—maybe forever.

My heart fell, and my hand with it. I turned.

Attila stood at the foot of the steps, her hands on her hips. "You really *are* a coward," she said, her voice like a knife. "I'm sorry I even bothered to tell you the truth, Mo. I deserve a better enemy than you."

I spun and knocked on the door like I could knock its head off.

Beyond the door, the shuffle of feet. "Who's there?" a woman called.

My heart jumped. "It's me. Mo. Miss Moses LoBeau. A sixth grader in her prime."

The door squeaked open—just one inch.

Two inches.

Three.

An old woman peered out at me, her face tanned and wrinkled, her white braid wound in a tight cap around her head. She stared at me, her blue eyes bright as a river's daydream.

She opened the door wide as Dale and Harm clattered up behind me.

"I'm . . . I'm Mo LoBeau," I said. She was too old to be Upstream Mother. "We're looking for . . ."

She glanced at my pendant and smiled. "You're looking for Josie Barrow," she said. "What took you so long to get here?"

The air went thin and rare.

Josie Barrow.

"Is she here?" I asked, trying to remember how to breathe. "Is she home? I mean . . ."

Dale trotted up the steps behind me. "If Josie Barrow is Upstream Mother, Mo's her girl," he explained.

She touched my face soft as a whisper. "Come in. I'll get us something to eat."

"Who are you?" I asked. "I mean . . ."

She laughed easy and quick. "Call me Miss Bessie. Josie did. I made a cake yesterday, I'll cut us a slice." She glanced at Attila. "What about your friend?"

Attila had perched on the yard swing. "That's my enemy. She ain't hungry. Neither are we."

Dale elbowed me. "Excuse me," he said, very polite. "I'm Mo's best friend Dale Earnhardt Johnson III, and this is Mo's other best friend, Harm Crenshaw. We'd love to have cake with you."

Dale is skilled in the art of dessert diplomacy.

"Have a seat, then," Miss Bessie said, smiling at Dale as we filed in. "We'll use the good plates. This is my aunt Mabel's recipe."

Dale trailed her to the kitchen.

Harm looked at me, his eyes puzzled. "Cake? Now?" he whispered as Dale said something in the kitchen and Miss Bessie laughed.

"It's the way people do things," I said. He folded onto the sofa as I walked the room, studying the polished upright piano, *The Last Supper* over the fireplace, the old jars lined up along the mantel.

I tried to look polite as Miss Bessie and Dale served the cake. Dale and Harm dug in and complimented the cook. I could barely swallow. Our chat died away. A silence stretched out long and soft as an old cat. "You want to know about Josie," she said.

"Yes ma'am," I said, scooting forward. "I do."

She looked down at her napkin. "Josie stayed with me

during the flood, but she doesn't live here anymore," she said. "I've seen some ugly nights in my life, but that first night was the worst. I was lucky. My yard's only a few feet higher than most, but that made the difference between the kind of damage men repair, and the kind can't nobody touch but God. Josie stayed with me for three days."

Just three days?

"Do you have her address?" I asked. "I know it's been a long time, but . . ."

Her eyes went a deeper shade of blue. "The hurricane swallowed the telephone lines, drowned the electricity. Gobbled up the roads. No way to call in or get out unless you had a boat. Helicopters flew over hour after hour for two weeks."

"Two weeks? But you said three days." Harm reached over and took my hand.

Miss Bessie looked at him, and then me. "All we had was us, and we had to stay put until the rivers went down, or the military came." I nodded. "A neighbor went out in his rowboat that first night, pounding on doors, looking for neighbors. He found Josie clinging to a timber, weak as a half-drowned kitten. Scratched up, mostly, bruised. A twisted ankle. I was the closest dry house. He brought her to me. She was a sweet little thing, no bigger than a minute. Slept all day the first day. Then she woke up asking for you."

Me. She asked for me.

She clasped her hands. "Second day she ate my soup, sat up in the bed. Got up and walked around the house. Sat right there where you're sitting," she said, and a chill whispered up my spine. "Ate at the table where we cut this cake. Looked out these windows. Didn't talk about anything but you."

She looked at me. "You have her smile," she said, and laughed. "And her hair, God bless you." She drew a breath and let it out slow. "That night, a fever came on her, from the floodwater, most likely. She asked for pen and paper. I did everything for her I could, but the next day, she was gone."

"Gone?" I repeated. I blinked very hard, trying to stay behind my eyes. "Gone where? Did the helicopters come, or a boat? Or . . ."

"Gone, baby," she said, her voice soft. "Gone, the way people go. I'm sorry."

Inside, I fell lost and sweeping, like a leaf set loose from its tree.

We sat for an eternity, maybe, and then she rose and took my hand. "Let me show you her room." She pulled me down the dim hall to a regular bedroom. Regular whitewashed slat-board walls. Regular blue-and-white curtains over two sparkling windows, regular bed. Regular chest of drawers, regular mirror, regular braided rug on a pine floor.

All of it regular, except Upstream Mother saw and touched and knew it.

I looked into the mirror, surprised by the pale of my face. Dale and Harm hovered in the doorway behind me.

"Take your time," Miss Bessie said, smoothing the bedspread—the old-timey kind, with the stand-up swirls in the center. "Stay as long as you like and come back often as you will. I only knew Josie a few days, but I wish I'd known her longer. And better. And I wish I could have done more."

She's gone, I thought, flown away without me. She left me in this crazy world alone.

I stared out the window, trying to breathe myself steady. I stood and I breathed, and I watched the orange sun dive for the horizon.

Who sped up the sun?

"Mo," Dale said, touching on my arm. "We got to go."

"We can come back," Harm said, his voice teetering. "Any day you want. But Lavender's waiting. People will worry."

"I don't want to leave her," I said, but I let them pull me down the hall.

Miss Bessie jumped up from her rocker. "Josie left something for you," she said, walking to an old jar on her mantel. "She knew you'd find her one day. I knew it too."

I stared through its bubbled, watery glass, at the note curled inside.

"Read it, Mo," Dale said, reaching for the jar.

"No," Miss Bessie said, her voice quick. She handed the

jar to me, her eyes kind. "Where's your family? I know you have one, from the way you walked in here like you own earth and sky. Where are your people?"

"Home," I said. The café felt a million light-years away and my heart felt small and fast as hummingbird wings.

She stared into my eyes. "Read this at home with your people."

Home. My people.

"Did she . . . did Josie ever hug you?" I asked, my voice wavering like a ghost.

"Yes," she said, opening her arms. "And she left this hug waiting for you."

Dear Upstream Mother,

Miss Lana read your letter to me and the Colonel tonight, her voice unhurried and sad and warm. We sat on the settee together, so close, we could feel each other breathe.

We thought about you for a long time.

The Colonel kissed me good-night and called me Soldier and Miss Lana tucked me in like she did when I was little. "You found her, sugar," she said. "And we all know The Law of Finders Keepers. What you find is yours to keep. Forever."

Mo

Chapter Thirty-two
Monday, Tuesday, Wednesday

Dear Upstream Mother

Miss Lana closed the café, to give our hearts time to catch their breath. She pushed the Treasure Opening back too.

Not even the sky's the right color in a world without you.

Usually we feed Tupelo Landing, but all day people came to our door bringing us food, in honor of you. Dale and Harm came just to say hello. Lavender brought a pie. I ate it when the clock said time to eat, but I couldn't find its taste.

Mo

Dear Upstream Mother,

Tonight the moon is slight. People say the dark of the moon makes time go thin, and shrinks the space between waking and dreaming.

Please come see me in my dreams. I will look for you.

Mo

Dear Upstream Mother,

My words have flown away with you.

Mo

Chapter Thirty-three
Thursday: The Comfort of Friends and Enemies

Tap tap tap. "Mo," Dale called, tapping at my door. "It's us."

I sat up on my bed and tossed Volume 7 aside. "Come in."

Dale stepped in, Harm easing in behind him. "Hey. Miss Lana says you're coming to school tomorrow." He held out a pie as Queen Elizabeth collapsed on my dirty sweatshirt collection. "Mama sends her love. Again. So does Bill. And me and Liz. And Lavender."

Harm set a potted pansy on my desk. "Us too," he said, and handed me a cold plastic-wrapped lump. "I made fudge. Gramps says come for dinner when you want."

I squeezed some Normal into my voice. "Thanks. Let's cut this pie."

Minutes later we settled in with plates and forks. "Bill made this one a snig Cajun but he says he'll make you a *boudin* sweet potato pie next," Dale said. "It's wide-open Cajun." He licked his fork. "Mama says I shouldn't ask, but Liz has been worried sick about your letter and I . . ."

"You don't have to tell us if you don't want to," Harm said, very quick.

My feelings scattered like faded confetti. I waited for them to settle. "I read it with Miss Lana and the Colonel when we got home that night, and I've read it myself every day since. I want to read it with you too. Only . . . not yet," I added as someone rapped at the door.

Harm leaned and swung it open. Attila stepped in like an Earth kid stepping onto Mars.

Her gaze flitted from my Charleston snow globes to my hair. "You have a lovely home," she said, stiff as Styrofoam. "Miss Retzyl asked Harm and Dale to bring your math homework by, but they forgot. So I brought it."

Harm and Dale would eat raw liver before they brought me homework.

"Great," I lied. "Thanks." She went quiet and still.

She hadn't said a word as we'd pedaled from Miss Bessie's to Lavender's truck either. As Dale whispered our story to Lavender, she'd combed her hair like she couldn't hear.

She climbed in the cab with me and Lavender, who put his arm around me. He smelled like motor oil and lemon drops. I wouldn't have cried except his breath went tight, and when I looked up at him, his eyes shimmered in the dashboard's glow.

Attila had sniffled too, staring out the window so we wouldn't see. Her reflection had given her away.

I set my pie plate by my Elvis in Vegas lamp. "Anna," I said, "thanks for . . ."

"I didn't do much," she said. "I had a minute while Mother was out, so I thought I'd bike by." She dropped my homework on my desk and headed for the door.

"Wait," I said, and took a deep breath. "Anna, your bike seat's too low. That's why you have such a hard time pedaling. We could raise it, if you want."

Her eyes went wide. "They're *adjustable?*"

It's amazing, the things people know and the things they don't.

"Right," Harm said, heading for the kitchen. "I'll grab a wrench."

Ten minutes later, she pedaled away on a bike that fit her but was still stupid. A little later Dale and Harm zipped home too, Queen Elizabeth loping at Dale's side.

Homework. Might as well get it over with, I thought, unfolding the pages.

She had filled in the answers for me, and added a green sticky note.

I am sorry for your loss. Attila

Chapter Thirty-four
Our Treasure Grand Opening

Grand Opening Saturday broke frosty and still, the grasses dreaming diamonds and the trees glittering jewels. The Colonel refused to wear an eye patch, of course, but Miss Lana went all-out pirate décor in the café: Coconuts by the cash register, black tablecloths, blood-red candles.

Lavender pulled up at nine, the copper-covered treasure cube weighing his rear bumper down. "Morning, mateys," he said, swaggering in. Miss Lana smoothed her dark Ava Gardner wig and swished her black skirt at him. Lavender touched her gold earring and gave her a wicked smile. "Is this a clip-on, wench?"

She laughed, took it off, and clipped it to his ear.

If any man ever looked better in a earring, he ain't been to Tupelo Landing.

Dale and Harm blasted in. "Get ready to be rich," Dale said, and vaulted onto the stool beside Lavender. "We can wait another week if you need it, Mo. We won't be popular, but we never are anyway."

"Sometimes the best thing for a broken heart is to keep moving," I said. "Let's roll."

"Hey, Mo," Bill Glasgow called, walking in with Miss Rose. "What's cooking?"

"Avast," I replied. "This morning we got a Shipwreck Special—a crash-up of eggs with stowaway cheddar, plus cat-o'-nine-tails sweet potato fries and ketchup."

"Perfect," Miss Rose said, and gave me a hug.

"Mo," Bill said. "I know you have reporters coming, but Blackbeard's treasure is history. I'd shoot photos for you, only I'm not old enough to use that box camera."

"I am," Grandmother Miss Lacy said, breezing in with Mr. Red. "Did you hear the news, dear? Red's in business again. He's starting a boutique distillery, using his old recipe."

"Red and Grandson Unlimited," Mr. Red said. "A lot can happen in a week."

Understatement, I thought.

The café filled. Joe Starr and Miss Retzyl at their usual table. The Azalea Women. The sixth grade. Jake and Jimmy Exum with Hannah Greene and her sisters. A carload of strangers who'd caught wind of our find.

Sal set up a projector on the counter, and Dale opened a screen in front of the jukebox.

At ten, Miss Lana tossed her apron to the counter and the Colonel closed the kitchen. "Showtime," she whispered, and

I hopped onto my Pepsi crate. The café rustled to silence.

"Welcome to our Treasure Grand Opening," I said. "I know you're all excited to—"

"Morning, people," Gabriel interrupted, sauntering in with Kat on his arm.

Weird. First he helps raise the treasure for free; now he turns up for the opening of a treasure that ain't his, and a possible trip to jail. What's he up to?

I looked at Harm, who shrugged. Kat unzipped her purple near-leather jacket and draped it on the back of her chair. "Congratulations, Desperados," she said. "I wish I was striking it rich today, but if it's not me I'm glad it's my son."

She wants a mother's slice of the treasure, I thought, looking at Harm.

Unlikely.

"Mo," an Azalea Woman called. "Did you *really* find a letter from your long-lost mother? The café's been closed, so we haven't had a chance to ask."

I gave her a faux smile and a double-dip of silence.

She turned to Attila. "*You* were there, Anna. Fill us in?"

Crud. Here it comes: the Upstream Mother Announcement I'm not ready to make.

"For heaven's sake, Anna," Mrs. Simpson said, looking at her daughter. "You were with *Mo?* On the cul-de-sac, we prefer not to mix with . . . some people."

Sal adjusted her beret and rose. "Excuse me," she said, "but according to my research, *cul-de-sac* is French for bottom-of-the-bag."

Mrs. Simpson huffed. Attila almost smiled.

"Focus," Dale whispered, and I dove into our case.

"Strange things have happened in the race for this treasure," I said. "Some said it was Blackbeard's curse. We borderline believed it ourselves—for a while," I said as Tinks pulled up outside. He smoothed his red tie and blue Sunday suit, and walked in carrying a Piggly Wiggly bag.

"Dale, our evidence box?" I asked. He thumped our crate on a front table and pushed the RESERVED sign aside.

I pulled out our plaster of paris footprint casts. I held them high. "We found these footprints outside Harm's window the night he was robbed. They're exactly like this Colonial boot," I said as Harm gently lifted Peg-Leg's boot onto the counter and tilted it, to show its tacked-on sole.

The crowd murmured.

"Was Blackbeard's ghost standing at the window? Somebody wanted us to think so," I said, glancing at Gabriel. "But Blackbeard wasn't there. These were a re-enactor's boots," I said. I nodded to Sal, at the projector.

She clicked a photo of young Tinks in his re-enactment uniform onto the screen.

"I wore them," Tinks admitted, and pulled the shoes out of his bag.

Grandmother Miss Lacy frowned. "Tinks, why on earth?"

"To scare us off the hunt," I said. "Tinks picked up pork chops for the café the day of the robbery. He used the blood from the butcher's paper to leave a bloody handprint on Harm's windowsill—also to scare us."

Sal clicked my photo of the bloody handprint.

"That was my handprint," he said. "I can't stand blood. I wore cheap plastic gloves."

Crud. Plastic gloves. Why didn't we think of that?

I turned to Starr. "You're a professional. Why didn't you think of that?"

"I did," he said, making a note. "Didn't you?"

Gabriel looked around the room. "So, thanks to our junior sleuths, we now know Tinks stole their clue. How nice. Arrest him, please, and let's open the treasure."

I smiled at Kat. "You may not have heard about the robbery, because you were sick."

"That's right," she said, her face lighting up like I'd given her a present. "I had a stomach virus that night. I was in bed a couple of days, in fact."

Gotcha, I thought.

Skeeter handed me a file. "Tinks made a mistake when he was in high school, but you didn't hear it because somebody kept it quiet," I said, pacing. "Still, the information was easy to find, for anybody who looked. And even easier for Kat Kline, who knew it from the start."

Tinks sighed. "I got in trouble showing off for a girl, in high school. In fact, I broke into a house to impress her, and I got caught—by Miss Thornton. Which was easy, because it was her house I broke into. And she was napping in her parlor."

The café erupted.

"Tinks?" the mayor cried. "A robber? Impossible!"

Tinks bowed his head. "Thanks to Miss Thornton I got off with probation, and even that wasn't on my record after I turned eighteen. She never told a soul except Mr. Red, and I never went wrong again—until now."

"Mo, I want to make a guess here," Harm whispered. He rose. "That crime wasn't on Tinks's record, but Gabriel knew about it because Kat told him. And *Kat* knew because she was the girl Tinks showed off for."

Good guess, I thought, watching Kat's face.

Tinks took up the story. "When Kat came back to town, I thought she liked me again. I wanted to help her find the treasure—until Gabriel started blackmailing me."

"Blackmailing you?" Starr asked, his voice sharp.

"A lie," Gabriel said.

Tinks looked around the café. "Gabriel said he'd keep my past secret if I did him just one favor. I was standing at the cash register the night Mo called the café and told the Colonel they'd found a mega-clue. I overheard her. I went to Harm's house and peeked in the window. And I saw the map."

"You're why the dogs kept barking that night," Dale said.

Tinks nodded. "I told Gabriel and Kat, and I went back to steal it. I wore the re-enactor boots and put the bloody handprint on the windowsill to scare you kids off." He hung his head. "I'm sorry."

"*Did* you steal our map?" I asked.

"No. I went to the back door, and I thought to myself, 'Tinks, this really *is* crazy.'"

"Crazy ain't crazy if it works," Dale reminded him.

"Exactly. And this *wouldn't* work," Tinks said. "Plus it was wrong. Breaking into a house didn't impress Kat twenty years ago, and it wouldn't impress her now. And it wouldn't settle the score with Gabriel, it would only make things worse."

Dale stood, Queen Elizabeth proudly rising by his side. "So you changed your mind, which is why your boot prints led up to the house and back," Dale said, and Sal clicked our footprints-by-the-door photo onto the screen. "But *somebody* went in. So you weren't alone."

Gabriel jumped to his feet. "This is an insult. Kat, let's go."

"Sit," Starr said.

Gabriel sat. So did Queen Elizabeth.

"Good girl, Liz," Dale said, and looked at me. "So who went inside?"

"Mom had a key," Harm said, his voice dry and lifeless as sand. He looked at her. "Mom, you took our map, and you took the box of old photos from the hall closet."

Kat crossed her arms. "It's a lie. Tinks did it. If the shoe fits, wear it, Tinks."

"Were they your boots, Tinks?" I asked.

He shook his head.

Skeeter clicked her briefcase open. "Not many people make Colonial boots," she said. "And none of them have made boots for Gabriel Archer or Kat Kline. I checked."

"See?" Kat said. "They were Tinks's. Just like in the photo."

And that's the reason you gave me those photos, I thought. Proof of Tinks's boots.

"Those boots rotted away years ago," Tinks said.

I nodded to Skeeter. "Were there orders for size twelve men's boots?"

"I found one rush order placed by Rhonda Baker, a week before she and Gabriel came to town."

Mr. Red closed his eyes and shook his head.

"A lie," Kat said over the café's cries.

I reached in our evidence box. "Is it? We also found this scrap of fabric on the dog pen, the night you robbed Harm and Mr. Red," I said, lifting out the thin strip of shiny, royal-blue fabric. "Can or may I see your jacket, whichever is correct?" I asked.

"No," she snapped, folding her jacket on her lap. "Not unless you have a warrant."

I turned to Sal's mom. She's short and dresses good, same as Sal.

"Mrs. Jones?"

Sal's mom stood and adjusted her beret. "I mended the lining in that jacket for Kat," she said. "The fabric I used is so close in color and sheen, only an artist could tell the difference." I passed the evidence bag to her, and she examined the fabric I'd found at the crime scene. "This is the original, Mo." She wrinkled her nose at me and sat down.

"Thank you for that expert testimony as a third-generation seamstress. And here's my photo proving the fabric was caught on the wire by the dog pen," I said as Sal clicked our next slide into place.

The café looked at Kat, who shrugged. "I used my key to enter my childhood home, I claimed some personal things, and I snagged my jacket. So what? I didn't take your map."

"Maybe you should have," Sal said. "A map just a few years younger than the Desperados' recently sold for $460,000. Of course, its art was better, but it wasn't written in poison ink by Blackbeard's ex."

$460,000? I went dizzy.

"You did take it, Kat," I said, reclaiming my legendary balance. "But Tinks wanted to leave it. You two skirmished by the dog pen," I said, and Sal showed our trampled-grass photo. "The map went flying, and you lost it in the dark. The dogs barked, Mr. Red shouted, and you ran, snagging the plastic wrap on the last piece of our map. The piece with the riddle. You ran away with the poison ink clue, Kat. And the ink made you sick."

Mrs. Little looked oddly pleased. "The ink worked. You've admitted being sick."

"Tinks? You were at the mayor's the night we unveiled the portrait of *Tupelo Mother*," I said. "The one that got stolen, along with the mayor's coins."

The Colonel stepped in. "Tinks didn't have to tip anybody off about the portrait," he said. "The mayor bragged to everybody in the café."

The mayor hung his head.

"Yes, let's discuss the portrait," I said. The Colonel headed for the kitchen, right on cue, as Tinks faced the crowd.

"First I want to say I made mistakes," Tinks said. "But when I saw a chance to make things right, I did. I helped the Desperados dig for treasure. I borrowed Gabriel's scuba gear and risked my life for them."

Gabriel jumped up. "He *stole* my gear. Arrest him."

"Sit down," Grandmother Miss Lacy snapped. "I refilled those tanks myself. You're not even out the price of *air,* you unctuous peacock of a man."

Unctuous? We all turned to Sal.

"*Unctuous* means he's a creepy, groveling suck-up," she said, her red curls glistening.

"Extra credit for vocabulary," Miss Retzyl cried.

Harm leaned close and whispered: "Why is Gabriel here?

It can't just be curiosity. He can read about our treasure in tomorrow's papers," he added as a reporter shuffled in.

Harm's right, I thought. Gabriel has something up his sleeve. But what?

"Gabriel Archer played us," I said, hoping to flush him out.

"He didn't play me," Mrs. Simpson said, filing her nails.

"*Especially* you, Mrs. Simpson," I said. "Gabriel came to town in a hotshot car, which impressed you, and said he was from an old family in Virginia. But according to Starr's background check, *this* Gabriel Archer is Gabriel *Smitty* Archer from Charleston, *West* Virginia."

Harm jumped up and paced. "Gabriel told us he worked with his young niece, so you knew he'd work with a kid—like Anna. But according to Starr's report, Gabriel has no family—and no niece. He conned you, Mrs. Simpson. You invested in his dig and he made Attila his intern. Every kid alive wants to find treasure—including Anna."

"That may be the only way Anna's normal," I added.

Mrs. Simpson shrugged. "Anna needs to learn responsibility. And she's getting chubby. I thought the exercise might help."

Attila's face went fire-truck red. "Mother, please," she whispered.

I hate Mrs. Simpson.

"Attila's the perfect size for a mortal enemy," I snapped.

"Leave her alone." I wheeled and pointed at Gabriel. "Gabriel needed your money. He's broke. Bankruptcy cases are public record," I added, and Skeeter flipped a file onto the table.

"Broke?" Mrs. Simpson said. "Gabriel Archer, you owe me ten thousand dollars."

"I don't," he said. "Read the fine print, sweetie."

Dale turned to Miss Retzyl. "Gabriel isn't the kind of person you want to marry."

"*Marry?*" she said. "Who on earth would marry a man like Gabriel Archer?"

Kat, maybe, I thought, watching her.

"Is that it, Desperados?" Starr asked. "I need time to sort these charges."

"There's one more thing," I said as the Colonel walked in carrying the rectangular bundle we'd saved from the aircraft at Gabriel's camp. Dale settled it on the counter, and whipped its cover away.

"Presto," he said. "*Tupelo Mother*. She's home from being stole."

Mrs. Little gasped, her eyes filling with tears.

"You stole that?" Kat said, glaring at Gabriel. "You didn't tell me."

"Because he didn't plan to cut you in," I said.

"I'd like to know where *my* finds are too," Attila said, putting her hands on her hips. "I'm responsible. I worked hard on this project. I found the buttons, a sword hilt, two pistols from those graves. Knives, coins . . . Where are they and when do I get paid, Gabriel?"

Sal placed a file on the evidence table. "All those things are valuable, Anna," she said. "Here's my appraisal of the things the Desperados discovered in the trunks in the Littles' attic. Clothes, tools, a peg leg . . . That little tapestry purse alone is worth thousands. As for this painting, *Tupelo Mother,* painted in 1727. It's homemade paints on poplar wood. With an unknown model, my appraisal sets the value around twelve thousand dollars. But if it's a portrait of Mary Ormond—Blackbeard's fourteenth wife—it's worth triple that. At least."

"As for your finds, Attila, they're being sold on the black market by a tall pilot with a bite mark on his arm," I said. "Detective Starr, did you run the airplane numbers we gave you?"

"I did. We found Gabriel's accomplice as he landed in New Jersey with Tupelo Landing's artifacts. Plus the things from the Littles' safe. I'll make sure it all comes home. And you," he told Gabriel. "Stay where I can see you."

"Everybody to the parking lot," I said. "It's time to open Blackbeard's treasure."

Chapter Thirty-five
Treasures

Moments later, Harm and me scrambled onto the back of Lavender's pickup, by the weird copper cube, as the crowd surged around us. Dale scampered up as Grandmother Miss Lacy snapped our photo.

I raised my hands and the crowd settled. "We'd like to thank everyone who helped us, including Miss Retzyl in case of extra credit," I said. "Harm?"

Harm lifted a hatchet from Lavender's toolbox. A few whacks later we peeled the cube's copper sides down, revealing a tangle of crumbly coconut fibers. We raked them away. The sun glistened on a perfectly preserved mahogany chest carved in a comet burst of *X*s and *O*s. "I've seen that design on your parlor chair, Myrt," Grandmother Miss Lacy said.

"It's Peg-Leg's signature pattern," Dale said, trying the lid. "No keyhole," he said, frowning. "Just a brass carving where the keyhole should be." He squatted and peered at it. "The reverse image of Blackbeard's seal—a skeleton stabbing a bleeding heart."

The reverse image? I lifted the ring from our evidence

box and pressed the seal into the carving. "Please work," I whispered, turning it. The latch popped open.

Grandmother Miss Lacy sprang to the running board as we opened the chest. *Click*.

Dale's shoulders sagged. "Another dress."

"Silk," Sal said, her eyes glowing. "An eighteenth-century party dress." She frowned. "With a square of calico pinned to it—with brass pins." She gasped. "Mo, this calico was cut from the attic dress. The calico dress is worth eight thousand dollars to any museum in the country. And this one is *silk*. This square of calico proves this is Mary Ormond's dress too," Sal said. "It's worth a fortune."

Harm whistled. "A dress too dangerous for Tupelo Landing, and too cherished to burn."

"Slippers," Sal breathed, peeping in the trunk. "From England."

I lifted a rectangular package wrapped in oilcloth. "Another portrait," I called, unwrapping it. A sharp-faced girl stared at me: hooked nose, green eyes, long blond hair. She wore the party dress we'd just found—and a necklace of glittering emeralds.

Harm read the name on the back of the canvas. "Mary Ormond, 1716."

I glanced at Mrs. Little, picturing Grandmother Miss Lacy's photo of her as a girl. Then I pictured the portrait of *Tupelo Mother 1727,* from the attic, and looked at this portrait.

The hair on my arms stood up.

"This is the girl from the first painting," Dale said, staring at the new portrait. "Only in the first portrait, she had short *brown* hair and wore a plain brown dress. Not long blond hair and a party dress with jewels." Dale looked at me, his eyes wide. "Mary Ormond went incognito. She buried this stuff to stay safe. She invented her own Witness Protection Program."

"Incognito! Excellent word choice," Miss Retzyl cried. "Extra credit."

"You are indubitably correct, Dale," I said, and looked at Miss Retzyl. Nothing. I pressed on. "Dale's right. Blackbeard's crew was looking for *this* Mary Ormond," I said, hoisting the new portrait high. "She cut and dyed her hair, going Colonial drab," I said as Harm lifted *Tupelo Mother.*

A big-haired twin scrambled onto the tailgate. "Mary Ormond probably used mayapples to dye her hair that mousy brown color, but there's no excuse for those eyebrows. Tweezers were invented in 3000 BC."

I smiled and said words I never expected to say: "Thank you for that expert opinion, Crissy or Missy."

As the crowd applauded the twin off the tailgate, Harm reached into the chest and lifted a silver cup. "Blackbeard's chalice. Just like Miss Thornton's book said."

We're on a roll, I thought, reaching in and untying a small oilskin bundle. Crud. Mary buried a doll in a death-trap treasure pit? Was she mad?

"Excellent!" I cried, holding it up. "A doll!"

"She's a beauty. And valuable," Bill Glasgow called. "That's French porcelain."

"Dolls aren't treasure," Mrs. Little shouted.

I looked at Miss Retzyl. "This doll's valuable, but it meant more than gold to Mary Ormond, a girl married off to a seadog sociopath. If I understand metaphor, and thanks to Miss Retzyl I do, this doll is Mary's childhood, kept safe from Blackbeard."

Miss Retzyl gave me a thumbs-up. Extra credit. Yes!

"What else?" Mrs. Little shouted. The trunk stared at us, empty.

"Mo," Harm whispered, "remember the attic trunk? Peg-Leg built this one too."

We examined the trunk's corners. "Thank you, Peg-Leg," he whispered as one gave way. A door in the trunk's floor scraped open. Mary's emerald necklace—the one in her portrait—sparkled up at us from a thick bed of rubies and gold jewelry.

I lifted the necklace, emeralds dripping from my hands.

"Emeralds," Gabriel said, working his way to us. "Magnificent."

Mrs. Little slammed her cane against the tailgate. "Don't touch it, thief."

"Hey!" I shouted. "Don't ding Lavender's truck." I grabbed her cane and whacked the chest, just like she hit the trunk in the attic. A hidden door scraped open in the wall, and a scroll belly-flopped to the trunk's floor. I unrolled it. "A message from Mary Ormond," I said.

"Please, not another curse," Dale muttered, closing his eyes.

"A confession," I announced, and the crowd went quiet as snowfall.

> Our Confession
>
> On this sad day—July 20, 1719—I, Mary Ormond, and my husband, Peg-Leg, make the following confession. Around noon we left our home and rowed across the river, for a picnic on the bluff. We landed at a low, friendly spot known for good fishing.

"The old fish camp," Dale said, and the crowd nodded.

> Another skiff soon came ashore carrying three of Blackbeard's men. They rolled water barrels toward the Sweet Water Springs, which all sailors know for sweet water, and mark on their maps, as it is excellent for long voyages.

"That explains your map, you twit," Attila said, glaring at Gabriel. "Those Xs marked springs! Not treasure! If I hadn't been out there finding our trifling little treasures with that stupid metal detector, we would have found nothing."

I read on:

The three pirates spied us–me with my long blond hair, Peg-Leg with his peg leg. They charged us, fumbling for their pistols, shouting, "Give up! Blackbeard put a price upon your heads for stealing his treasure, and if he can't pay us in this world, he will pay us in the next!"

What could we do?

Peg pulled two pistols from his belt. I tugged mine from my cute little tapestry purse that goes with everything. We fired together, dropping all three pirates in their tracks and also killing the parrot Sweet Bart, whom I knew in happier days.

I am so, so sorry about the bird.

Dale blinked back tears.

We buried them in a nice spot. And we made a plan to bury our pasts by the springs, to keep us and our little son safe. We used Blackbeard's own devilish technology as we dug.

So, to the brave soul reading this now: We assume

you are family who found our attic clue and that you need funds. So here lies the last of Blackbeard's treasures, the ones that put our own lives in peril but that may enrich yours. The vast unmarked treasure we kept hidden in our tidy little home—the gold coins, doubloons, and pieces of eight. We hope you've spent it well.

Love,
Mary and Peg-Leg

"Brilliant," Dale said. "The coins they kept would have been like unmarked bills to them." He frowned, tapping his lip. "I wonder if they changed their names when they went incognito. Daddy's side of the family would have."

I looked into Mrs. Little's flashing black eyes. My blood went to ice.

Harm gulped. "Desperados, are you thinking what I'm thinking?"

"No," Dale said. "Not unless you're hungry too."

"I'm thinking *exactly* what you're thinking," I said, and we rushed the evidence crate.

"Wait," Dale whispered, burrowing between us. "What's going on?"

"Here it is," Harm said. He opened Mary's blank journal and turned to the pressed daisy. He read the script underneath, his voice low: *"A rose by any other name smells as sweet—William Shakespeare.*" He looked at me. "We were right, Mo."

I felt the blood fall from my face and heard myself swallow.

"Mo? Are you okay?" Dale asked. "Because you don't look good. You never look neat, but now you don't even look . . . *right.*"

I opened my clue pad and scrawled a note: *Myrt Little = spawn of Blackbeard.*

Dale read it and gasped. "What?"

"Mary and Peg-Leg never left Tupelo Landing," I whispered. "They changed their look and changed their name—to Little. The Little family has been frittering away Blackbeard's unmarked treasure for three hundred years."

"I'll take that silver cup," Gabriel Archer said, striding forward. "And those jewels. It's mine, and here's my proof." He reached into his pocket. "A map sketched by JRA," he said, unfolding a copy of the same map Kat gave us weeks ago.

Finally, I thought. A book report pays off.

"JRA," I said. "John Rose Archer, Blackbeard's quartermaster on the *Queen Anne's Revenge.*" I looked around the crowd. "Book report on a fat book. I even read the index."

"You *only* read the index," Dale said.

"Shhhh," I said, glancing at Miss Retzyl.

Gabriel frowned. "As a former crew member, John R. Archer was entitled to his share of treasure. He was a distant relation of mine. Blood is blood, and I'm here to collect for him," he said. He looked at Grandmother Miss Lacy. "Sorry, dear."

"I wouldn't be sorry yet, *dear,*" she replied.

"Back off," Mrs. Little said, swishing her cane. "The treasure's *mine.* By thicker blood than yours."

"Allow me," I said, and she nodded. I projected. "The Desperado Detective Agency is proud to present Blackbeard's great-great-great-grandbaby—Myrt Little."

The crowd gasped. Sal screamed.

"Finally, everything makes sense," Grandmother Miss Lacy said, looking from Mary Ormond's portrait to Mrs. Little's yellowish face and hawkish nose.

"Put the treasure in the Jeep, son," Mrs. Little said.

"Hold it," Gabriel said. "You can't prove anything with an ugly face."

"Take that back," Grandmother Miss Lacy snapped.

"Actually we *can* prove it," I said as Starr pushed between Gabriel and the treasure. I reached into the evidence crate and snagged Blackbeard's curse. "This curse," I said, "is sealed in Blackbeard's blood—with his signature ring."

"And here's Mrs. Little's childhood oath, also signed in blood," Harm said, pulling it out.

"And if that isn't good enough, I'll open a vein," Mrs. Little said.

I smiled. "Either way, I'll bet your Jaguar it's a DNA match, Gabriel."

Skeeter stood to face the crowd. "Landowners own half the treasure by law, and then the Law of Finders Keepers kicks in. The Desperados and the Littles are rich!"

"Sixth graders who did extra credit pirate reports win too!" I shouted, and they cheered.

"Treasure's worth nothing until you sell it," Gabriel said. "I can set that sale up for you—for a percentage."

"Piffle," Grandmother Miss Lacy said. "History belongs to everyone. That treasure belongs here." She looked at her old friend. "Myrt, we're the richest people in town. I say *we* buy out everyone who wishes to sell, donate our own treasures, and start a museum."

Brilliant.

"The Mary Ormond Museum of Blackbeard History," I said.

Mrs. Little wavered. "Mother, it's an election year," the mayor whispered.

"Deal," Mrs. Little said, and the crowd roared.

The Buccaneer Bash thundered into the night. "Welcome to pirate night," I told table after table. "Tonight we got Barbaric-que, Psycho Potato Salad, and Blood-Red Slaw."

"Devil's food cake for dessert," Harm called, swaggering by with a dessert tray.

As people dove into seconds, Detective Joe Starr stood to address the throng. "Attention, please," he said. "This is a complicated case, and I want to thank the Desperados for their help." He scratched his eyebrow with his pen. "Lana, Tinks trespassed on the inn's property. Would you and Miss Thornton like to press charges?"

They shook their heads.

Starr flipped a page in his pad. "Mr. Red, Kat broke into your house. The charges probably won't stick if you gave her a key, even if it was twenty years ago. But you can try."

"Ask Harm," Mr. Red said, very even. "He's the detective in our family."

"No charges, thanks," Harm said, putting cake on Hannah's plate.

"Desperados? Charges against Kat and Tinks for stealing your map?"

I hesitated. If Harm didn't want charges against Kat, I didn't either. On the other hand, I ain't as highly evolved as some people think. I slipped over to Kat and whispered, "I'm not pressing charges because Harm loves you. And because I thank you for saving the photos that took me to Upstream Mother, even if you were just trying to set up Tinks. But mess with Harm again and I'll kick you so hard, I'll roll you up like a window shade."

"Metaphor," Dale said.

"Smile," Sal said, and squeezed his hand.

I smiled at Starr. "No charges, thanks."

Starr looked at Harm. "You have good friends, Harm.

And you have a well-loved son," he told Kat. He looked at Gabriel. "I have a feeling you won't be as lucky.

"Mrs. Little? Charges? Breaking and entering? Theft?" Starr offered.

"I'd like to blow Gabriel's kneecaps off," Mrs. Little said. "But I guess that's the Blackbeard in me."

"So are the five engagement rings from your safe," Dale said, and she nodded.

"If I can't shoot him, I'll settle for pressing charges," she said, and Starr pulled Gabriel's hands behind his back and cuffed him.

"This is outrageous. Miss Thornton," Gabriel cried. "Do something."

"Certainly." She lifted her camera. *Click.* "For the museum. Good luck, dear."

Miss Retzyl watched Starr lead Gabriel out and stuff him in the Impala. "Dale," she said as Dale and Sal each stuck a straw in Sal's milkshake, "why did you think I was interested in marrying a man like Gabriel Archer?"

Dale wiped his mouth. "He sent you flowers at school. And he called the café to apologize for standing you up. I heard him. And treasure hunters are romantic," he added, and Sal blushed.

Miss Retzyl shook her head, her normal auburn hair shining in the glow of the Winter Tree. "Dale, *Joe* sent me those flowers. And I *did* call here one morning and Gabriel *did* stand me up—on a school visit. I thought the class would like to hear him speak. Besides . . ." She looked at Starr as he walked in. "I couldn't marry Gabriel if I wanted to. I'm already married. To Joe Starr."

Miss Retzyl and Joe Starr? Married?

"Our valentines worked!" Dale shouted, high-fiving me.

"The cards were sweet, Dale," she said. "But Joe and I got married on Ocracoke Island. In a civil ceremony."

"Quicksand weekend?" Dale guessed, and she nodded.

"Took forever to get things set up," Starr muttered. "Sorry to miss the robbery at your place, Red."

"We'll have a church wedding here," she added. "And you're all invited."

When the party wound down, I pulled Dale and Harm aside. "We got one more treasure to open tonight, Desperados," I said, and led the way to my flat.

Harm took the rocking chair, and Dale and Queen Elizabeth plunked down on the floor. "You're the first to hear this after Miss Lana and the Colonel," I said, pulling Upstream Mother's letter from its jar and pushing the curtains back, to welcome the stars.

"It's an honor," Harm said, his voice going crooked.

I read slow and soft, the way Miss Lana reads it to me.

By now, we've read it a thousand times.

Dear girl,

If you are reading this, you've found me. I knew you would.

Letting you go was the hardest thing I've ever done. Watching you spin away on that sign broke me a thousand ways. Every moment since I've prayed you'd come home to me.

Now you have. And you wonder how I survived.

As you swirled away, a wall of water swept me off our roof. I went under once. Twice. As I started down forever, my arm scraped something half floating. A timber. I clung to it and my world went dark.

I woke up in this bed, in Miss Bessie's house, saved by a stranger who pumped a half-life into me.

Did you live? I know you did. I can feel your heartbeat in mine.

My name is Josie Barrow. Josie for my grandmother, Barrow for a river in Ireland—a river she knew and loved as a girl, but that I've never seen. I wrapped you in her sweater. I am 20 years old. I sing but can't carry a tune. I wear colors that clash. I'm hot-tempered and I am strong.

When I love I never stop. And I do love you.

I wish I had something wise to tell you, but this

is all I know. Love is both infinite and rare. Give it like there will always be more—because there will be. When someone offers it, grab it and don't let go.

I am yours and you are mine, wherever we may go. My love for you bends my rivers and scatters my stars.

Your loving mother,
Josie Barrow

I put the letter back in the bottle that brought it home to me, and we sat together, wrapped in the courage of starlight.

Chapter Thirty-six
In the Loop

Dear Upstream Mother,

How are you? Tomorrow Miss Retzyl and Joe Starr get married in the Episcopal church, the church that played "Blue Suede Shoes" the day the Desperados decided to look for you.

I know you will be there because I will be.

The Colonel will stand up for Joe Starr. Miss Lana's walking in for Miss Retzyl and so am I— Miss Moses LoBeau, Emergency Bridesmaid. A lifelong dream.

Grandmother Miss Lacy put flowers in the church, in honor of you.

Miss Rose will play the piano and Dale will sing Have-A-Maria. The rest of the sixth grade has a special place behind Miss Retzyl's family, who's coming from Rural Hall, just outside Winston-Salem.

Thank you for your letter, which I treasure. Thank you for bringing me into this world, which

I love. Everything in my life flows from you. I am yours in any shape the universe takes until our paths cross again.

Today, in my messenger bag, I found the card Harm tossed on my desk Valentine's Day. Inside he'd written a bad poem. When I thanked him he said, "I also brought you a pansy and fudge, LoBeau. Poem, flower, candy—check."

Miss Lana says we will be a power couple by the end of the week.

The Desperados have a new case within our Bicycle Radius, and we still got one photo of Always Man to track down. I promise to keep you in the loop.

I love you like starlight loves star.

Your girl,

Mo

Acknowledgments

SO MANY PEOPLE TO THANK!

A lot of people helped with this book, and I thank you all.

Thanks to my husband, Rodney L. Beasley, who puts as much energy into these books as I do, for your love and support.

Thanks to the folks who understand when I disappear into the writing cave, and welcome me when I come out. My brother and sister—Michael and Allison Turnage—and their spouses, Susan Bowyer and Johnny Woodall. My nieces and their families: Karen, Alan, Vivian, Julian, and Lillian Boyd; Lauren, Elvis, Olivia, and Harrison Schreckengost; Haven, Nick, and Taylor Krarup.

Thanks Claire Pittman, Lauryn & Eric Sawyer, Mamie Dixon, and Catherine Walker.

A salute to my cousins, who understand barbecue can double as lip gloss, and who always show up for me. Thanks in particular to ace librarian Mary Jo Floyd and her students at Fuquay-Varina Middle School in Fuquay-Varina, NC.

Thanks to novelist Patsy Baker O'Leary and her Pitt Community College creative writing class. It's good to have a writing tribe, and you are mine.

Thanks to Eileen LaGreca for the great maps, and to Gilbert Ford, for the cover art.

Turning now to sheep and yarn: Thanks to Ann Fay at Rising Meadows Farm, Liberty, NC; Jane Plaugher in Boone, NC; and Jeanne Shrader at Knitting Addiction in Kitty Hawk, NC, for sharing your thoughts and expertise with me.

And to Jo Ann Reed, thanks for talking sweet potato pies with me.

My gratitude always to my editor and publisher, Kathy Dawson, who loves Mo and Dale as much as I do. Thanks to so many people at Penguin Random House, but especially Claire Evans, Jasmin Rubero, Cerise Steel, Regina Castillo, Doni Kay and the other amazing sales reps, Jennifer Dee, Venessa Carson, and Carmela Iaria.

Thanks to my agent, Margaret Riley King, at WME, for the exciting projects on the horizon.

And finally back to family again: Thanks to my father, A. C. Turnage, Jr., whose story of his first kiss inspired Dale's, in this book. And thank you to my mother, Vivian Taylor Turnage, who showed me how to stand up, speak up, and think for myself. I miss you every day I open my eyes.

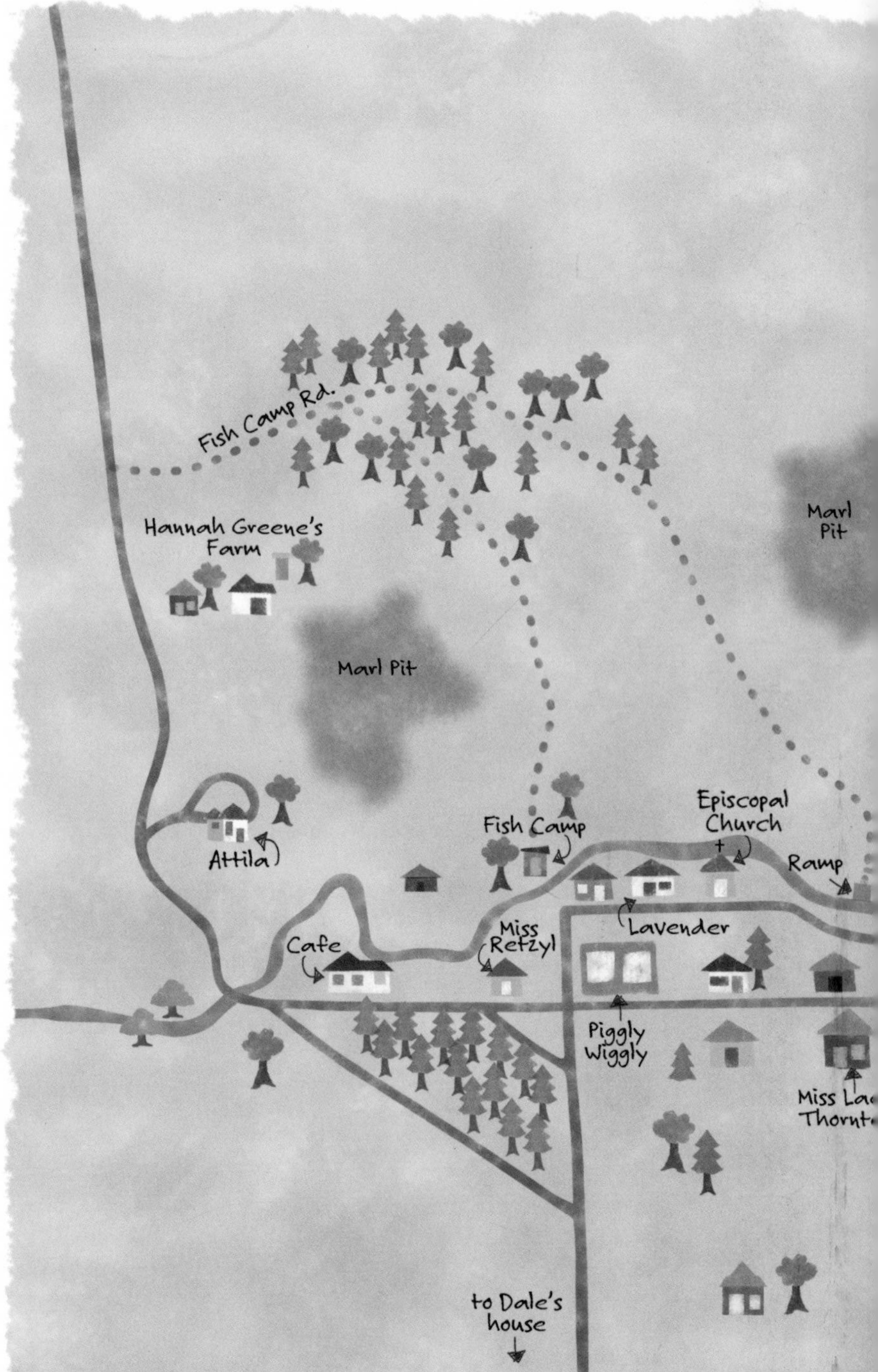

Fish Camp Rd.
Hannah Greene's Farm
Marl Pit
Marl Pit
Attila
Fish Camp
Episcopal Church
Ramp
Lavender
Cafe
Miss Retzyl
Piggly Wiggly
Miss La
Thornt
to Dale's house